T0113314

PEOPLE IN DARK PLACES

bryan g salazar

authorHOUSE®

AuthorHouse™
1663 Liberty Drive
Bloomington, IN 47403
www.authorhouse.com
Phone: 1 (800) 839-8640

Published by AuthorHouse   10/26/2016

ISBN: 978-1-5246-4736-0 (sc)
ISBN: 978-1-5246-4735-3 (e)

Library of Congress Control Number: 2016917832

Print information available on the last page.

Contents

To Ellene Cabajar, who keeps all my monsters in check.

Afterglow

Every day—every single day, the old man would walk down the street on the way toward the cemetery. Every single day since his wife was buried there, one gloomy Sunday afternoon. The cold fingers of pneumonia took hold of her for days before it eventually took her away from him. It had been the saddest part of his long life. Long it is. He is already seventy-five years old.

He kept a house a few blocks away from the cemetery. It was a small house, but ever since the death of his wife, he started to see it seemingly grow in breadth. The desolation of being alone, of being apart from the one dearest to him, it made him see the world as it really is—vast, empty, grieving.

He knew he always wanted to be with her. At times he would think about cutting his time short just to start sharing the peace she had found. It was a lonely world without her. It was a damn lonely world. Sleepless nights came and went, and thoughts of her always ran around his mind. Restless thoughts. Oh, how he wanted to be with her during those times!

Yet in the end, he would take a step back, and think. He knew his time would come very soon now. So he continued waiting.

He goes to the cemetery every afternoon. It has become a fixed schedule. He takes a seat for hours beside his wife's grave until sunset, and when dark starts to steal into the afternoon, he starts his way back toward his lonely home. He sleeps the night over, wakes up, passes the morning through noon, and then walks the steps to the cemetery again afterward. His remaining days, for him, had been meant for these afternoons.

He was walking toward his wife's grave when he caught glimpse of a man standing on top of another one nearby, a couple of meters away from his wife's. Shovel in his hand, the man stood there digging through a hill of mud which had built up over the tomb. The man was apparently middle-aged, and seemed strong enough to dig even through the concrete tomb itself. When he finally noticed the old man, he smiled. But the old man didn't even alter a bit of his bleak countenance to mirror the apparent pleasure of the young man seeing him. Since he was a stranger, the old man felt no obligation to repay the smile. He walked on and took his usual seat beside his wife's tomb, and the other man continued digging.

The old man had already noticed the mud building up on the tomb days before, but took no heed of it. Now, watching the young man digging through it, it finally caught his curiosity. "That's a pile," he said.

"Yeah, it is," the young man said. "Had almost covered everything. This is my grandfather's, by the way."

"I see. I'm here every day actually, every afternoon. This grave right here is where my dear wife is buried. I don't think I've seen you around here before."

"Oh, yes. I've just arrived in the city. I worked abroad for quite some time."

"I see. You go on. I won't be a problem." The old man finally smiled.

"No, there certainly won't be."

"My name is Feliciano Marquez, by the way," the old man spoke after several seconds.

"I'm Lorenz. It's a pleasure to meet you. Well, at least there's someone I can talk to while I get this thing done. This place sure is very, very quiet."

The old man nodded his head in agreement. They stretched out each of their hands to shake, and the moment the old man took hold of Lorenz's hand, he suddenly felt a flash of odd feeling within him, a feeling that seemed to be a mixture of eerie and familiar. It seemed like slipping into a brief moment of déjà vu. When he sat back he took a scrutinizing look at Lorenz. A smile brushed into the young man's face.

Later when the sun began setting, and the old man stood up to make his way home, he saw the progress Lorenz had arrived with the digging. Half of the mound had already been cleared off from the top of the tomb. The darkness slowly settled in.

"You're going home?" Lorenz asked, pulling the spade out from the mud.

"Yes," the old man replied. "I am guessing you are too."

"I am, too. How about some company on the way?"

The old man complied with a smile. Quietly they walked out of the cemetery and on until they stopped by the old man's house, where they both bade each other farewell. So the day ended. The darkness had completely enveloped that part of the Earth.

The old man submerged himself into the usual atmosphere of his little house, but this time his thoughts did not dwell on his wife, as per usual to him upon getting home. This time, it remained upon the stranger he had met in the cemetery. For some reason quite strange to him, it seemed that he may have already met this man somewhere in the past, that this man likely belonged to some sort of important part in it.

He poured himself a drink of a glass of water before he lied on his bamboo bed. *Who was that man, and why does he seem so familiar?* Something bothered him, something trying to slip into his head. Something that he wanted to pursue knowing.

He fell asleep with these questions circulating his thoughts.

The weather did not look good on the afternoon the next day. Heaps of dim clouds blocked the entire sky and occasional sounds of thunder burst from them. The wind blew around in a steady scale of vehemence. Looking at the skies, a storm could possibly be lurking just a stretch behind.

This was not a first time for the old man nevertheless. Apparently in the number of months he had been doing these daily visits in the cemetery, there had been at least a day when an afternoon was showered by rain.

When he arrived the weather had broken off the usual stillness of the cemetery. Alternating noises from the trees swaying and thunder rumbling went about the place. Lorenz was already there, resuming yesterday's pending work. When he saw the old man, he flashed the same delightful smile at him. The old man repaid it with a smile of his own this time, before once again taking his seat beside his wife's tomb.

He then noticed that Lorenz was now almost done with his work.

A short but louder peal of thunder erupted from the sky, and Lorenz paused digging upon hearing it. Looking up, he said, "Looks like it's going to rain a lot."

"Looks like it," the old man answered. "It's already too dim for this hour. How long have you been here?"

"Today?"

"Yeah. Digging."

"An hour now, I guess. This digging's almost done."

The old man looked at the mud once more and shared an approving look with Lorenz. A square epitaph by the head of the tomb was almost visible now, only covered by a handful of dirt that seemed to have hardened already. Lorenz was about to drive his spade on to these remaining traces of dirt when the rain started to drop a more voluminous shower. The speed of the raindrops escalated rapidly in a short span. Along with the precipitation traveled a stream of howling winds, slapping through the leaves of the trees around them. The old man quickly opened the umbrella he brought over his head, while Lorenz ran beneath a nearby tree, putting the spade leaning against the trunk. Only a few paces separated the two.

They looked intently at one another, for a string of minutes, waiting for the other to speak. The rain fell in a splash between them. At last, Lorenz spoke, "This rain knows the most perfect time to fall." A grin pulled out from his lips.

The old man laughed, feebly. "Yeah, it sure does. I guess you would have to push back on that digging you got there." They both slipped into a fleeting laughter, and a consequent feeling washed over the old man, a feeling that somehow he knew a lot about who the young man was, despite them acquainted only the day before. There was something about the young man screaming in his head, seeming to tell him something, that perhaps there already had been a point in time before when he had met and known him. Apparently he just could not recall when that was and whatever consequent circumstances occurred that caused him to lose his grasp of it. Something. Somewhere.

Slowly, he receded into thoughts that were not usually present in his head. He found it difficult to remember certain moments in his life. All of a sudden, he felt unfamiliar with his own self.

Lorenz stood under the tree observing the old man. From there he noticed the change in the old man's countenance, right to the apparent ponderous state it was painted with now. The grin that had both touched their faces a while back had dissolved. Lorenz began to delve further into his own mind himself. But unlike the old man, the thoughts he had were shy of any doubts.

The rain gradually abated, eventually reduced to a drizzle.

"Who are you?" the old man asked, as soon as the noise of the falling raindrops receded. His voice was mixed with some trace of reluctant emotional outburst. His eyes had turned cloudy.

"You know me," was the answer from Lorenz. He picked the spade up from against the tree and climbed back on top of his grandfather's tomb. "You know who I am." And then he continued scraping off the remaining mud.

"I feel like I have met you before," the old man said. "Please tell me who you are. Tell me why I have been having these thoughts in my head, these confusing questions. I can't even be sure of who I really am!" Tears began to cloud his eyes, tincturing their sides red.

Lorenz looked at him and grinned, and he found the grin even more confusing. The young man finally cleared off the last traces of mud from the epitaph of the tomb and threw his eyes back to him.

"You have met me before," the young man said.

"I don't understand."

"We go a long way, really."

The old man stood frozen, his face mired with haze and questions. A jumble of chaotic thoughts filled and swayed around his head, bouncing wildly against the walls, concocting disoriented mix-up of feelings he was not sure he ought to feel. How much he understood what Lorenz was talking about: nil. How much he wanted to know what he meant: infinite. He stared at the young man and found a complete stranger in him again.

Lorenz shifted his eyes back toward his grandfather's tomb and suddenly a bright, blazing illumination shot out from the epitaph. The light streamed out continuously and its intensity became so blinding that it swallowed up everything from the old man's sight. He could no longer see Lorenz, nor his wife's tomb, nor the rest of the cemetery. The light had wrapped him in a burning embrace. Later he felt being buoyed up into the air. He screamed, he called out Lorenz's name, for he knew there was nobody else around to call out for. But no answer returned to those screams. He continued rising aloft.

And then somewhere, as he felt afloat in midair, a voice came into his ears. A familiar voice.

"Won't you want to come home to me, my dear? I have been waiting for many years. I have been waiting for us to be together again."

The voice then broke into a series of weeping sounds. He knew the voice. How could he ever forget the music of his dear wife's voice?

It went on: "It's very wonderful here, my dear. The fresh air. The trees and the birds, the mountains, the clouds: they are all such a sight to see. The sun shines at you with a pleasant morning smile. At night, these sights continue to mesmerize me. Add the moon and the stars and this place becomes so much perfect. When it rains, I don't drop myself in the corner and cry. The rain is as wonderful as the sunshine. This is a home so perfect, my dear, and it would be so much more perfect if you're here with me. Come home, my love." The sound of tears came again. There was pain in the voice, a hurt that had come from years of solitary waiting. The voice slowly faded, letting go of its grip around the old man's heart. He cried. He missed his wife so much, and he felt an equal pain. Now he felt completely determined to follow her, share her happiness and peace in that perfect place.

But the light, he seemed lost in it. The voice was gone and there was only him submerged in this mysterious blazing glow, floating like a kite in a summer sky— floating without really going anywhere. He called out the name of Lorenz again, and still came no answer. Soon a familiar smell wafted through the spaces within the light, a scent he somehow knew. It was a scent that came from a past he had but which he could not quite recall. The familiarity of it struck him more vehemently. It turned his eyes into cloudy orbs.

Soon, one by one, pictures of reminiscences dropped in line inside his mind. He finally remembered. That was his scent. It came from a perfume he used to wear years back, many years back. It was a birthday gift from his daughter. It had been so long ago. Now he imagined himself in front of a mirror, spraying the scent all over his body. A bright smile touched his lips. He felt happy, tremendously happy.

He let that short flood of happiness course through him. Amidst the feeling of disorientation and being lost submerged in the blinding light, he conjured some hope of being happy. He wanted to be so. Oh, how he wanted to be happy!

The light began to fade and turn into a sea of white smoke. He could feel a solid ground under his feet now. And then when the smoke finally cleared away, he found himself at the moment standing on the tomb of Lorenz's grandfather. Lorenz was gone.

The old man cast glances around for him, but he was already nowhere to be found. The cemetery had turned in a silence that was unusual and unnerving. He felt a surge of fear come into him. He had been visiting this place for a long time—even doing so alone—and yet now he felt scared.

But, scared of what?

He looked down at the tomb beneath his feet. It looked fragile, very old. There were numerous branches of cracks on the sides and the supposed cross at the head just above the epitaph had no more but one arm left. His eyes fell on the epitaph, and in an instant he stood aghast at what he saw. The name etched upon it was Feliciano Lorenzo Marquez. That was his full name.

He heard a voice from behind him, another familiar voice.

"It's time to go home now, Lorenzo," Lorenz said.

"What is this?" The old man's voice trembled from confusion.

Then another voice came, one bursting up from his wife's tomb. "It's very wonderful here, my dear. Come now. I have been waiting so long for you." A blaze then suddenly rose up from the tomb, slipping through a vine of crack that had run the whole width of it. The fire grew immensely making the whole place look as if it was suddenly set in daylight, though beyond them already lay the evening. The familiar scent of his perfume wafted through the air again, but soon it turned into that of putrefaction.

All around him the voices chorused in screams, in sounds that seemed to come from a long, dark tunnel.

"Remember, Lorenzo? Remember the fateful night you rose up beyond your diabolical mind? Remember how you hacked us to pieces!"

"Get out of that fabricated fantasy, old man," the distinct voice of Lorenz went. "This is your evil reality!"

The voices whirled around the air. It was driving him mad. It was driving him out of his senses and casting him into his familiar ones. The scenes from many years came back to him in vivid imageries. He loved his wife, he loved his daughter—he had loved them both. He only wanted to be happy. He only wanted them to be close to him all of the time. He did what was just right, because *they are trying to leave me! They say I am turning mad! I love them both! I make love to them both! I only did what was right! I axed them so they can't leave me. Is it that so hard to be happy?*

CLARISSA

One. Quijano.

She sat on one of the reclining chairs in their terrace one afternoon, reading a book.

Her name is Clarissa, and all across the town she was known most by her comely face. Many had sought for her attention. Many had wanted to go on a date with her. Every man knows her name and knows well enough to mention her beauty. The expanse of its reach wasn't even restricted to geographical breadth, but socially as well— even married men want to become adulterers by her.

Clarissa was twenty-one years old. She finished her degree in Nursing last month in one of the universities in the city, and now she was in preparation mode for the licensure exam. She had gone back here in her hometown to review, wanting a place far from the bustles of the city, far from any distractions, where she could immerse herself in a dozen of Nursing books and reviewers for a whole day in a string of days.

But this afternoon, she inched back a little from her Nursing books and decided to read a novel.

Overlooking the terrace was a street that had forked from the main highway connecting the town to the city.

It barely held width for two cars to fit, basically for the two opposing lanes, and mostly empty of passersby—a typical street in a rural community. Darkness completely flooded it at night. There were no lamp posts on the sides where there normally should be when in the city, even an overabundance of it. During that time, the street would owe its light from the scarce rays coming from the lamps in some of the houses. It was a quiet and dark street, and Clarissa liked the way it was.

Clarissa seemed to like the quiet and the dark.

Clarissa had read a few pages of the book when the street suddenly began to be filled with people, whose subsequent clamoring soon caught her attention. She closed the book in between her fingers and stood up to see whatever was going on down the street.

There seemed to be a parade commencing. A young man in formal attire stood at the back of an open-type multicab coursing through the street, moving along in a snail's pace. He was waving his hand to the people already collected at the sides of the street. By the minute they gradually grew in number. Across their faces could be seen looks of delight fairly at the sight of the man in the motorcade. And Clarissa turned out to be equally delighted herself as well, excited even so.

She caught herself smiling like a teenager at a first snapshot of puppy love. But she knew this as more than just a shallow tender attachment. She knew who he was, and she knew all about her romantic desires for him, dating back to her pre-city years.

The man was Robert Bermudez, the son of the incumbent town mayor currently finishing a last term in the mayor's office. Robert was to run for the same position, hopefully to sit after his father, as the old man would try to win the governor's seat. Robert had been a licensed civil engineer working in the city before taking a complete turn toward politics. He had a steady life practicing his profession to every standing structure in there when the old man called and told him to bring his ass back in town and do what a Bermudez is born to do, adding that "Politics is the only real job worth a real man." He tried to refuse at first but was eventually made to reconsider it, a threat and inheritance talks later. He got back in town and filed the candidacy.

So there he was now, roaming around the town, plastering his face all over it, bidding the people to write his name on their ballots beside the designation "Mayor," and smiling every minute just so people would stay delighted with him. Not that there was no other way they could get the people to vote for him though.

The town people seemed to like him so far, and they regarded him with respect. Perhaps because he was an educated professional in the city, and a face of a promising character that could capably lead them and the whole town. Or perhaps because the family's going to buy their votes and that would be extra money on election day. Little did they know that behind his gleaming face hid a secret darker than the secret of where the funds of his education and his family's fortune had been obtained. The term of Robert Bermudez's father had been a time where greed lurked in every corner of the town hall. He scammed all the benefits that were ought to be spread about the town, and hid behind the shadows of the people's naivety, letting himself be known as a sympathetic mayor who has his heart for their welfare.

Clarissa smiled at the campaigning mayor-to-be as his ride inched closer and closer to their house. He continued waving his hand to the people, who were cheering at him like the man was instead a movie actor. When the vehicle at last got in front of the house, all of a sudden he looked up toward her direction by the terrace, and locked his eyes there for several seconds. She saw herself dumbfounded by such sudden turn of event, if an accidental glance was a big event ordinarily. But to her it was. She knew. She had her reason to treat a simple glance, accidental or not, as more than ordinary.

Robert saw the smile in her face and felt a sudden flash through his mind. I didn't expect this town to have at least one beautiful fish, he thought. He obscured a sly grin on his face, but it came as a sweet one to Clarissa's eyes, something that meant more than just him campaigning for her vote. He waved his hand at her and she found herself smiling wider than her lips could stretch out. He saw her cheeks blush.

He stood beside another young man at the back of the mini truck. This man had been a long-time helper of the Bermudez family—a "boy"—and a childhood acquaintance of Robert. His name was Benito, but Robert had been used to calling him Ben.

Robert glanced at him and whispered close to his ear, "The woman in the terrace. Do you know who she is?" He furtively pointed his lips toward the terrace.

Ben followed it and led his eyes toward the woman in subject. Of course he knew who she was. That was Clarissa, the constant subject even of his own frequent lustful thoughts.

"Who is she? Do you know her?"

"Ah, that woman," Ben said. "That's Clarissa. She's a beauty, isn't she?"

Robert's smile didn't falter as he threw one glance after another at Clarissa. The woman seemed to notice this and couldn't help but keep smiling herself. She smiled through this nascent brand of happiness without consciously perceiving the fact that his smile wasn't the kind that she thought it was.

Clarissa's eyes completely followed Robert until he had eventually passed by their house and forward to the town plaza ahead, where he was to give a campaign speech. The people who had conglomerated in the street during the motorcade had gathered again at the plaza upon his arrival. There he was met with the same cheering and the same hopeful eyes. Robert felt an excitement within him, not mainly by the thought of the sure shot win for the seat in the town hall's office, but also of the thought that his stay wouldn't be as dull as he had expected it to be. He had Clarissa fill his mind.

Clarissa, he thought. Clarissa, his mind pondered. What Robert wants, Robert gets. That was a fact. His twenty-six years alive had been years ran along by that single line.

And in time, the simple what's became who's.

Clarissa became a want.

(The story that Clarissa was reading in the terrace was Nick Joaquin's "May Day Eve." In it was told a myth that when a woman stands before a mirror, in the middle of the night, holding a lighted candle, the glass would show her an image of the man she is to marry in the future. Though it is after all dismissed as a myth, others still can find no hurt in trying their own version of it. But the twist in the story is that the mirror may show a different image. The mystical reflection can either be the man of your future, or the mirror can conjure the image of the Devil.)

It would probably be a risk to try, but Clarissa didn't think so. She sat on a chair by her study desk lit by only a single lamp. The light was a bright yellow, like a blazing candlelight in a middle of a completely dark room. She was lonely, but she didn't think so again. There was a stock of candles in the storage room, she knew there was, and she was thinking of getting one and do her own version on the mirror here in her room. The twist, she wasn't thinking of it. She was too buoyed up in hopes to think of seeing the Devil in the mirror instead. For an educated woman, you'd think she would be better than playing real dice with a myth.

She set herself before the mirror with the candle in her hand. She had lighted it and had turned the lamp on her desk off, and right now, she was smiling at her own reflection. A silk night gown flowed over her body as she stood there. The flame of the candle danced on the wick as if the darkness had played a piece of music around. On the mirror she could see that her shadow had also swayed along with the light, like it was dancing tango with the flame.

But the real music was just about to be played.

She began to whisper, "Show me the man I am going to marry." Silence followed at the sways of the candlelight. She let it last a minute before whispering again, but still the same silence ensued. Nothing happened. Nothing showed on the mirror save for her reflection and the rest of the room that went in and out of the light. She stared blankly at herself on the glass.

"Please show him to me." Her voice started to sound a little desperate, apparently skidding loose from her natural tone of voice.

She began to apply some tune to the plea, thinking a chant was what was ought to be done instead, and repeated it a couple of times. The flame had now eaten up a quarter of the candle. Her desperate eyes looked as if they were apt to start a fire. She was getting a little impatient now. "Show me Robert Bermudez, for God's sake!"

Then she heard a short snapping sound from the mirror, and saw that one of the four sides of the rectangular glass now bore a small crack. Instantly she turned from being a little impatient to being a little crept out. For a fleeting second she stood in disbelief and somehow thought she had caused it. Then came a soft gust of cold wind blowing around the room, putting out the tiny flame of the candle. Darkness immediately settled in, around Clarissa and around the whole room.

What happened next was to leave a large blot in her mind and never to leave it until the end.

The sound she heard a while ago resounded in the next few seconds, before the room was suddenly filled once more with light. But it was coming from the mirror. Clarissa saw clouds of smoke on the glass gradually slipping out of it through the crack that had now crossed its sides. Her reflection on the mirror was wrapped around in flames.

She stood aghast from what was happening. The candle slipped out from the grip of her hand. But what followed next made the terror more terrifying. The fire wrapping her reflection on the mirror was creeping toward the entire room seen on the background. Then a pair of claws began to move up over her shoulders, five fingers on each with extremely long and pointed nails. Clarissa's surging fear had maxed out of her control.

A voice followed along the horrifying sight. It came from behind her, seemingly from a long way underneath the ground. It was the Devil slowly making an entrance into the picture. The voice mumbled something, but Clarissa couldn't make out any words discernible.

"Who . . . who are you?" Clarissa's voice was shaking. She closed her eyes and quietly hoped someone would pull her out of this nightmare now.

"I am the Devil, of course," the thing answered. "You called upon me."

It was real. Clarissa began to sob.

"Oh, hush, my darling," the Devil resumed. "Why don't you open your eyes and take a look at me? Come, Clarissa." She felt the Devil's hands touching her closed eyes, but to her amazement, she didn't feel the pointed nails or the burning skin she expected. The hands were warm and harmless.

She slowly opened her eyes and the hands retreated away from them. She looked into the mirror and felt relieved. The smoke had gone, the crack on the glass disappeared, and the abominable thing was no longer standing there behind her. Instead, she saw a man, a smiling man, the man she had so wished to see since the start of that all.

"Clarissa," the man said.

"You . . . I . . ." Clarissa was too much at awe. She reduced herself into tears again, and this time it was out of relief.

"Why? What is it, Clarissa? Come, don't cry anymore. You don't have to be afraid of me."

In a sudden, as if from a quick impulse that she lost control for the moment, she wrapped her arms around Robert Bermudez. She had her face away from the direction of the mirror lest she would see the Devil again. Her fears had grown to extreme a while ago. She would have that mirror thrown, smashed, burned, whichever would make it devour its own horror.

The surge of fear seemed to be lost inside her, but one could see that it had been a better thing that she decided to face away from the mirror, because on it, what she was really embracing was the Devil itself, and she was burning, naked, and bloody all over.

Two. P. P.

It ended up as a dream. It was, she thought. The last thing she remembered before the time she thought she had fallen asleep was wrapping her arms around his body, refusing to look at the mirror, and finding warmth in that surreal sequence of events. Perhaps it had only been a dream—the Devil, the blaze on the reflections on the mirror, her own bedroom being swallowed by the furious conflagration, even the presence of Robert Bermudez inside that very room. That could have been nothing but just the frantic motions of her thoughts encased in a deep slumber. It had been both a nightmare and a sweet dream.

She jumped out of her bed and glanced at the mirror. It all felt so real, all felt like it wasn't a dream at all. It was a picture of the highest resolution. Maybe it had been real after all. Her mind couldn't discern whether her eyes were shut at those moments she felt so terrified and then so relieved at the end. She was at a loss for judgment.

But it didn't seem possible, all of it, supposing it was set on the plane of reality. The Devil and his pointed claws, the horrifying voice, the scorching fire that wrapped her body, the sound of the crack creeping over the glass like a lightning fork, the darkness itself. There was intense fear in her mind as she allowed these thoughts to parade inside. But none of it seemed really possible.

Then the conflict arose.

These thoughts formed a line. Robert Bermudez standing behind her, the embrace she gave him while her heart was beating in the melody of her dissolving fear, the feeling of being safe in his arms. They all felt so real too. The same highest resolution. With them, she wanted to discard her initial wish that what had happened was just a dream. She could smell him, a scent so manly and seductive that she was willing to give him the night, only if she hadn't fallen asleep. She felt quite bad for that near chance and how it had slipped away, even if it could be just a make-believe. But how would she ever hope that those weren't all real?

She looked at the mirror. Her thoughts, those passing pictures in her mind, were just fleeting signals through her nerves. It didn't take a minute for them to come and go. Now she had fixed her eyes on the mirror, and then she thought she saw something . . .

There! It was really there! Instantly she stopped thinking of anything else when she saw it. There was the very proof she both wished and not, whichever tide of emotion she catered while thinking. There was the tell-tale crack screaming at her of how dark the previous evening had been, and how bright it had been as well. She drew a terrified smile on her face.

She wondered if that was enough of a proof. The smile slowly faded from her lips. She shifted her look around. And that ended it all. How could it all be true if she could see that the room, while it was devoured by fire during last night's episode, showed no tell-tale signs of it presently?

This time sadness outweighed her relief. He had not been here. It could have been just a dream after all.

Close your eyes, dear.

The voice had come from behind her, and she could feel the breath of it brush against her nape. She wasn't afraid though. She began to move her head immediately to face whatever or whoever was there, but her neck suddenly wouldn't turn, as if some force had locked it in its position.

You don't have to be afraid, dear. I came here not to cause harm. I am here to help you rather.

"What do you mean?" Clarissa asked, not from a fearful tone, but from excitement. "What help?" For a brief moment she thought it was a Genie, or a fairy godmother.

Anything.

Anything, she thought. It rang around her ears. There are so many "anything's" that she wanted help for. Her nursing licensure, a successful career of it possibly, a lot of money. Just basically everything the world could offer her, and perhaps, especially perhaps . . .

Especially Robert Bermudez.

Yes, in her head she was quick to respond. The nursing licensure, the career, the wealth, the material happiness were all lost so hastily. Yes, of course, that man.

"I don't know if you can help me on that one," she rather said. "Robert Bermudez is not an ordinary person in this town. Surely there are a lot of other women out there who equally desire him, the whole population of women in this town no doubt . . ."

And why would it not be you?

The interruption immediately brought her to silence. She repeated it in her head: and why would it not be me? Yes, why would it not be her after all? Who in the whole town was more beautiful than her? Who in the whole town has finished college like she did? She was an absolutely different fish than all these other women in this town. Robert Bermudez could be hers. Why would it be impossible?

She started to make up her mind. Of course, a little help would do.

Close your eyes, dear.

Yes, I will, she said to herself, almost unwaveringly. She closed her eyes and saw a series of pictures in the darkness of their lids. She could see Robert Bermudez, smiling, coming up to her, as if they were in a romantic movie and he was her leading man. She could see the seaside, and they were walking along it, hand in hand. They were sharing an endless flurry of smiles. And then she saw a huge sphere of what turned out to be the Earth. They were floating somewhere in the space, and she held his hand, thinking, I could live in a vacuum if we were together.

Yes, you could, dear. And you can open your eyes now.

She opened them.

She opened her eyes in a dizzy state, and felt very feeble. She felt as if she had come from a whole day of running. Haze enveloped her vision.

She lied on a bed where sheets of blanket—off-white hued and some soiled—were wrapping her legs up to her torso, missing and revealing her flat stomach, and then covering her breasts. As she tried to get up, a fleeting sharp pain struck her belly. Right now, she was all confused.

This is no more a dream.

She insisted on getting up, fueling her attempt with the need to know what was going on, where this place was, and who had brought her here. She looked around in slow glances, feeling her neck ache with every movement. She felt as if her head was filled with water. Some nerves in it throbbed painfully.

It was dim inside the room, while her vision continued to be blurred with haze. There appeared to be a window on the nearby wall, but the set of wooden jalousies in it was all but shut closed. Few rays of light managed to pass through the slits between them and bounced on the wooden floor. It was the only illumination serving the room and Clarissa's scant vision.

She hoped to hear the voice again: the one that had commanded her to close her eyes and then open them to this hazy scene. Once more she struggled between deciding whether to believe that what she's currently in was all real or that she's merely being played by her own imagination. The pain and the weakness possessing her body were too unbearable to dismiss thinking this wasn't real.

"Good morning, princess," was the words of a voice that suddenly went through the cold air. Soon, a shadow of somebody fell onto her sight, onto the bed, and onto her limp and nude body. The palpitations of her heart leapt into a crazy rate.

"Where . . ." she tried to speak but that first word sent a shrill ache in her throat, and she felt discouraged from speaking again. But she badly needed to speak. "Where am I?"

The man's face became clear to her at last after he took a few more steps toward her and sat on the bed just beside her naked body. Suddenly she lost knowledge of what to feel.

"Robert Ber . . ."

"Hello, Clarissa," Robert Bermudez spoke, a grin creeping up his lips. He reached for the hand of Clarissa which she put over her legs. When she finally realized that they had been bare open to the eyes of the Bermudez boy, she drew the blanket up to conceal them. To this the man grinned a much wider grin.

Clarissa tried to remember what had happened before she had opened her eyes and found herself inside this room. Yes, the night before, she recalled, she had seen the Devil in the mirror, the fire eating up her room and her body, the crack creeping on the opaque glass, Robert's sudden appearance after she had closed her eyes from fright, the embrace . . .

And then waking up again, the conflict she had with her thoughts over deciding to believe if it was all a dream or not, and the voice telling her to close her eyes, which she did. *Which she did without hesitation.*

Her mind blew tempest within itself. How could I have closed my eyes to the command of a voice that came out of nowhere?

I am here to help . . .

And help it did. "Did you hear that?"

"Hear what, my dear?" Robert asked.

"Someone . . . something." Clarissa couldn't say things straight. She repeated "someone" and "something" almost a dozen times after. The nausea she felt a while ago which had waned down came up to her again.

"We're in a room." Yes, she could see that. "And we made love like we really cared." Yes, we did. I am stripped, and you are here. With me. On this bed. Yes, we did, my Robert, my love . . .

Like we really cared.

It was the voice's turn to speak.

Watch what happened, my dear.

One by one, the scenes of what had taken place flashed like in a projector inside her mind. From the bed in her room she got up, she walked toward the mirror, she talked to her reflection, she ran out and went back holding a candle, she lit it up, closed the light on her desk nearby, she watched herself in the mirror, she sang like a crazy woman, she screamed, she sobbed, she closed her eyes, she stretched her arms forward as if to embrace someone but all there was and what she embraced was dead cold air. And then she walked lifelessly back to her bed and slept like nothing happened, she woke up the next day and walked again toward the mirror, and "Was it a dream?" and "It's real. I hugged Robert, he was there" passed, someone knocked on the door, she opened it and saw her mother, they talked but she couldn't hear what it had been about, and then she walked out, into the living room, into the terrace—

Someone was there. She recognized him. It was Ben.

The voices were faint. "Robert wants to see you." "Now?" "He wants to ask you out for a date." Smiles. "Tonight." Smiles.

Happy Clarissa.

And then the scenes her memory had skipped. She found herself sitting across Robert, dining in what looked like a classy and expensive restaurant. He was talking to her but his voice was inaudible. She smiled all the time. He poured some wine into her glass, and then into his. He gave one more quick motion to her glass, but she didn't see it. She was distracted. Nothing seemed to catch her attention but the eyes that were gazing at her and what words his lips were saying to him. She just smiled, all through the moment.

Sleep. Sleep, Clarissa. This is what you wanted. This is what you asked. This is the starry side of your dreams. Sleep. Feel it, my dear. Drink the emotions. Feel its sweetness in the palate of your mind. Sleep, Clarissa. Think of dreamy thoughts.

Clarissa's head swirled around. Her half-closed eyes danced around a carousel. She was smiling momentarily, frowning at times, and then laughing hysterically as if she was on a comedy show on TV. Two people were sitting beside her, she in between. She would look at them and smile. She had been like a wasted woman who had imbibed a whole tank of liquor.

From either side she could hear murmurs and whispers. But she had fallen into unconsciousness.

When the drug had gradually slipped out of her system, she opened her eyes slowly to a sight of two naked men standing nearby. She found she was lying on a bed, the same one in fact upon where she lay the last time she had awakened. Her strength was not enough for her to fully open her eyes. Her nauseous mind was still beaten up and any chance of questioning what had happened and where she was still denied her.

Still she didn't give in to her current feebleness. She had strength, a meager one, enough to open her eyes a fraction wide of the widest their lids could stretch. She could speak perhaps, she could ask the two men, naked and standing beside her, to tell her what had happened, where she was, and why they were . . . and why she was bare and stripped as well? A rush of fear swiftly possessed her, absorbing her scanty strength, taking hold of her.

The two men started another round of her.

But there was not enough of that little strength she had to stop them.

Three. Voices.

"What shall we do with her now?"

"What else, of course?"

She had a dream. She was standing on the edge of a cliff looking over a very deep abyss. There was a continuous gusts of wind slapping against her face, and when she moved her eyes downward, she had seen how close she really was from a very bad death. A very bad one it would be.

Still the voices managed to enter her ears. She was alone; she was solitarily looking at the vastness in front of the cliff. Who was there to hear the voices from?

But then there already had been voices from absent sources at the start of all this horror.

It was the two men, now clothed, who were talking in the midst of her dream. It faded gradually, and soon she had gained some sort of awareness, although still a little hazy as ever, of where she was, and who they were. This was not the help she wanted from the voice that talked to her before. She didn't wish for fear to consume her, she didn't wish for this nightmare.

Let me jump off the cliff.

"Where are we taking her?"

"You're taking her somewhere," Robert Bermudez said, sitting beside Clarissa in her dark-tainted car, "and I have to go to my campaign rally. You already know what to do, Ben. Don't be a fool."

"Are you sure about this, boss?" Ben asked. He sat on the front seat beside the Bermudez family driver. The latter had been shutting his ears for many years. So many things had knocked on his conscience at that length of time, but seeing the image of his poor wife left at home, and his starving children, he had been reduced to a life of all drive and no talk.

"You dumb rat! Of course I am!" the young man screamed from the rear seat. "Do you plan to get behind bars and have me lose this stupid election?"

"No, boss. Of course you're sure about this."

Robert finished with the last button of his long-sleeves polo and said, "Drop me off at the corner." The car stopped and he went out. Ben switched seat to where his boss had sat beside the seemingly unconscious Clarissa, falling in and out of her dream. There seemed to be a thick mist in her vision and in her thoughts, but her fear had been very vivid, stinging her heart.

Jump off the cliff.

It was the voice again. The words came in clearly through her ears, as if it came from an entity that did not belong to the scene inside the car. Clarissa feebly mumbled a reply, "Bring me back to that dream. I want to be alone. Let me jump . . ."

"What?" Ben said. She spoke in a low voice and failed to imply any meaning in her words to her audience inside the car. But she had intended them to be heard by the other one.

"Let me jump off the cliff."

"Cliff? Oh, yes. We are on our way to the cliff."

The car speeded out of the town onto the remote mountainsides. Yes, there were cliffs, hundreds of them, and Clarissa could jump on each of them if she wanted to. There were no more houses along the road where they drove, a perfect choice of a place to clean up their mess. One more turn and they stopped. Beside a very deep cliff.

In less than a few minutes from now the most beautiful face of the town will be rolling down into the drop toward her end.

Ben grabbed her by the hair and pulled her out of the car. She screamed in pain through the drag, letting the noises echo through the mountainous terrain before them.

"You can scream all you want, Clarissa." Ben wasn't bothered. He knew it was impossible for anyone other than him and the driver to hear her from where they were. They were in a different world. This was a world where the Bermudez could silence even the winds and tie the mountains shut from bringing the echoes singing against them.

Don't scream. Jump, my dear.

"Help me. You told me you will. This wasn't what I was asking for."

Ben could not understand her from since a while ago, and he paid no care this time. It wouldn't really matter now whatever the woman says.

Clarissa's mind turned numb. She couldn't feel anything anymore. Not the vehement grip of Ben's hands on her hair, pulling it so strong the strands were apt to get loose from her scalp, not even the cold wind slapping her face. She was about to lose her consciousness again.

Tell me the things of your fancy.
Tell me everything you wanted.
Tell me. Sing it to me.
Give me your soul.
"I will . . ."
Bang!
What do you want?
"I want to live."
Why?
"I will . . ."

It was all dark around her. Her eyes were open, she was sure they were. But there was not a strand of light that they could perceive. Full dark. She suddenly got afraid she might have gone blind. She stretched out her arms into the deep dark in front of her but her arms, she found out, had been gone, seemingly ripped from her body. She tried to walk forward but her feet had been going stiff, although she felt a fleeting relief knowing that she still had them connected to her body. In a second that feeling was gone. All emotions surging in her heart, she started to cry.

No noise around but her sobs.

"I want to die . . ."

You will be.

"Then where am I? Why can't I see anything? Where are my arms? Why can't I move my feet? Tell me! Is this death already?" Sobs.

Yes, my dear. But you're here for a purpose. You're arms aren't gone. I'm holding them. I locked your feet. I snatched your eyes. You are good as dead, my dear.

"Purpose?"

A deal.

"What are you talking about? What deal?"

Your soul. That miserable soul of yours. That wreck of a soul that's clinging helplessly onto your dead body.

"I want to die. Please end this." Sobs.

Wait until you hear of the terms.

"I don't understand you. I won't listen to you anymore. Please end this and leave me alone!"

Robert Bermudez.

The name floated like smoke inside the mind of Clarissa. She felt fear. She felt panic from the thought that Robert Bermudez was just around lurking in the dark, ready to aim at her again. She wasn't afraid to die anymore, but it still horrified her thinking that the man could still be anywhere near and that she was just within his striking distance. He had become an image of terror now unlike the fanciful image she perceived of him before these long dreadful days.

Won't it be unfair to you, my dear? He's probably on a merry cruise right now, after all he has done to you. While you're here dying like a wretch.

Clarissa did not answer, though she had heard the Devil very clearly.

You drink your own blood while he drinks the finest out there. You sob and beg to die while he lives like a king, as if nothing had happened, as if none of this had happened. As if he didn't take away your life and throw you like an animal. Helpless. Miserable. Blind. Mutilated. Futile. Dead.

Clarissa just wept harder. She was wailing loudly. Yes, they were true. The truth hurts.

And you won't answer.

Her wailings began to lighten, and in the dark she seemed to be able to see the face of Robert Bermudez, smiling, throwing a sarcastic stare at her. She could see his lips move, uttering some words but without conveying them with a sound. She read them and she can make out the words, "You're dead, you filthy cat. Ha ha ha."

"You are! You are! You piece of . . ." She went on throwing forceful strikes into the air, to the hallucination of a face she had on the blanket of darkness around her.

Do we have a deal?

"I'll kill him first. I can die after I've killed him!"

Is that an affirmative, my dear?

"You can have this wretched soul once I've burned his with my hands!"

Then sleep, Clarissa. Sleep.

Robert Bermudez was at the veranda of their huge house, talking with someone on the phone. It was more screaming than talking, peppered by occasional curses. This made the man who was walking up toward him cease his steps, turn a few paces back, and feel a slight hesitation to go on approaching him. He had a look of worry on his face. And fear.

"You clean that filthy whore, Chief, or I'll take back everything from you! Do you understand me?" Robert Bermudez cut the call before he could hear any answer from the other line. He had noticed Ben slowly coming up.

"Sir."

"You don't 'sir' me, you useless rat!"

"I killed her, sir, I swear. I shot her twice in the head and pushed her off the cliff. I saw her roll down dead. I saw her she broke her neck at the bottom. Sir, I . . ."

"Shut your dirty lying mouth, Ben. Who do you think is that woman waving in the news right now, huh? Does that look dead to you?"

"I'm sorry, sir. I can do the job again. I promise I'll have her chopped to pieces this time."

"No, no, no. It's too late. She's sung everything. The whore's attracted the whole town, and you know what'll happen next? My father will kill me. He will turn my body inside out. He will have my head on a platter. You know that, don't you? Don't you, Ben?"

Ben tied his lips together, refusing to allow the anger of Robert to swell. He knew there was no more explanation needed. Not to this man.

"But you have to know much first, you worthless rat. Before I'm dead I'll make sure you get your grave first. Hear me? You are going down first!"

He stared sharply at Ben, almost aiming to eat him up any moment. But before any course of violent action could ensue, someone made a stop. One of Robert's bodyguards stepped into the veranda, carrying the Bermudez landline telephone and informing him of a call waiting.

Robert took the phone and whispered to the bodyguard, something like, "Kill him off."

But it happened so fast. Ben saw the service firearm of the bodyguard tucked on his side and made a quick move toward it. He snatched the gun in a split second and pushed the bodyguard toward Robert.

"You rat!"

Six gunshot sounds whiffed through the evening air.

Four. The Other Side of the Deal

The deaths made the headlines the next day. Robert Bermudez and his bodyguard were shot dead by the family helper, Ben, who then shot himself in the head afterward.

Words were exchanged among the townspeople. This became more news than the previous one Clarissa had brought the past days. But everyone knew that both had been connected, only that the deaths had fished more sympathy from the people than hers. The buzzing of the sad news rang around the whole day, and the Bermudez family declared it a day of mourning.

And who didn't mourn?

She sat on her bed, crying. The windows had been kept shut since the day began, and the lamp was rendered out of use. She sat there amidst the dark, as always, because she liked it, and that was where she lived. In the dark her soul resided. She had it on a scale with the Devil.

She cried very hard, had burst into tears for more than an hour now.

Why aren't you happy, my dear?

Sobs.

He's dead. You have nothing to fear now. He won't be there in your fears anymore. Why are you crying?

"Didn't we have a deal?"

Yes, we did. Yes, we did, Clarissa. Now, we shall go to the other side of that deal.

"No! This is not in the terms of our deal." She screamed like a woman losing her sanity. Perhaps she was going insane. She was a more terrifying sight to perceive than the Devil itself. "You said I'd kill that animal! You said I would!" The screws in her mind seemed to be falling off and it was obvious that there was no more hope she could turn them tight into that crazy mind of her again.

You can see how terrified the Devil was.

Don't be mad, my dear. I understand you.

"Well I am not giving my soul to you!" Her scream measured the whole interior of the room and almost shook it from the volume it was conveyed. This completely astounded the Devil.

Alright, let us rearrange the terms of the deal. Of course you can reconsider that one, my dear.

Clarissa stood up in complete disarray of thoughts. Her tumultuous screams abruptly died away into the air. Her eyes dropped from the burst of tears she let fall, her hair doodled to make a nest out its dry strands, and her weak body seemed to be just a puppet walking with strings hooked to her limbs and controlled by somebody on the ceiling. But it was just her own devastated mind holding these strings together.

She went to her desk, not minding that she was pacing through the dark. Her mind was in control of her, seizing her completely, pushing her off the brink of sanity, into the deepness of the cliff. She didn't give a thought about struggling through the blindness of the room.

Let me jump off the cliff, her mind was telling her. How sweet it was to die than to go on living in this miserable world.

Please step off from that death, my dear.

"Why do you care?"

Because you can do more than kill yourself right now.

She was delirious. Things were coming in and out of her mind. There were other things her eyes were picking up while she was submerged in the darkness of the room. And then two white figures started walking around her, stepping up on her bed, and jumping back down. But they did not reach the floor. They ended up hanging from the ceiling by nooses that suddenly had encircled their necks. They had been Robert Bermudez and Ben when she looked up.

"Burn in Hell!" Clarissa screamed in a sudden. She stretched out her arms and grabbed their suspended feet, pulling them down in a succession of vehement screams, "I'll break your necks, you pieces of shit!"

They crashed down to the floor, and, grabbing a penknife from her desk, she stabbed them rapidly a thousand times, a million times relentlessly. She was cursing, up to their broken necks. She took out their visceral parts and squeezed and threw them scattering in the room. She became a picture of insanity mingled with macabre.

More. More. More.

Then an immediate thought seized her hands to a halt. The Devil was right, there was something more that she could do than wishing to die in misery. Her eyes met the Devil's and she let off a terrifying grin.

35

Tell me what the matter is.

"Bring me his soul."

And what shall you do with it?

"To possess me. To let him have my body. Take my soul and let his reside in this miserable body."

The Devil laughed. *I know. You can have it, if I can have yours.*

The day of mourning was over. The news spread out across the town like any other news could be spread. At the request of his father, Robert Bermudez was scheduled to be interred the next day after the shooting.

A strong downpour of rain greeted the fateful day, but the interment was still a go. It was expected that the whole town population would be attending the funeral rites, and they all did so, despite the torrential shower that had begun to wash over the town. Anyone from a plane or a helicopter overhead would think there was an umbrella festival going on. But a festival is not supposed to be this gloomy, and mournful.

Audible sobs and wailings and lamentations filled the weather of the town. They loved that man, perhaps maybe even worshipped him to a point. It was an intense throng of emotional people that maybe Ben had in fact done a perfect move shooting himself dead after he had taken the beloved man down. Otherwise, he would probably be hanging on the town hall front entrance right now, with a marred face, or quartered, or perhaps burnt alive. Watch the grieving children of the corn—

They filled the cemetery. Men, women, even children. The funeral car had to stop for almost ten minutes when it reached the gate. There were too many people standing on the way. People from every corner started shouting, and pushing each other to get the perfect spectator spot and the perfect view by the time they take Robert Bermudez's coffin out of the hearse. But, as of the moment, a lot of them were blocking the road.

Two gunshot sounds dashed through the air, and a yell followed: "Okay, anybody who doesn't step aside will have a ticket to the ground right where he is standing. Who volunteers?" Instantly the sea of people parted in half, revealing the road they were blocking only a moment ago.

The march commenced. The wailings went on. The funeral car passed through the gathering of sad faces of men and women before stopping by a tent. The whole Bermudez family sans Robert now was seated on chairs beneath it, everyone clad in mourning black.

Four people hurried to the back of the funeral car to take out the coffin. Another man pulled out the bier and started to set it up near a square dug hole across the Bermudez family under the tent. The people started to move close but carefully not closer. The rain began to slow.

The downpour made some parts of the cemetery soil moist and muddy, and when one of the four men who carried the coffin stepped on one, his feet got buried a few inches down into the murky cake and made him lose his balance. He fell on one of his knees and lost hold of his corner of the coffin. It fell down with him, on him, and had he not stopped it with his soiled hand in time, its weight could have crushed his chest. The lid flipped open and the whole incident shook the corpse inside, its face smacking against the glass. The mourners around immediately rose to an uproar.

And when they saw Robert's dead face slumped on the glass panel, everyone gave out a loud unanimous air of gasp. Its eyes were bloodshot and wide open, like someone who has seen a ghost. The old Bermudez ran immediately to the area and ordered them to close the lid, shouting monstrously. Then he picked the man who had lost his balance up vehemently to his feet and pushed him aside to the lookers-on. They soon punished him for being so clumsy. After several seconds his face had turned red. The rites continued.

An old woman from the throng was making the sign of the Cross about three times and saying to herself, "Bless those eyes. The windows of the human soul."

Clarissa was stripped naked. In her room she stood before a mirror—the same mirror that had showed her the root of all this mess in her life, the same mirror that had cracked and burned and had scraped off the sanity of her mind, the mirror that had become the door that ushered her life from serenity to utter misery. *This is the wonderland that seized the lust of those men.*

There were about twenty lighted candles standing in line on her study desk, their flames reveling in different directions to the music blowing around the dim room. Scattered on the floor were her ripped apart books. There were two handcuffs and a bowl of what appeared to be several pieces of red pepper lying on the remaining space on the desk.

She held the penknife by the handle with her right hand and the fingers of the left one wrapped around the small but sharp blade. They were squeezing it. Soon blood oozed out from that hand, streaming like a red-tinged river as her fingers continued to apply more pressure to the blade, and yet her face did not show a bare trace of pain in it. It was as if her mind was not even there at all. Gone to someplace else. Insanity had numbed her entirely.

With the fingers of that same hand she pressed the wick of one candle standing on the desk, immediately extinguishing the flame. A thin line of smoke rose up from the wick like how they would portray a soul seeping out of a newly deceased body. She held the knife high up to her shoulders and threw another blazing stare into the mirror. Her eyes were looking there, seemingly imploring her heart to just shut its valves and let her wonderland just die. But now was not yet the right moment to die. And then in slow motions she chopped the nipples of her breasts. The blade slashed into those dangling pieces of flesh in a manner of movement like it was not tied up to her nerves. No pain at all. Blood trickled down her body. After this torture, she grabbed some of the pepper in the bowl and stuffed them "down under," where many men had wished to stuff their own "down under" before. Before she became the woman who grew the guts to accuse the most respected man in town a crime he was too pure to ever commit. She pushed it the farthest that she could inside of her. She put out two more candles afterward, in a similar way as she did on the first. After all these, she still showed no sign of being in pain. She then broke and sliced three fingers of her right hand, put out another candle, and for the next moments that followed, she had wounded her body enough to make the Devil skip lunch at a sight of her. She squeezed the remaining pepper in the bowl until its juice spread over her palm. She held it up high and then wiped it in her eyes, those bloodshot eyes, those windows of a soul so miserable and cold.

Only one candle left.

She stepped onto her bed and reclined against the headboard. "Cuff me to the bed."

As you wish.

The handcuffs floated through the air and went to each of her wrists, cuffing them to the post at each side of the headboard. The pepper in her eyes seemed to have set them aflame. She was completely drenched in her blood.

And with all the strength and breath she had had left, she screamed at the top of her lungs, "Go to Hell, Robert! Go to Hell! Go to Hell where you belong!" The wind blew around the room and hit the flame of the last candle. It went out.

What followed next was someone shouting tumultuously in the blind.

Mickey, Dead at Sea

He opened his eyes. Slowly, slowly, slowly. And like a computer waking up from sleep mode, the pending thoughts inside his head prior to the brief stint he took in the dream world popped up back along with his regained consciousness. There are thoughts that just wouldn't die, you know. Sleep isn't a murderer of thoughts. He wished he had thrown his head against a hard concrete wall instead so that perhaps these thoughts would be annihilated for good. But here he was, waking up to those nerve signals again, consuming them all in his chaotic little brain.

He rose up from the couch he had slept upon to a sight of a cluttered table in front of him. Empty cans of beer, ashes of cigarettes and cigarette butts, pieces of papers, and photographs. These photographs, at the sight of them, made up the most of the weight of his thoughts than the rest of the things around them. The photographs! These damn photographs! *Why haven't I thought of burning them?*

But, no! He still needed them. He still needed these loathsome frozen images. Beside them was a bottle of household poison. He had contemplated drinking from the bottle last night before he thought better of it and pushed himself to pass the rage off with some other liquid to drink. The bottle of poison remained there unopened. The madness had seized him, but at that point there still had been a space in his mind for a piece of rational judgment. A dark piece of it, it was.

He stood up and walked to the kitchen. The little window above the sink told him about the morning daylight. The wall clock on the other side said it was already nine. His stomach grumbled, like it was gurgling of the tank of beer he had put in it last night. That time he readily transformed into a thirsty camel and he answered his thirst by letting red horses kick him out of unconsciousness. He looked at his stomach, and said, "You want me to cut you off this body and let you find your own food?"

He turned his eyes to the stack of knives beside the gas stove on the tiled sink. *Slit you? Or maybe not. There is another one more delightful to slit than you.* He could hear himself laugh maniacally as those words slipped soundlessly out of his head. The intangible laughter only died down when the thought of Mickey once more entered it. In an instant the entire breadth of his mind got seized by Mickey, the smiling Mickey in those photographs.

The stack of knives appeared like gold bars as he let his brain consume the images of Mickey and Sandra. It was a pensive thinking, and the void picture of the kitchen sink before him projected vivid scenarios of the two: laughing happily, throwing mocking glances at him, their tongues entwined in a kissing scene playing to stir his already disconcerted mind. The rage just lurking inside him grew into storm clouds.

Now, where are they?

He remembered immediately about the trip she had told him in passing. At the time it came to him merely like a whistle, now it sounded like a trumpet horn blown right into his bare ear. A team building, she said. A stupid team building. That had been before the photographs. A month ago, he skimmed into some emails in Sandra's inbox. Work related stuffs, and the like. Nothing really interesting to him. She is an office-girl working in an outsourcing company, in night shifts, two cities away. He scrolled down the messages, his eyes starting to feel heavy then, when suddenly they caught blaze upon one message he immediately thought had no business being in a work email. The subject was "Babyluv."

Babyluv? He jumped out of slouching on his chair and clicked the message open.

Hey there, munchkin. Want some milk with your coffee? My pipe's got all you want. Call me.

A nuclear bomb detonated inside his head. He was about to click the reply button, already enraged, deciding on confronting the sender of the email, but a click in his mind stopped him. *I got to be sure. Got to be.* He clicked the reply button and typed:

Babyluv, my phone got soaked while I was in the shower. Can you send me your number again?

He clicked the send button, fired up in his seat, eager for a reply. *Give it, you son of a bitch. Give it.* An hour after, a blazing hour it had been, the reply arrived. From the *babyluv*. A cell phone number. He saved it, but decided to put what he called the investigation on the hands of a friend. Find proof of Sandra's affair with this *babyluv*. After a month of painstaking wait, and pretense of still being blind of the suspected infidelity, a news came. Mickey, the cockshit *babyluv*, had been moonlighting with his girlfriend, Sandra.

He heard his stomach grumble, wanting of food. As he stood there in the kitchen, in a sinister pondering, within the sceneries of his imaginative mind, the time fleeted by like cigarettes alit. He opened a can of corned beef and stacked it all inside his mouth, eating everything of the stuff in one raving mouthful.

His head buzzed like bees on fire. *Babyluv, milk, pipe*, team building, the beach. Yes, the beach. They were going out on a trip to the beach. She and his boss, the *babyluv* Mickey.

He ran to his room in a flash, thinking nothing else now but killing. The claustrophobic room ran down to his nerves as he quickly sought his way underneath the bed. Oh, how he could smell the scent of his Sandra on the bed! But under it, he could smell the fumes of a dead Mickey's body. He spent the next minute under the bed and got out and up on his feet with a .45 in his hand.

Let the show begin.

He rode his motorcycle sticking the needle to a constant hundred. No time to waste after all. The beach was only an arm's length away now. He could smell the breeze already, smell the fire and the smoke bellowing out of his gun. Smell the sweetness of one good revenge.

When he got there, the party was just starting. It seemed like a small gathering, a mental count of fifteen souls in our Kiddo's head, to be a point less later. He hid behind a parked multicab, and quietly observed the ongoing event. The .45 tucked in his shorts went along with a tattered sleeveless top and a pair of Spartan's slippers. Dressed to kill.

Later he caught sight of Sandra. And guess who she was with, sitting next to each other, cuddling maybe: our *babyluv*, good-as-dead friend. He slowly slipped out of his hiding place and walked toward them. The to-be assassin tiptoed on sand behind the two, their eyes toward the sea. Slowly he pulled the firearm out from his side, now and then watching around for intruding eyes.

When the steps left to be taken were reduced to a good two or three, his tiptoeing escalated to a full-speed run, and at the end he grabbed the bastard Mickey by the neck. He shot one bullet up the air, and screamed: "Hey, *babyluv!*"

Mickey fell to the sandy ground and looked at his attacker with startled eyes.

The party began to trickle into the circle made by the three, nevertheless reluctant to squeeze closer upon the knowledge of a firearm involved, which had now been recklessly swung from side to side by its slinger.

"Anyone desires to stop me, you're free to join this boy here!" he said, pointing the gun now at the stiffened Mickey's temple.

Mixed protests and verbal restraining attempts rang out from the crowd. But he had already gone mad. Mickey couldn't pay for a struggle. The gun had been pointed at his head like how he had pointed his pipe at the wrong hole, and anytime it might puke a bullet into his skull, should he try to move anything provoking. The horror was just beginning, nevertheless.

"Hey! Hey! Guys!" he, the gunman, screamed. "I'd like to tell you everything first, before we continue with the show. Lend me your ears, people. This here boy, and that there girl. They've been playing hide the pickle behind me for months! See that! See that!" He grabbed his crotch and shook them, with the gun on his other hand still on Mickey's head. "Silly boys. Who wants milk in their coffee? And you, girl, I have them all you can have. I'm pretty rich, you know."

"Stop this madness now," Sandra answered, weeping. "Put the gun down. Let him go."

"Oh, so now you're crying? Why start now?"

"What do you want?" Mickey spoke.

"Can't you tell by the hand cannon up there at your stupid head!" And then he shot both feet of Mickey and dragged him by the hair. He took him toward the sea, where a *banca* was docked by the shore. He took the screaming Mickey, now attempting a struggle, into one of them. "I'll pay the rent for this when I come back!" He screamed behind them, apparently to no one.

He laid Mickey on one end of the *banca* and took a seat on the other, and then he started rowing. The people ran frantically toward the shore, as if to stop them, when they most likely could not.

He rowed as fast as his adrenaline could fuel him, and in a couple of minutes they had gone out a long way from the beach. The people seemed only dots from where they were. A little later, he stopped rowing and pointed the gun again to Mickey's face.

"How does a mermaid taste when you're eating it on another's plate, *babyluv*?"

"You're crazy!"

"Oh, let's talk."

"What do you want from me, you lunatic?"

"I have told you already. And don't forget who's looking at the end of barrel."

Mickey sealed his lips.

"Good. Good."

They fell into an uncomfortable silence. He, the gunman, looked out to the shore and caught a glimpse of a flickering light coming from afar. Sirens wailed afterwards. The police were coming.

"They're coming now," Mickey said. "Why don't you just let me go?"

"That sounds fun." He grabbed the feet of Mickey with each of his hands and lifted them. The *banca* was rocking over the unsteady fabric of the sea. "I am letting you go now." He lifted Mickey's feet out into the water.

"No, please." Mickey gripped on the wooden sides of the *banca*. So he, the gunman, shot both his hands.

"You did say I should let you go." He pushed the remaining part of Mickey's body still on the *banca* out into the sea. "There. There. Swim, you bastard! Swim! Go forth!" He shot Mickey in the head.

He saw the body pulling out of its life, slowly descending into the depths of the water. He reclined back on his seat, and smiled at the clouds. How pretty they seemed. The sun was blazing in his eyes. Oh, what victory! What feeling of bliss it is to be served by a platter of one fulfilling revenge.

"I think a smoke will do."

Bang! goes the .45.

Awards Night

It didn't come as a surprise when he got nominated for the Best Actor in a Leading Role category for this year's awards. This was the third nomination he received in a row. The first one he won, convincingly so—the fifth win in his fifty-year acting career, all in the leading role category. But the second one he lost, unexpectedly, in the acting hands of a young, up-and-coming actor for a role in a romantic comedy. And that was what pissed the veteran thespian off.

So it didn't come as a surprise either that his manager and long-serving friend, Dom, had been waiting for an hour in the awards venue for the old actor to show up. He had thought about the vast chance that the actor would boycott the ceremony, but he had talked to him, and pleaded with him beforehand, so it gave him a little bit of an optimistic probability that the actor would grace the awards with an honored presence, and he had leaned on that minute chance. Now, after a dozen unanswered calls and a score of most likely unopened texts, he finally decided to drive down to the old man's house intent to drag his ass out to the awards venue himself.

It was astoundingly quiet all around the premises when he arrived, and similarly the countless knocks he had dealt the door with came unanswered. Thence the silence surrounding the place made him reconsider what he thought a while ago was keeping the old man at anchor inside his house—that he was still butt-hurt and embarrassed by his last year's loss and had made a decision to give this year's awards a cold shoulder. Now he was thinking maybe—and it came to him as a tremendous blow given the old man being old or given his being possibly depressed or sunken from shame—maybe the actor was . . .

"Oh my, God," he muttered. He ran around to the back of the house thinking the back door leading to the kitchen was open. And, by heavens, it was.

"Kirk?" Silence. He entered the actor's room and was met by its dim interior only lit by the erratic waves spewing out of the television monitor displayed on one corner. "Kirk, are you asleep?" *Kirk, are you dead?*

The old man sat on a large reclining chair facing the TV set and his back toward the door, a hand dangling over the armrest so Dom could tell he was there even though the recliner's backrest had completely concealed the other parts of the old man's body from view. Dom stood motionless for a second, still overwhelmed by his macabre presumption. There was a small table beside the chair and on it, seemingly looking straight at him, was a revolver. His feet caught fire immediately and brought him stooping between the chair with the old man and the flickering TV set.

He was fearfully expecting blood to be smeared all over the actor's body, but felt immediate relief upon seeing the otherwise. "Kirk?" he said, looking at the old man closely for a second. For that brief second, as he scrutinized the seated figure, he saw what looked like an eternity of its motionlessness. But soon the movement of his breathing came, and all turned well with Dom's racing feelings. Now he had to pull the old man out of his slumber, tell him to get his ass in the awards ceremony, and also ask what business had the gun had in the vicinity of his room.

"Kirk, wake up!"

The actor shook for a moment, attempted to return to sleep, and thought better of it when he seemed to remember something. He opened his eyes and saw the familiar face of his manservant, as he sometimes called Dom. "What are you doing here?" he asked.

"What are you talking about?" Dom returned. "Wait, tell me something first, why do you have a gun in here?"

"What?"

"The gun! What the fuck is it doing in your table?" Dom picked up the revolver, felt its weight. "Is this real?"

"Of course it is. Put it down before you hurt somebody."

Dom laid the gun back on the table, careful but quick. "What are you thinking about having a gun, Kirk? Get rid of this shit."

"Calm down, Dom. It's a prop gun." The old man took his turn picking up the revolver and proceeded to make it waltz around his palm and fingers, like a cowboy, tricks and all.

"Shit, put it down, you jackass."

"Keep your cool, will you? It's not even loaded, and I don't have anything to load it with."

"Loaded or unloaded, you throw this away. You wait to be seventy before you turn into a jackass? Where did you get this anyway?"

"I thought I have always been a jackass? Well, Susan gave it to me."

"Susan?"

"Yeah, Susan. The producer. She let me keep it."

"She let you keep a prop? You should have kept the diapers." Dom let out a laugh, to which the old actor didn't ride the wheels of.

"Ha ha. I'd die before I resort to such disgusting degradation. What the hell are you doing here, by the way?"

"Oh, shit. I forgot . . . No, shit! You forgot."

"What?"

Dom looked around the old man. "Where's your remote?"

"Why?"

"Ah, forget it." He walked toward the TV and pushed the program button a few clicks before stopping at the live coverage of the awards night. "There's where you should be right now, Kirk! In fact, you should have been there two hours ago, but it seems you have forgotten. Must be the age."

"I didn't forget about it, Dom. I simply don't give a shit."

"Old man, you are up on the best actor race this year, once again, and looking at your competition . . . I mean, they had better just handed it over to your ass right after your movie wrapped. And that would be the sixth under your belt, and that's one more than the late Peping Uno had gathered of the shit."

"Four of my five winning roles were up against Peping's."

"Exactly! I mean, no, the point is tonight's award will make history for you. No one's won the award six times, and much more all in the leading role category."

"The point is I'm a better actor than Peping was—bless his dear departed soul—and I'm a better actor than anyone you can pit against me, and no history-making award can further prove it, so I don't care about what's going to happen tonight in the awards, who's going to be the best dressed, and who's sound mixing was the most audible in the final cut."

"What are you talking about, Kirk? This is your career. This is your life's achievement. You've been acting your ass off for many years, and believe me, you have been the best there was to ever grace the country's film industry. You deserve all the recognition they give."

"Gee, you make me teary-eyed, Dom. You have your points, but my career really had ended last year. What they are doing to the film industry, their "showbiz," they're turning it into a freak show. And I'm not going to be a part of it."

"Then why did you take the part, Kirk?"

"You mean my movie for this year?"

"Yeah. Up for best picture as well."

"Well, the only thing that keeps it out of the trash—recyclable, I'm sure—is that I was in it. And as for your question: you know, just for old time's sake."

"Last year, huh?"

"Yeah."

"You were nominated last year."

"I was, and the year before it. Won it, if you forgot."

"And you lost last year."

"Yes, and wherever you're going to lead with this—"

"It's George Devanteer. You're still bawling over the travesty, and you're being like this because you, the five-time winner, lost to a newbie last year."

Kirk kept mum, fighting between admission and denial. "Well, okay! And that's what I've been trying to send, Dom. I've been working so hard in this profession, I've been playing parts the best and only way they should be played, I've been building a legacy and maybe hope for our dying industry . . . and all of it only to be derailed by a . . . what's that boy got anyway? Devanteer? He's not even a Filipino—"

"Half."

"—He grew up abroad, Dom! I bet you he doesn't even know how to take a bath with a dipper. And the son of a bitch can't even speak a word of Tagalog. What he does is wink, smile, and flirt with the supposed teenage girls comprising his viewership, and calls it acting. He isn't acting, Dom. He doesn't even deserve to be mentioned in the same sentence with acting or actor or films, for God's sake!"

"He played an Amboy coming here in the Philippines for the first time, Kirk. You can't expect him to rap like Gloc-9 in the movie. He played his role within the designated setting and the plot as it was scripted, and he kinda nailed it."

"Nailed it? What, you handling him now?"

"Ugh, listen to you. That loss will never shake the truth that you are one of a hell actor, the finest there will ever be, I would say. If it affected your name as an actor, it should be so little and so ignorable that I'm sure the year that passed had wiped it to molecular traces already."

"Well, it did affect me, Dom! I mean, the industry . . . as a whole, you know."

The television coverage showed that the guests were already requested to enter the venue and the ceremony would be kicking off in a minute. Dom heaved a sigh.

"Come on, Kirk," he said. "Attend this one, just for old time's sake. Then you can do whatever you want with your career afterward. I'll let you off your remaining contracts."

"I wish I could muster up the acting prowess to show interest toward the ceremony tonight, Dom," Kirk said. "But this profession has been my life, you know. I've respected it, for years I have dedicated so much work in it. It is more than just playing roles to make money. This is art for me. And knowing that for these past years, these ass-clowns have more than just did everything they can to disgrace the profession I so hold dear, makes me want to finally not want to be around any of these people anymore. I'm sorry, Dom. You're part of the industry, so I can understand if you won't take my words with light. Just go to the awards without me, pal. You can keep the award if I win."

The intro music of the ceremony flushed out of the TV speakers, and Dom heaved another sigh. "I won't deny feeling the same way as you are. If this wasn't my job, I'd have slammed the current status of the film industry of this country just the same as you do, Kirk. I mean, we deserve better quality of films." He moved to the bed an inch behind the chair where the old man was seated and took a space for his own.

"You should go back, Dom," Kirk said.

"Nah. I'm not up for anything. What were you watching on the TV before I was here, anyway?"

"I was going to watch a PBA game. Manila Classico."

"Manila what?"

"Manila Classico. Marketing nomenclature for the supposed rivalry between Purefoods Star Hotshots and Ginebra."

"Are those really basketball teams?"

"Well, have you watched a single PBA game before?"

"You tell me, old man."

"Well, I can tell you haven't."

Dom fumbled on the remote control. "What channel is it?"

"I can't remember the number. The cable network's got around 200 channels. Numbers just go over my head. Just flip on the channels till you find it."

"You want me to flip over 200 channels to find it?"

"Yes, how will we supposed to find it then? Just . . . just flip on them, will you?"

Dom started clicking on the program button, and it took him about a minute of clicks before finally chancing on the PBA channel. The game was still going on. "Second quarter."

"Yeah, and Ginebra's giving the new coach of Star a beating. See, this is just like that Devanteer kid. You give some new chap on the block an honor, or responsibility as large as, say, coaching a whole basketball team, and they think they own the game."

"One of the team's got a new coach?"

"Jason Webb."

"The actor?"

"No, the actor is Freddie. This is his son. He used to be a commentator, then sat as an assistant coach for Star for a year, and then was assigned as the head coach the following season—bypassing the other veteran assistant coaches for the job."

"So I'm assuming it didn't go so well with his team."

"You bet your posterior it didn't. Man, it pisses me off!"

"Which team are you siding on, anyway?"

"Purefoods."

"There's no Purefoods in there."

"The Star one, right there."

"Purefoods? Then Star? How come?"

"Well, the full name of the team is Purefoods Star Hotshots."

"Only 'Star' is written in there."

"Dom, if they put the whole thing in there, it's going to block the whole TV screen."

Dom let out a brief laugh, trying to imply that he had just been messing with the old man. "So, you've been having these ill affections about the films that keep going our way every year?"

"The film industry's on life support, Dom. These studios, they never risk their asses for a chance to innovate our films. Whatever formula is working to fill the theaters, they stick with it and milk it year per year to drought. They never cared for quality."

"Yeah, something's needed to be done. If we could just gather all these studio heads in one room and hold an intervention."

"These film festivals, I don't get the point of these events aside from all the studios' equal desires for big box office returns. We are one of just a few countries holding a film fest and what do they do with it? They keep parading these crap films during that time of the year when the rest of the world is apt to take a peek on our filmmaking capacities."

"If they could just use these events on films that are actually worth it."

"My point exactly. I mean, they don't even honor the veteran players of filmmaking. Many of us actors just grow old and die in obscurity. No wonder many of us resort to utilizing our acquired fame and celebrity status in barging our ways to other fields—politics, mostly. What do we know about public service? We have lived the numerous years of our lives in front of cameras, speaking another person's words. How does an experience in crying in front of a camera at will make any of us effective in serving the public?"

"I agree with you, Kirk. We should have some governing body, or organization that helps actors who have been out of employment—"

"It sickens me, Dom. We used to be magnificent people. Now most of us are just sell-outs."

Somewhere a telephone began to ring.

"Somebody's calling, Kirk," Dom said.

"Oh, it's just one of my old pals. He's been trying to contact me all day. He plans to run for the mayor's seat this coming election again, and wants me to endorse him. This is not the first time, as this isn't the first time that he has intended to run for mayor. I turned him down every time."

"Why? Endorsement seems easy. He's your pal, anyway."

"I don't want to dabble into politics. It's dirty, it's complicated, it's all noise." The old actor picked up the remote control. "This game's going nowhere pretty. James Yap's playing is such a pain in the eye."

"Wait, you won't finish the game? No hope for the Star?"

"They're getting beaten by the second, Dom. And I hope this Ginebra team wallow all they can in this 'success' with all the sacrifices its sister teams have made for them. The cry-babies!" He switched the channel back to the awards coverage. "I might as well see the outcomes of this freakshow. Want a drink or something?"

"Yeah, I could use some drink or something."

"I have a bottle of rhum on the cabinet." He pointed to the furniture on the other side of the room. It had been dim in that spot Dom didn't notice there was a cabinet there the whole time.

"What are these DVD's?" Dom asked when he had walked over to the cabinet and seen a stack of DVD cases beside the single bottle of rhum on there. He saw they all had the same cover.

"Reunions. You know, the TV show. It's written there."

"Yeah, I see it. You bought these? Or did Susan give these to you also?"

"No, I didn't buy them. And yes, those are from Susan. I asked for them."

Dom went back to his seat on the bed with the bottle in hand. "Anything special with that TV show?"

"Nothing much. I just liked the concept. Reuniting separated family members."

"Ah, a little tickle to your sentimental nerves." Dom chuckled. "But I'm not judging. To each his own."

The old man refused his every turn of the *tagay* that Dom ended up finishing the whole bottle himself. The next minute he passed out drunk on the bed. Later he woke up from a loud noise he became sure as soon as he picked up enough consciousness was something exploding right by his ear. He put on a defensive stance with his arms when he saw the gun Kirk was holding in front of his face.

"What are you doing, Kirk? Damn! Do you intend for me to go deaf?"

"I'm sorry, pal. It's just that . . . it had to go off. Rule says."

"What rule is that?"

"Well, never mind. It was a blank, anyway. Listen, I just got the best news today, Dom." The old man was smiling delightedly.

Doom took a glimpse at the TV monitor and saw some director speaking on the stage, holding a trophy and spewing out relentless barrage of thank you's. "What? Did you win?"

"Did I . . . no, the Devanteer kid won again. But that doesn't matter now. This is much, much better than that."

"What is?"

"My old pal just called again, and having nothing to do, I decided to answer it. You won't believe what it was he had to tell me all this time."

"The endorsement?"

"No. I won't be the ass-clown singing jingles on campaigns, Dom. My old pal has offered me the spot to be his running mate. Imagine me as a vice-mayor, man!"

Goddamn, Kirk!

O'er The Same Soil

There must be some wonderful story behind that lighted window on the third floor. Or the three roses growing on three different pots right on the ledge of that other window. Or perhaps I could write some good material from the swaying curtain hanging by that window on the fourth floor. Oh, I still believe that good old-fashioned short stories are better entertainment than any movie in those big malls.

I can't sell a story, the truth is, not anymore in this time of times. Well, if this had been ten years ago, where newspapers apparently contain more substance than they do today, then maybe I could still sell three or four stories per week. But, really, for the last three years or so, I haven't had sold a single story to a single magazine or newspaper.

My name is Tobias Vergara. I am still quite young, at thirty-two, though I have already been writing fiction since my teenage years—and was a long time ago making a good living out of it. Short stories were the gold mine of publication back then. Across the town I had once been hailed as a celebrity for my ingenious ability to churn out pretty-well received short stories, and boy did I savor every moment of it. I was a feisty and optimistic young man, and my ability to weave words was akin to how

Spiderman weaves his webs. Similarly so, with the works my busy hands produced, I flew and swung around the city's skyscrapers.

But those days apparently were already behind me.

I walked past the building with those three windows, dismayed as ever I would be. You may think that I was just taking a leisurely writer's night street walk perhaps to get my head clear, but this wasn't one of those walks. This here's actually one of the desperate walks I had been taking since the past countless nights, watching and making do with every detail I could see in this dreary part of the world. I wish I was really just taking a leisurely walk, I do. Smoking cigarettes, taking note of everything there was to see, and then forgetting them soon after, unless they sparked something in me. But as much as I really don't smoke, I really wasn't out walking for leisure. Truth be told, I walked in every chance for hope that some night, this or another one in the nights ahead, something might just suddenly impact me so imperatively I could churn out a good short story, or a novel even, by it. Some work that was finally worth something—some work that might get me ahead of the line once more.

But so far, after numerous nights now, nothing had yet struck me.

I walked the highway now, watching the beaming lights all around me—from all these cars and motorcycles, and all these tall buildings that had sprouted out of the city premises so rapidly as if they were once just monggo seeds somebody had scattered around the place. In every direction I looked, I could see busy people walking and talking and working. A lot of them seemed happy, seemed optimistic, and seemed successful. They had all the things that had eluded me for a long time now. They were doing well, doing fine, and they weren't starving.

The snare drummers inside my stomach had gotten to work. When was the last time I ate, by the way? I hadn't had dinner, and stretching farther back into the day, lunch had also been skipped. The last time I had something in my stomach was last morning—a breakfast of lukewarm coffee and stale bread I purchased for half the price of freshly-baked ones. For the love of Ray Bradbury, give me something to eat!

I stopped in a blinding stream of light, and found myself standing in front of the entrance of what appeared as a push, almost glittering restaurant. Through the glass partition I watched as the busy goings-on inside—the guests eating in the midst of conversations, rattling percussion of utensils and porcelain, and waiters moving around taking and serving orders—made the snare drums in my stomach gradually escalate into a whole orchestra. The luxury, the richness, the appetite, and the mood of the evening inside beamed before me like a flame in an oil lamp where I'm the moth keenly watching. Here before me now was a picture of the city full of businessmen, of people of note, of a populace that differed from most of us by the carats of their sweat. And as I looked at them, a sudden flush of a lifetime's regret and despair crept into me. I should have been somewhere inside this place right now.

As I continued to watch the scene, suddenly I had this out-of-the-blue auditory hallucination that God greeted me a good evening. Such a surreal imagining, like someone lost in space. Then it came again, "Good evening, sir." It didn't sound dreamy this time. This time it felt human. I turned my face about and saw the God I thought the greeting had come from—but it was rather a man, dressed formally and neat and looked as someone out of the people inside the restaurant.

The stranger smiled at me, a welcoming one.

"Me?" I asked, pointing to myself.

"Yes, sir. Good evening." The smile lingered in the man's lips, and the look of his eyes complemented the congeniality of it. "How do you do, sir?"

"Just fine, I guess. Have I . . . have I done anything?"

"No, of course not. I just came to you to ask if you're available for the night. Mr. Leonard Mendoza would be delighted to have you as his guest for dinner." The man concluded his statement with apparent pleasure, and the welcoming smile was still on his lips.

"Mr. Leonard Mendoza? I don't think I know the man."

"Well, you will have the pleasure to get to know him shortly, sir. Will you oblige the invitation?"

I sank quietly into my thoughts, actually contemplating the offer—of course I did! Just the plain opportunity to at last fill up my rumbling stomach was more than a reason to consider the invitation, plus the equally enticing fact that I'd be answering those rumbles with a grandiose meal in a grandiose restaurant. Screw the fact that I'd be sitting with a stranger during it, or that I'd be indebted to him afterward! If I didn't eat tonight, I sure was prone to murder some unwary stranger ahead and . . . now, that's something abhorrent that was surely due to my hunger. Refusing free meals was a luxury I couldn't have.

But who was this man, anyway? Out of all the names I could recall in my past, even a stifling sense of familiarity with a Leonard Mendoza wouldn't come to me. Or maybe it was the other way around. Maybe this Leonard

Mendoza had been a fan, one of the throng of readers who formerly hailed me on a pedestal. But whoever he was and whatever he was up to with this bizarre offer, one thing was for sure for me—a full plate of sumptuous dinner would hail me on a pedestal tonight.

I heard the man heave a fleeting sigh, which brought my attention back to him immediately. "Sir?" The welcoming smile continued to touch his lips.

"Can you . . . usher me to the table then?"

He led me on toward the entrance of the restaurant, and shortly before we were about to step in, suddenly I remembered to take a look at myself, particularly the way I had been dressed. Although my clothes had been rather proper, to this restaurant, I may very well look like a transient from a decade ago. I stopped shortly, and looked at the man and back to myself. He seemed to understand my predicament, and quietly told me that it shouldn't matter. Well, then again, to be bothered by such thing was a luxury I couldn't have. I followed him through the spaces between tables and diners toward a far corner of the restaurant. He ushered me to a table, and seeing how everything had been set and made to look, I was genuinely taken aback by how earnest this Mr. Leonard Mendoza had been to this unusual arrangement.

Two waiters stood near the table, and when I looked at them, a welcoming grin appeared up in their faces. One of them gestured a hand to me, beckoning me to a seat. The other one took a bottle of wine from an aluminum bucket placed on a small table beside him. He poured some amount from it into a glass and placed it on the table in front of where I was to be seated.

I noticed the set-up of the dinner was made for three people, and one of the three chairs had already been occupied by a man, his back toward me and the usher as we came. I reckoned he had been prepared for this dinner—unlike the terms that had brought me here—since he had been dressed appropriately. For all I know this could be the generous host. He turned his head to face me, but unlike the usher and the two waiters standing nearby, this man's face showed me none of the same congenial welcome. After that brief glance, he returned his eyes back to the table and took a sip from his glass. I readily thought this might have been a wrong decision, that I might be going in for some trouble here.

The waiter greeted me a fine evening as I took my seat, and all the while I carefully eluded the momentary glances of the other man. I tried not to have to look eye to eye with him. Once seated, I took a sip from my glass, the taste bringing a fleeting nostalgia around me. After a galaxy of years, I had once again tasted an alcohol of fine taste.

Everything seemed to be set already, and apparently we were just waiting for the occupant of the last empty chair—the host of the dinner himself, Mr. Leonard Mendoza, I assumed.

A couple of minutes afterward the man finally arrived. He was rather old, but seemed to be quite energetic nevertheless. He had an enormous volume of beard down his chin and the same with the mustache up above his lips. When he had taken his seat on the table, the two waiters standing behind us abruptly went into a room on the other side of our area—the kitchen, I presumed—past a large double door, apparently to start serving our meals. The congenial smile I quietly expected beamed on the face of the old man. He glanced alternately at us two men before him as he did so.

"Good evening, friends," he said, not letting go of his smile.

I answered him the same greeting, although it came out barely audible. The other man just nodded his head once, and on a normal day, maybe backward to years ago, I would have scorned him for being such impolite to such congenial greeting, but tonight I paid no care.

"I'm glad you took my invitation," the newcomer said. "My name is Leonard Mendoza. And you, fellows?"

I felt relief to have confirmed my assumption, and I told him my name—Tobias Vergara—and the other one followed with his—Paul. His years in the street wandering completely alone, he said, had long made him drop his surname from use. To everyone, he was just Paul.

"I'm sure you're both wondering why you're here," Mr. Mendoza said. "I would regale you with the reason why I've invited the two of you to a dinner with me, a complete stranger, but I'm really starved out right now. I have just gotten off from a busy day and to tell you honestly, I was looking forward to this dinner. Do not be doubtful, do not be afraid, we're all here for a special reason in which, as I said, I will regale you with later. Just treat me as a long-time friend." He smiled as pleasantly as ever.

I got to like him instantly. The notions of mingling with a stranger didn't get in between us, except maybe for Paul, who stayed faceless in front of Mr. Mendoza. But he did seem entirely in for the dinner all the same. Three complete strangers around a single table.

The waiters arrived shortly with our food, and for the next half hour they served us with a sequence of palatable dishes that I had never had for maybe an eternity until now. I ate generously but remained reserved nevertheless. If these men had been here in the city for the last decade or so, then there was at least a fair chance that they have heard of my name, back when I was still a celebrated author. If so, then I wouldn't want them to realize the dire truth of my financial failure by weighing out table etiquette against my starving stomach. But the way things turned out after introducing myself to them told me I didn't have to concern myself with it in the first place. They didn't seem familiar with me, or who I had been in this city before.

When the meal was over, main course, desserts and all, Mr. Mendoza proposed a toast—to whom the honor was for he was to talk about in the next minutes. We drank each of our glassful of wine and seemed to begin regarding each other like long ago acquainted comrades. This dinner had turned out just fine after all.

As soon as Mr. Mendoza's blissful laughter had faded, the apparent mood of the coming sentimental recalling started to set in.

"I know you'd think me silly for what I'm about to tell you, my friends," Mr. Mendoza said. "There's something special about tonight, in fact I have been doing this every year, in this same restaurant." He paused, taking it in. "A friend of mine has his birthday today and, silly it may be, I've been celebrating it for him these past two years."

I looked at him in awe. *All this for some friend's birthday . . .*

"His name is Jose Rivera," Mr. Mendoza continued. "As old as I am, I believe. An established businessman. For thirty years and until two years ago, Jose and I had been very close friends, very close allies in the prison. I was incarcerated a long time ago for the murder of my former boss at one of my employments. I was young and daring then. I didn't back down on things that I deemed unfair or oppressive, and in this case, that boss of mine had been one hell of an oppressor. I loathed him and although I kept my emotions reserved for years, eventually it got to the point where I publicly protested against him. So when he was found dead in his room a few weeks after, they knew right away who to point a finger to. And as you might probably know, money works in ingeniously plumbed ways. They accused me, tried me, sentenced me, and then to that damp cell I subsequently ended. To tell you honestly, friends, may this have a bearing on your impression about me or not, I didn't kill the man. But our animosity made it all rational that I could have a motive. And maybe that's what doomed my whole defense in the court. Though I pleaded for my innocence, my face could not hide my satisfaction of his fate.

"I got to accept mine somehow. Years after, I became fully institutionalized and washed out of the glorious days I had when I was still a free man. I had accepted the bars as the edges of my world. I worked my ass off on prison labor, stayed the good man that I am, lived life as normal as I could. I didn't even realize I was becoming an old man inside.

"Jose Rivera came into the prison on my tenth year. Oh, he's a hopeless mess at first—paranoid, extremely terrified, unable to accept the new world he had been sent into. He was there for murder, two counts. He killed his wife when he found out that she had been cheating on him for five years. He killed the other man as well. Can you imagine the guts of that? Five damn years!

"He pleaded guilty, albeit the remorse that he felt about it. If only he could take it back, he said he would never do it. But life's been rough on my old friend.

"He was the one who told me all about this dinner tradition that he planned to do once he gets out of prison. You see, this was the very restaurant that he and his wife had first met. And to pay back, in his own way, to the dreadful act he had done to her, he planned to dine here on the night of their wedding anniversary, every year as is fitting, and invite two complete strangers to dine with him. Two people it is—because aside from the anniversary, this day was also his birthday. It sounded silly, yes. What can an annual dinner with two strangers do to appease his remorse over his guilt? But that's just his way. I won't judge. Who would judge a kind act anyway? When I was released two years ago, I told him that I was going to try out his plan on my own. I told him about it, and he gleefully agreed.

"So that same year on this very date and evening, I set up this same dinner with two complete strangers—two interesting strangers they were, indeed. That experience meant something valuable. Similarly, I told them all about my old friend, and that the dinner was his idea. And that someday, come the day when he'd be free again, he'll have the chance to do for himself this noble act. And maybe we could dine in here together—just two old pals who once shared friendship, bitterness, and time behind bars."

Mr. Mendoza lifted his glass on a signal to the waiter standing behind him. As soon as our glasses were filled again with wine, the old man beckoned us quietly into another round of toast. At that very moment, my liking of him had risen to an absolute admiration.

"Do you have a family, Mr. Mendoza?" Paul asked, immediately after we had brought our glasses back on the table. The tone with which he delivered the question seemed to me to be out of sincere and solemn curiosity.

Mr. Mendoza smiled at him before he answered, "I don't have any, Paul." Pause. "But my friend has. He has told me all about him also. A son named Anthony."

"Have you seen him?" Paul asked.

"I haven't. But I would be very glad to meet him one of these days. I'm sure he has a lot of things to know about his father in prison."

I cut in and asked, "A lot of things? Why, hasn't his son visited him there?"

"No," Mr. Mendoza said, "ever since his first day inside, Anthony never paid him a visit. But my old friend said he understood why so. The child must have been angry at him, I'm sure. They had never talked to each other again after the death of his mother, in fact."

"That's very sad," Paul said. "I'm sorry to hear it."

"But my friend didn't give up on him," Mr. Mendoza said. "You know what he did? Every month, on the date of his boy's birthday, after every frustrating month that's passing without him getting to see his son, he writes him a letter, telling him everything—his life inside the prison, his regrets, his hopes, his optimism, his desire of seeing him again—everything. For three decades, he never missed a single month of the letters, hoping that one day, Anthony would answer him, and he would see him again. My friend was always hopeful, and I know he is still now. Unfortunately, his efforts are still in vain."

What followed next was a long silence. Each of us seemed to look at each other with waiting eyes. Both of them seemed to wait for the other to speak. As for me, I waited for Mr. Mendoza to tell the further details of his story, or just anything that he wanted to speak of. I thought of keeping my own story to myself. Although the old man had been honest about his past to us, who were barely a pair of total strangers to him, I thought of regaling my failures in the past and probably still in the future a thing I should spare them with. Also, they would only look down at me with pity afterward, and I wouldn't want that.

The next thought that entered my head was the fact of me being here. It was the enticing offer of food that pushed me to agree to this dinner, but now I started to think there may be more to this dinner than the food. All things else aside, there was a story—an interesting story, a story and that was what I was walking the street earlier for in the first place. If this was the spark of inspiration that I was looking for, then maybe, just maybe, I may have already walked the right steps on the right street on the most perfect time of the year.

I felt a little out of composure with the sudden realization spinning around my head. I excused myself from the group and went to the men's room, planning to gather myself before anyone of them would think that something wrong was happening with me.

Facing the mirror inside the men's room, I began to flutter back the pages of the story that Mr. Mendoza had related. It was a subtle line, sure—it contained the factor of interest that most usually makes a story a good one. One by one I put all the details in a row, deciding on whether to use the same names, or mask them with fictitious ones. I could add some details perhaps, a little twist, or a slight tweak in some of the corners to surely make the story a one big fishing hook into a sea of readers. The glimpse of the hopeful coming days started to burn bright in front of me. I went out of the men's room feeling like a man reborn.

But Paul was no longer there when I got back to the table.

"He said he had to be home for some urgent matter," Mr. Mendoza said when I asked him. "It's something about his daughter, I think. Too bad, I still have something important to say, and I had to say it with you two together."

I sat down, timidly, wondering whatever important the old man intended to say to us.

"I owe both of you an apology," he said when I had settled down. "I really do hope I'd see Paul again. He fled too soon. Anyway, I'll just have to do my explaining to you, Tobias. Just listen, alright?"

I nodded, albeit spun in hazy thoughts.

"Would you be mad at me, perhaps, if I tell you that there were parts of what I told you a while ago that aren't true?"

I stared at him in dumbfounded silence. The feeling of betrayal surged in almost in a sudden. Of course, I felt betrayed and somehow made a fool of, and the dinner may not weigh a reason for me to rather not feel them so. But I kept the growing temper inside me and thought of asking him which parts of the story he had fabricated. I looked at his face and found a trace of concern in it.

"I'm sorry—"

"Hold off," I said. "Can you instead tell me which parts of your story were true?"

"Sure, my friend," he said. "Anthony was real, and the letters. They were all true. And the story behind Jose Rivera and his incarceration were also true."

"Where is he imprisoned?" I asked.

"Was imprisoned," the old man answered with due emphasis. "I am Jose Rivera. I killed my wife and the man she had been having an affair with."

"What? I don't understand. Who is Leonard Mendoza then?"

"You are talking to him as well. Leonard Mendoza is the identity I had conceived back when I was still in prison. His back story is a complete fabrication. I had to protect myself when the time of my release comes. I still have a son to look for, Tobias."

"Protect yourself from what?"

"I am not entirely certain, as a matter of fact. But I have a solid reason to think it could be from the man I had killed. He was from a circle of very dangerous people. Last month, as my term neared its end, a stranger paid me a visit in the prison and told me—no, he threatened me—that as soon as I was free again, they'll have me killed. And he meant it. There was a blaze in his eyes when he said it to me."

"Last month?"

"Yes. I was released yesterday, and I carefully hid myself right after I got out, assuming the fabricated identity of Leonard Mendoza. A colleague of mine helped me retrieve the savings I had outside while I was imprisoned. The dinner idea was also true. The anniversary, the birthday, this restaurant which I told you was where I met my wife. I conceived it while I was within the prison walls, and that was what I meant to do right after I get out."

"Why? It doesn't make sense . . ."

"Anthony agreed to a dinner with me."

A brief, meaningful silence ensued, before I broke it up with a question, "He has talked to you?"

"I invited him through a letter, and the next day he sent me back an answer, agreeing to the invitation."

"He didn't show up?"

He reached into the back pocket of his pants and drew out a leather wallet. It had already swelled from apparently a lot of ID's and receipts. Some of them were sticking out, and I wondered if all of them were for his fabricated identity. He opened it and pulled out a square photograph. "There's Anthony right there."

"This is . . . this is Paul!"

"Yes, that is him. And I just thought that I may have no need to hope to catch up with him anymore for this explaining. I think he may have already recognized me."

"You should go after him. Don't you want to see him anymore?"

"Well, I think I'm over with trying to get him to accept me, Tobias. I mean, I'm literally exhausted of words to tell him how I wanted to be part of his life again. The last few years I spent in prison, I spent them in the sole hope of just being able to see him again for once. Just once and I'll be fine with it. I'm finally calling it a day. Or rather, a life."

The old man laughed generously. Happily. And it was an amazing thing to see and realize, being the man that I was presently, that it only took a speck of time for happiness to completely outweigh the decades of the old man's sadness and hopelessness in waiting. And I think that happiness thus is the only thing, aside from change, that is constant.

Mr. Jose Rivera bade me a joyous goodbye before we ultimately parted our ways. If there was something that made this night a one hell of it, it was that I could see that there finally may be a chance for me to change my own fate. I decided to start walking back home and to begin with whatever I could make of this night in paper.

I continued walking until I reached a small park located a few blocks away from the highway. On one side of this park was a small lake, where on the pathway beside it were scattered a number of benches overlooking the still water. A number of sodium lamps scantily lit the area. On one of the benches I saw a figure sitting alone and apparently looking out quietly into the lake. A lamp post beaming just above the figure made me recognize him immediately.

"Paul?" I said, walking toward him.

"Oh, it's you," he said, after glancing at me. "Sit down."

"Well, I mean, Anthony, isn't it?" I took a seat on the bench a short distance from him. A kind of silent astonishment appeared in his face when he heard what I said, but it soon disappeared.

"So he told you the truth after all," he said.

"He said he's going to tell it to both of us, in fact, but you had left before he had the chance to do so. Anyway, he thinks maybe there is no more need for you to be told about it."

"I thought he'd never recognize me. You know, after all the years he didn't see a light of my face."

We both fell into a brief silence.

"I've got to tell you something though," he said.

"What is it?"

"Well, I'm not just his son anymore."

I shot a confused look at him when he paused to look at me.

"I've been under the employment of a very dangerous man for about five years now," he continued. "My job description is quite simple, if you think about it, but morally, not so much. They call me a hitman. An on-call hunter. They give me names and relevant information about certain persons, and then I go out, look for them, whatever and by all means necessary, and then I kill them. They've kept me under strict protection from the authorities. Eluding the police has never been a problem for me. Through those five years, there have been many unsolved murders around this place, and much of them are all my doing.

"These are big men, Tobias. These men control a whole lot of gears around the city, and every time anyone ever gets in the way of any of them, they contact me and make use of my services. At least those were my speculations, actually. They don't include the reason why someone they specify should be killed. But one thing's for sure: I have already become an expert at what I do. But you don't have to be afraid of me.

"Two days ago they approached me with another target: Jose Rivera—my father, unfortunately. I didn't inform them about that, no. When I first heard the name, I didn't know what to respond to them. All I know is that refusing the job was out of the question—as a matter of fact, refusing to kill their intended target would never be an option for me. I was torn not because I had to choose—I had nothing to choose from in the first place—but because I wasn't sure if killing my father would do me good despite my bitter hatred toward him.

"I have all his letters. I kept them. I read every single one of them, every night, I repeat one or two letters—trying to understand for myself why I can't let myself go from this hatred. And though his words would sometimes take a grip on me, at the end of the night I would still lie on my bed dazed and unsatisfied. This bitterness has latched itself on me. In the last letter he told me that I could finally live my life without him trying to become part of it again, but that he only wanted to see me for the last time. One last good look at me, and then he'll be gone, for good.

"He's got what he's wanted now." Anthony stood up. He looked straight to the lake, had been doing so the whole time he spoke. "The water is so calm tonight, don't you think?"

I didn't answer, and I just stared into the water like he did.

"It's nice to meet you, Tobias," he said, showing me a smile that was however difficult to comprehend. "I've never been this open to a new acquaintance. Guess I won't consider you a stranger anymore." He moved a few steps on his way before I interrupted him with a question.

"Don't you want to see your father again?"

He turned his face back toward me. "I have bosses, Tobias."

Before I could contemplate a chance to speak, he started walking again, and a couple of steps ahead, the darkness of the place had swallowed him completely into the night.

The Children of Anne de Luna

A large truck had stopped by the newly moved neighbors' house while Julie Sy, whose house stood adjacent, was watering the plants in her garden. Two large men hopped out of the truck and walked around at the back, opened the sliding door, and proceeded to take out a wooden table, four wooden chairs, and a small lamp. These they then brought apiece into the house of Anne de Luna, the lady of the new neighbor family, who just moved in town yesterday. She arrived with two young girls, apparently her children.

While the two men brought each of the furniture inside, Anne de Luna stood by the door supervising them. Julie had held off with her gardening to observe, quietly and closely watching Anne. Yesterday, as the members of the new family were coming up toward the house, Julie saw what had been an empty expression in each of their faces, but this time, Anne appeared very excited, smiling as her furnitures were brought in piece by piece. She handed each of the men a couple of bills afterward and thanked them profusely. The energy Anne had shown today and the one yesterday lie at both ends of the scale.

As she moved toward the door, Anne caught Julie's eyes looking at her.

"Hi," Anne said, a smile beaming up in her lips. She walked toward Julie, who also flashed a smile herself. "We're your new neighbors."

"Hi, I'm Julie." They both extended their hands for a shake.

"We've just moved here yesterday," Anne said. "The house is still empty save for an old couch the last owners had left. Well, you know, free furniture. Also, getting new ones is pretty exciting." She glanced at the side of the street where the truck had only a while ago stopped.

"I agree to that. Been there, about five years ago already, when we first moved here."

"We?"

"Yeah, I live with my ten year old daughter, Abby. She's in school right now."

"I have a ten year old too! Matilda. And Rowena, my eight year old. They had to stop school midyear in the old city. I'm planning to enroll them in that public school around the corner next year."

"Are they in your house now?"

"Yeah, they're probably playing through a tea party upstairs. You know, kids' imagination. They have this role-playing tea party they do with their dolls. Plastic table, plastic chairs, plastic cups, plastic kettle, imaginary tea. I had to buy them this whole set last month." The two women slipped into a fleeting laughter, before Anne spoke again, "Hey, why don't you and your daughter come over for dinner in the house tonight? You can get the first crack at trying the new chairs."

"Sure, we'd be glad to. We'll be there."

"We will see you then."

That afternoon, Julie decided to let out some of the strain she had had so far that day. After the little gardening, she had sat through a couple of hours in front of her computer to work. She went out into her garden and bummed a stick of cigarette, looking out at the almost empty street of the neighborhood. Residents there had little to interact about with each other. In fact it would only be her who paid notice to the new neighbors.

Not a little long afterward, the same truck from earlier came again by the de Luna's house. This time, only one man got off and brought out the furniture Mrs. de Luna had ordered for delivery. And there she appeared instantly by the doorway, the same smile flashing from her face. She saw Julie and waved, and Julie waved back.

The man brought out two chairs—the same as the ones delivered previously—from the back of the truck and carried it inside Anne's house, under the woman's supervision as per usual. When he had gone, with a generous tip from Mrs. de Luna and all, the woman glanced once more at Julie and smiled. At that instant, out of the blue, Julie thought something was amiss with her.

Julie got back on her chair across the computer, a blank Word document sitting idly on the screen. For months she had been struggling to finish writing the follow-up novel of the first one she published two years ago. That debut novel managed to break into the bestselling lists despite the minute readership of local fiction in the country, and only the past few months, talks of adapting the book for the screen had even swirled around. On her end, Julie expected to finally sell the film rights any time from now. So while perusing on the waiting stage, she decided to craft a sequel.

She raised her hands over the keyboard without actually having something in her mind to type. She hoped the mere action would spark something in it. She played the last scene of her novel the prequel in her head, and the events that she wanted to be in this draft she aimed to write. She actually had planned the sequences beforehand, but she doubted they would stretch to a book length. As the writing would progress, she hoped she would be able tinker more action and narrative to cover all the spaces of this nascent project, print it for national consumption, cash the money, and perhaps write another sequel to lock in a trilogy. That and the hope that the first book would finally get the green light for a movie adaptation. But at the moment her hands were stuck on air and the lines of thread interconnecting the story events in her head were still in a chaotic tangle.

She closed her eyes so she could vividly picture out how the plot should start. As her imagination began to play around her head and go on for the next couple of minutes, the telephone in the adjacent room rang. The noise did not really pull her out of her mental play with a surprise. She slowly opened her eyes and waited for the next instance of the ringing. When it came, she stood up hastily and walked into the other room, hoping this call would be that important to sabotage her little mind movie . . .

"Hello, is this Mrs. Julie Sy?" the caller on the other line spoke.

"Yes, speaking," Julie answered.

"I'm your daughter's class adviser. We want you to come over here quick, she's running a high fever."

"What? I'll be there right away."

81

Julie had no time to change, and she went on to a running race toward the door. When she opened it there stood the last person she expected to see on her doorway. Anne de Luna looked at her with the same smile printed on her face, not a bit fading while she saw the stricken countenance of Julie.

"Hi again," Anne greeted.

Julie could only look at her in her stricken face.

"I just came by to borrow something," Anne continued.

Julie stayed silent, though in her mind she had already screamed at the woman.

"Julie?"

"Anne, yeah. I'm sorry, I'm really in a hurry right now. I got to get going, my daughter's sick in school— "

"Well, sure. Though I have to ask you: Can I borrow your hammer? I've got this little fixin' to do in my house and I'm not sure if we have one. I am sure though that my husband's not even a little bit into carpentry and that stuff."

"What? Yeah, sure, I have one . . . Wait here, I'll go grab it."

When Julie returned less than a minute after with the tool in hand, she found Anne clearly in some sort of blissful anticipation. And it now really did it for her. Julie became finally sure this woman had the bugs in her head. "Anything more that you can trouble me for?" She couldn't hold back bringing out this question without a little sarcastic tinge.

However Anne proved to be incapable of reading it, and, with the same annoying smile on her face, said thanks to Julie for the hammer and headed back to her house. Julie got out and slammed the door behind her in the slight hope that the banging sound would slip the "I hate you" card into the head of the woman. But she went on with her way without bother, even making Julie seem to see her stupid smile through the back of her head.

Abby was in the school clinic, lying on one of the two beds in there, when Julie arrived. When she saw her, the little girl almost jumped out of the bed and threw her arms around her mother's neck. Julie carried her, waltzed about where she stood like she always does when she makes baby Abby go to sleep before, and tried to hush her down when she heard that she was crying. Abby hugged her mother tight and her breath felt to Julie's nape like a steam from a kettle of boiling water.

"Abby's fever has gone down," the nurse said from behind them. "There's nothing to worry about. She just needs some rest and glasses of water. You should take her home now."

"Thanks," Julie said, and then to Abby, "Let's go home, sweetie. Do you have your bag with you?"

Abby nodded and pointed toward the foot of the bed, where her small stroller bag was placed. "I'm sorry for calling you here, mama."

"What are you talking about, sweetie? Of course I should be here for my sick princess. Do you want anything to eat?"

"No, mama. I want to go home."

"Of course, sweetie." She picked up the bag with her other hand, and thanked the nurse again on their way out of the clinic. Abby had gone to sleep on her shoulder.

When they arrived by their house, Julie saw Anne through her house's window, sitting and looking out at them. And sure enough, at the sight of the mother and child, Anne drew out her trademark smile from her lips.

Julie gave her a nod and immediately turned her eyes toward the door of her house, absently picking up speed. That was when she remembered her promise to her new neighbor of their presence for dinner that night.

Maybe I should decline right now, she said to herself, as soon as she had put her daughter to bed. She thought of making Abby's fever an excuse. Although she had already thought that Anne may be a little hard to deal, she was quite sure the new neighbor would understand Abby's situation at the moment. And she might also add work into that excuse. Tonight may just see her able to crash out a few pages of the new book.

The de Luna's house burst out with blinding lights through the windows. When Julie stepped out of her door, she felt like Nick Carraway looking at the mansion of Gatsby beaming out streaks of light. After a while a stream of classical music began to flush out of the house.

Julie gave the door a string of soft knocks, at the same time her heart gave her chest a string of heavy pumps. Dinner invitations around the neighborhood had always been rare, and so would declining one be. In fact, this would only be the first instance that she had to do the latter. And to a new neighbor. And to Anne de Luna. Her heart only made it worse in her head beating even faster.

The door opened to a sight of two very little children.

"Hi," Julie greeted.

"Hi," the two chorused. The taller one continued, "You must be Mrs. Julie?"

"Yes, I am," Julie said. "If I am not mistaken, you are Matilda. And this is your younger sibling, Rowena?"

The two girls nodded in unison. The scene of the ghost twins in Stanley Kubrick's film version of "The Shining" suddenly popped in Julie's head, which she decided to hastily wipe out.

"Where is Abby?" Matilda asked.

Julie spared a second to recall if she had ever mentioned her daughter's name to Anne during their conversations earlier. "She is at home right now. Can I speak to your mother?"

"Mama!" Matilda cried before picking up into a sprint.

Rowena stood in front of Julie, pensively staring at her. "You are pretty," she said.

"Thank you. You are pretty too." She brushed the little girl's hair with her hand.

"Mama's cooking in the kitchen. She says you and Abby are gonna join us for dinner. Mama cooks very well."

"I'm sure she does, sweetie."

"Come in, Mrs. Julie. We have new chairs." Rowena burst out with enthusiasm at announcing this.

"Um. I should speak to your mother first. There is something I have to say to her."

Just then Anne came out of the kitchen and saw her visitor.

"I told you she's here," Matilda said, running behind her mother. "She said Abby's at their house."

"She's a pretty girl, mama," Rowena said.

"Julie," Anne said.

"Hi, Anne," Julie greeted. "Can we have a minute?"

"Sure," Anne said. Then she whispered something into the ear of Matilda, who subsequently took her younger sister. They walked hand in hand upstairs.

"Where's Abby?" Anne asked after they had gone out in front of the house.

"She's asleep, Anne. She's running a fever. I had to get her early from school today, and the nurse told me that she needs to rest. I got to look after her, Anne."

"But, but what about our dinner?"

"Can we do it some other time?"

"Oh." A long pause ensued, long enough for Julie to remember that the classical music playing from inside the house was Pachelbel's Canon.

"Abby really needs to rest, Anne," Julie spoke at length.

"Yes, of course," Anne said, sounding like she had been holding her breath during the long pause. "Of course, Julie. You should see to Abby right now. I guess we can have the dinner some other time."

"Thank you, Anne. I'm really sorry this had to happen at the last minute. Some other time." Julie wasn't wholly sure she wanted that "other time," but she thought she had to give that to Anne, seeing that she had not broken into that usual smile since hearing about Abby's fever. "Say sorry to Rowena and Matilda for me."

"Of course."

Julie's heart had leaped out of her chest.

Abby was still fast asleep when Julie entered her room. Her body from her neck down was covered with layers of blankets. When her mother sat by the side of the bed, she opened her eyes faintly. The light from the fluorescent bulb on the ceiling made it harder for her to open them fully, and she turned her head toward her mother and tried again to open her eyes on her.

"How are you feeling, Abby?"

"Hot. It's like I'm in a pot of boiling water. Where did you go, mama?"

"I went over to speak to Anne, our new neighbor. Are you hungry? Do you want something to eat?"

Abby shook her head no very slowly, and then spoke, "The one with the two girls?"

"Yes, that's the one. The two girls are her daughters, Matilda and Rowena. Matilda's about your age."

A tiny smile showed up on Abby's lips. "Can I go play with them when I get okay, mama?"

Julie thought of Anne, and what she had been making in her mind about her lately. She thought however that the children might not have inherited the bugs in their mother's head. After all, she had already seen their charm earlier. "Yes, sure. They can come here and play with you, sweetie." She kissed her child's forehead and felt the temperature on her lips. "I'll get you some soup, sweetie. You need to eat, and then medicine after."

"Okay, mama." Abby closed her eyes and pulled the blankets up to her nose.

While Julie prepared the soup in the kitchen, she checked her email for some news, hoping that one would be about the book deal finally coming through. But there were no new emails to open. She checked her phone to see if she had missed some calls, but there were also none.

Three swift knocks came on the door, and at the fore of her mind she immediately thought of her agent standing at the doorway—the good news finally sitting on her lips. Usually she would peer on the window beside the door first to see who had knocked, but this time she went straight to opening it.

The visitor turned out to be a usual face despite being only a new acquaintance, only she really didn't need to see that face right now.

"Hi again, Julie," Anne greeted, in her once again beaming smile. "I would just like to return your hammer. Very useful, I should get one for my own." She gripped the hammer by the end of its handle, like she was going to use it at that moment. And it's what had been Julie had thought about, in fact—and why she had stood speechless on her ground since she opened the door for Anne.

But Anne held the hammer in place after she had held it up in front of their faces. Julie was about to flinch, and was glad she didn't, thinking how it would have turned the table around for the both of them.

Anne had no idea about these current proceedings inside Julie's head. Apparently for her, it was just the normal way to hand over a hammer to somebody. Julie took it immediately before Anne could change her mind and maybe go on bash her brains in with it. Did she think she was going to say something to her now? She didn't think so. All she wanted to do thereafter was to slam the door on Anne. At least that was what she wanted to do if she could do it.

"Thank you, dear neighbor," Anne said.

"Welcome." She closed the door slowly behind her, peacefully, yet trying actually to fight the urge to slam it. She almost had turned her body about on the way to the kitchen when there came knocks from the door again—three swift knocks.

"Julie!" Anne cried through the closed door. "How about we have the dinner tomorrow night?"

Julie decided to keep the door shut between them. "I will have to check my schedule, Anne!" she cried back. She paused for a second, waiting for a response. "Look, I'm cooking in the kitchen and I need to go check on it now. You should probably go home, Anne." She paused once more, waiting for an answer, though she wasn't sure if she really wanted one. When the silence from the other side of the door persisted through the pause, she peered through the window and saw that Anne had already gone. She heaved a sigh of relief and ran hastily into the kitchen.

The soup turned out fine, and after she had spoon-fed half a bowl of it to Abby and brought her back to sleep, she went to her computer to work. She knew writing's still a bit hazy for her to commence doing right now, as she didn't even have the faintest idea of how to start. But should the film talk about the first book not push through, at least there would be a second one out in the bookstores for the reader's consumption. She had readers, not fans. She always refers to them as readers.

The Word document on the computer screen remained blank for an hour. She ended up staring at the blinking cursor for minutes, then switching windows to check her social media accounts, and then back and forth and back and forth for the whole duration. Glued on the chair, she sat wandering aimlessly around her head as the sand continued to pile up above her. Some of the sand even started to work magic on her eyes, and before she knew it, she had fallen asleep in front of her computer.

Around midnight she was woken by the ringtone of her cell phone. It was her agent calling.

"Yeah?" Julie said, managing to say it through a yawn. "I'm working on it . . . Yeah? Really? They want me in their office tomorrow?" Life had taken complete hold of her now. "Of course. Thank you very much, Leila . . . I will see you tomorrow. Thank you. Buhbye."

Then as if earlier she had not aimed at writing at least a paragraph of prose for the night, she shut down her computer and lulled herself into sleep, this time in her bed.

Abby's fever had gone down considerably the next morning, but Julie decided to keep her at home for the day. She prepared breakfast for the two of them, sending Abby's into her room so she can eat right in her bed. And she cooked an extra plate for Abby to eat later, if ever the appointment she had for the morning would extend past lunch. This might be a big day for Julie, one that she had been waiting for ever since.

She called Abby's teacher to inform her that her daughter was not coming to class, and then she told Abby about the appointment she was going to have with the studio head.

"Are we going to see a movie about your book, mama?" Abby asked, excitedly.

"Hopefully, Abby," Julie said, although a little reluctantly. Her novel was a suspense thriller that had scenarios of murder, sex, and graphic violence. She wouldn't even let her daughter near her computer when she was writing it.

"Wow. Congratulations, mama."

"We are still hoping. But thanks, sweetie." She kissed her daughter's forehead, and smiled at not burning her lips this time. "Listen, stay indoors while I am out, okay? If someone comes and knocks on the door, don't answer if it's a stranger." She paused, suddenly pondering on something. "If Mrs. Anne comes, don't open the door. Just tell her that I'm not here."

"Why not, mama?"

"She . . . she . . . she gets pretty annoying, Abby. Well, she is a sweet woman, but you really need a lot of alone time to rest today. Alright? You understand me?"

Abby nodded yes.

"Call me if there's anything. You know my number?"

"Yes, mama. I have memorized it."

"That's my princess."

Julie got home by 12 o' clock noon, downcast and frustrated. The meeting she had with the studio head didn't go as she had hoped. On her way home, she thought of passing by a bar and chug on some beer, but thought better of it and went straight toward home to attend to her daughter.

Jimmy, an old man living across their house, saw her on the way and approached. She wasn't entirely in the mood for a chat, but the old man had already stopped behind her when she saw him.

"Julie," he said.

"Hey, Jim," Julie said, trying to sound delighted.

"Is anybody in your house?"

"Why? I was on a meeting this morning. Abby is in there. She didn't go to class today."

"Well, she must have been asleep. Is she sick?"

"She had a fever yesterday, and just gotten better this morning. What's the matter, Jimmy?"

"I saw the new neighbor, the woman. She has been coming on your doorstep for quite a number of times. She knocks first, then when nobody was answering, she goes back to her house. Then she'd come back, and she'd just stand across your door, or took a peep in your window. I didn't see Abby come up by the window to see every time that woman comes."

"I told her not to answer her if she knocks."

"Have you met this woman, Julie?"

"Yeah, I met her yesterday. She actually invited Abby and I for a dinner last night. We couldn't come because of Abby's fever."

"Well, I think it rather fortunate that you didn't come to her dinner. She's a bit odd to me, if you ask me what I think."

Julie agreed with him in her head, deciding not to voice out what she had thought of Anne herself to the old man. They would become two neighbors gossiping about another neighbor, and she had never been like that. After a while she said, "I'll go talk to her. She must need something."

"You better be careful, Julie."

"There's nothing to worry about, Jimmy."

Of course, there is something to worry about, Julie said to herself. As she walked the pathway leading to the door of her house, she glanced at the window of Anne's house. There she caught a glimpse of Anne standing. Anne was not smiling this time, just standing there looking at her. She didn't even realize she had picked up speed while walking. No, she was already running.

She raced toward her daughter's room, relieved to see her lying on the bed and reading a book.

"Mama," Abby said.

"Abby, are . . . are you alright? Did someone . . ."

"You look tired, mama."

"Did Anne come in here?"

"No, mama. But she knocked on the door this morning. And I did what you told me. I didn't answer her."

"Did she know you're here?"

"I looked through the window when she came, but I think she didn't notice me. She just went away after."

"Oh, good. Listen, sweetie. Do you want to come over to grandma's today?"

"Yes, yes! I want to see grandma!" Abby leapt on her bed and kissed her mother on the cheeks.

"Okay, go get dressed. Quick. We're going there now."

Abby ran to her closet to change her dress, as Julie went to the window to look over anything from the neighbor's house. Her heart had been racing since her feet had a while ago. It was too trifle a reason to stay the hell away from her new neighbor now, but Anne had really messed up with her head to deny thinking that there really was nothing to worry about. Julie was a writer, and for God's sake, Anne could make a solid character in a suspense novel, say, a crazy neighbor who had just moved in town wanting to kill the mother and her daughter residing next door.

Julie saw Anne's house flashing off bright lights through the windows, like last night.

"Oh, my God," Julie gasped, then to Abby, "Come on, sweetie. We should go now."

She carried her daughter out of the room and rushed toward the door. All the disappointing news she received last morning, all the hopes of writing a sequel to her successful first book, all of it had dissipated out of her mind. All she thought at the moment was to get herself and her daughter out of that house right now.

Only there was a little problem she had to face. When she opened the door, there stood Anne on the doorway, smiling at them, and in her hand was clutched a small beretta. She looked larger wearing an oversized and thick jacket.

"Going so soon, Julie?" Anne said. "I hate to interrupt you and Abby but I was hoping we can have our postponed dinner right now."

Julie pulled her daughter toward her back, looking horrified at the gun in Anne's hand. "I have to take Abby back to a doctor, Anne. She's having a fever again."

With her free hand Anne touched the little girl's forehead. "That's odd. She isn't hot. Julie." She paused and smiled at Julie's terrified face. "Julie, why would you lie to a woman with a gun?"

"Listen, Anne, if there's anything going on in your mind right now, let's talk about it. Just put the gun away."

"That's a terrific idea. Why don't we go through it on a dinner?"

"Please, Anne. Not like this."

"I insist, Julie." The crazy woman lifted the gun pointing at Julie's stomach toward Abby's head. The little girl started to weep.

"Alright, Anne. Just keep that gun away from my daughter, please."

Anne hid the gun with the flap of her jacket, but was still pointed at Julie. She scooted to the side to pave a way for the mother and daughter. "Walk, and take it easy or you'll see how crazy this day will seem to become."

They walked slowly to the other house. Several meters away from the door, Julie heard the same melody from Pachelbel streaming through the open windows. She could see the dining area through one of them, where Rowena and Matilda had already seated, completely motionless. Another buzz of fear crept into her seeing the backs of those two children sitting next to each other. They seemed very stiff.

"They are so excited to see you and Abby," Anne said from behind them, realizing that Julie had taken a look at her children in the dining room. "Especially Abby."

The music flushed on louder when they had stepped through the door, and instantly Julie smelled the pungent odor working inside the house. Her fear was at last confirmed as she and Abby slowly walked into the dining room and saw the faces of the two children seated by the table. Their eyes were open and bloodshot, and fixed onto a large bowl placed on the center of the table, where soup filled to the brim was steaming off. Across each of them were two smaller bowls containing the same kind of soup, but apparently not from the one in the large bowl. It seemed to have been cooked much earlier. Dried vomit was streaming from the slightly open mouths of the two girls.

Abby buried her face into the bosom of her mother, who herself was stricken by the sight. She felt her consciousness gradually seeping out of her mind but tried to fight it off. Passing out inside this house with Abby in tow would be the last thing she'd do around Anne's presence.

"Matilda and Rowena couldn't wait," Anne said, "so they just started with their soup without you."

"Anne," Julie spoke, barely making herself audible. "What did you do? What did you do to your children?"

"Shut up!" Anne exclaimed loud enough to almost shake the table. And then in a lower voice, she continued, "Sit down, Anne. Abby. I bought these new chairs especially for the two of you."

"Please, Anne."

"Sit down!" She pointed the gun right to Abby's head, and Julie quickly took a seat across the two dead girls, carrying her daughter on her lap. Abby's face was buried on her mother's shoulder now.

"Whatever reason this has got to do with us, please leave my daughter out of this, Anne."

"You don't understand, Julie."

Julie had never had a hint of understanding of any of what was happening. "Tell me what it is, Anne. Let's talk it over. Keep the gun away from Abby, please."

"You are not talking your way out of this."

"What did I do, Anne?"

"Shut up."

"Please, Anne. Please."

"Shut up."

Abby began to cry louder, feeling the continuous surge of fear inside her.

"Shut her up!" Anne screamed.

Julie hushed Abby, whispering into her ear that everything was going to be okay. She doubted it would be.

Anne had seated by the adjacent side of the table. She looked at the Madonna-and-child in front of her and smiled, feeling triumphant. "Feed your little girl, Julie," she said.

There was another smaller bowl in front of Julie which Anne pointed with her glance.

"Feed her," Anne said. From her pocket she pulled a wooden spoon and handed it to Julie. "Let her taste the greatest soup she will ever have in her very brief, meaningless life."

"No, Anne," Julie said, her voice breaking to make way for a burst of tears. She knew it was the soup that had killed Matilda and Rowena. "I beg of you. Please let us out of this. I don't know you, I didn't do you anything."

"But I insist."

"Anne, tell me what this is about. Let's talk about it. Please don't let it go on like this."

Anne looked steadily at Julie for a whole minute. Her breaths had been heavy. "You're right, Julie. You don't know me. Probably you don't know who I am . . ."

"Let's settle this."

". . . but you were wrong. You did do me something."

"What is it? Is it about the way I talked to you yesterday? Is it about the dinner?"

Anne drew out a maniacal smile. "You think that is all what this is about?"

"What is it, Anne?"

"You stole someone from me." Anne put the hand holding the gun down onto the table and her face turned from wrathful to one that seemed grieving. It was the telltale sign of the string of memories that was going to burst out of her. "You took him away from me, Julie. Raoul and I were happy and you took him away from me."

"Raoul?"

"We were the happiest people in the world before," Anne said, in a rather dreamy voice, like a girl who was relating her romantic story. "I met him in a bookstore, and she saw me with a smile in his lips. We looked at each other for a long, long time, and before I knew it, I was falling in love with him.

"He took me to a lot of places. He gave me a lot of gifts. He promised me that we will be together for the rest of our lives. I gave my whole heart to him. I wanted him forever. He gave me two beautiful girls to love just as I love him. It seemed like all the happiness he gave me would never end. But then you came, you snatched my dear Raoul from me, you cunning bitch!"

Anne stood up fervently and pressed the barrel of her gun on Julie's head, screaming a series of curses.

"No, Anne, please!" Julie said. "Don't shoot. Listen to me. Listen to me."

"You're a thieving son of a bitch and a bitch yourself!"

"I didn't steal Raoul from you. Please, just listen to me."

Breathing heavily and in quick successions, Anne moved a step back and held the gun with her both hands now, still pointed at Julie.

"Raoul and I didn't love each other. It was just for one night. We were both drunk."

"Don't lie!"

"I swear to you, Anne. Please listen. I'm sorry. I'm sorry. I didn't know that he had a family when we met. I didn't mean for anything of it to go beyond that night. We were both very drunk. Anne, we didn't have what you two had. It was just a mistake. And I'm sorry."

"A mistake?"

"Yes."

"Where is he, Julie? Where is my Raoul?"

Julie found herself suddenly still, sunk deep in a thought. That morning during her meeting with the studio head and her agent, there was another piece of news that came to her aside from the rejection of her book's movie deal. Since the birth of Abby, her father and Julie had been in contact with each other, albeit rarely—once or twice every year, mostly just to talk about Abby. Julie had refused any financial support from the man, and for ten years he and Abby had never even once seen each other. Julie herself had no plan introducing him to the girl.

During the talk with her agent, Julie found out that the man had been involved in a car accident the night prior. He was able to reach an emergency room and stay through the night, but earlier that morning he was declared dead. Raoul, Abby's father and only now Julie learned had been Anne's husband, was already dead.

And now in the midst of all this horrible happening, Julie knew that the news of Raoul's death would only add fuel to the fire. The certainty that Anne would finally shoot her and her daughter if she learns about the news was absolutely undeniable.

"Is he dead, Julie?" Anne asked, bursting into tears now.

Julie only looked at her, without a word. She wanted to lie, that Raoul was in someplace and fine, and that maybe they could start life together all over again. But under the flooding eyes of Anne, no word would come out of her mouth.

Anne buried her face in her free hand and the one still gripping the gun. She was crying with all her breath now.

"I had a deep-seated fear that he's already dead," Anne said, in a broken voice. "And now that he's gone, I guess that is it for me. My girls are gone, the love of my life is gone, what purpose do I still have in this world?" Slowly, she pointed the gun to her own head.

Julie looked away from her and held her daughter tighter. She expected a gunshot in the next second, but after a couple of it, she heard laughter instead. Anne laughed her crazy head out.

Jimmy, the old man neighbor, was taking the trash out when he noticed that the door of Julie's house was open with nobody there to be seen. The house looked empty, so his suspicion suddenly rose after looking at the open door. He walked over to check.

"Julie? Are you there? Abby?" He stepped inside, slowly, not quite used to entering a neighbor's house without an expressed welcome. Nobody answered. "It's Jimmy. Anybody home? Julie?"

He spent another minute looking around. Afterward he decided to go out and inform the guardhouse in charge of the security within the neighborhood. For all he knew, a burglary could have happened in the house. Unless, he suddenly thought as he stood outside the house, the new neighbor had something to do with it, given her peculiar behavior last morning. He glanced at the house of the new neighbor and noticed the bright lights coming through the window. That only added to the earlier notion of Jimmy about the woman being odd. He thought of charging in there, though he decided to keep off being aggressive. But if the need to be aggressive arises—that if the woman really should have something to do with Julie's house empty and the door unclosed—he knew he could be aggressive.

From a distance he could hear the classical music playing inside the house. Not long after he also saw the dining area through the window just as Julie had seen it earlier. From where he was he could only see the backs of Matilda and Rowena and a very slight glimpse of somebody sitting across them. It could be Julie, he thought.

When he had arrived by the door, he noticed that it was ajar. He stood there for some seconds, actually hesitant to knock. He was thinking of what to say once the new neighbor comes to answer. Then he heard the laughter—that same laughter that made the insanity wrapping Anne's head most evident. He thought he'd only hear this kind of laughter in the movies, and in them this meant something bad most of the time.

He pushed the door ever so slightly, squeezing half of his body in.

"Hello?" He looked around and eventually landed his eyes on the dining room. The new neighbor, with her back toward him, was pointing a gun to her head. "What the—"

"Jimmy!" Julie exclaimed.

It happened in a span of a second. Anne turned around to see the man on the door, and along with the turn was the quick motion of her hand with the gun. She pointed it to Jimmy and pulled the trigger in an instant. The bullet went clean through the old man's shoulder, pushing him down to the ground.

"No!" Julie stood almost immediately she forgot that Abby was on her lap. The little girl fell on the floor. But Julie's adrenaline rush this time didn't include looking to her daughter. She dashed toward Anne and seized the hand that held the gun. They struggled for some seconds before Julie slammed Anne's wrist on the table, forcing her to let go of the beretta. It slid toward the opposite side of the table and stayed on the edge, only an inch away from a drop to the floor.

Anne tried to push Julie away but the force didn't throw her even an inch. Julie was able to stand still on her ground despite the push, but realized she was a split of a second late against Anne on running for the thrown gun. Anne had already dived atop the table, reaching for it.

Julie thought she had already lost the option of outstripping her, nor would tackling her at that distance fare better—Anne could very much keep her hand away from her and leave enough space for her to use the gun. But she did have something to reach that Anne would not. She picked up the large bowl of soup from the table, poured its contents over Anne, and slammed it on the back of her head. Anne had already taken hold of the gun, but the hit on her head had depleted all the strength from her body. Nevertheless she was still conscious, without Julie realizing.

Julie stooped down to check on Abby, who had passed out on the floor. She prepared to carry her on her arms, but a sudden scream burst out into the air: "Julie!"

Anne was able to get a grip on the gun and had turned her body to face the woman stooping on the floor. For a second Julie thought this would finally be it. She realized she could not summon some more strength to confront the crazy woman.

But Jimmy had barged through the scene in a sudden, carrying a vase with one hand. With a little support from the hand connected to the injured shoulder, he raised the vase above his head and threw it down toward Anne's bare and bloodied face.

"You shot me, you son of a bitch!" Jimmy screamed.

The vase finally brought Anne out of consciousness. Jimmy pried the gun out of her hand and helped Julie and Abby up.

"Let's get the hell out of here," Jimmy said. It was only just then that he realized the two dead girls sitting nearby. And without looking back they ran out of the house.

When the police came later, they told Julie and Jimmy that Anne was found dead sitting with the two girls around the table, in contrary to how they had left her. Fresh vomit was streaming from her mouth, suggesting that it was the poison in the soup that finally killed her. For the last time, Anne shared a dinner with her children.

Junior

"The man's got a hell of a house," Eddie said, looking up at the highest part of the roof.

"Of course, he's a billionaire," Old Billy said, after puffing out smoke from his nicotine-infested mouth. "Owns a thriving business in sea transportation, has built three large malls in the heart of the city, controls a number of small profitable businesses, I am not surprised if the man is now worth a gazillion of gold bars."

They stood by a lamp post a short distance from the main gate of Mr. Lincoln Fajardo's enormous house, just behind a large parked vehicle. They were there concealed, to check and observe the terrain of their next target.

Old Billy and Eddie had been a duo of master burglars for a string of years—running about the city with already a number of crimes behind them. Ingenuity and cunningness, and with luck sometimes, were skills they had profoundly utilized to amass an amount of fortune from time to time—though fleeting however—and to consistently elude the authorities who had always been consistently short behind their tracks. Throughout the record of burglaries the duo had committed in the years, circumventing arrest had never been a problem to them.

Old Billy was not literally as old as his name suggested him to be. A fair count, he was barely shy of running forty-four years. It was the police who supplied him the name after he pulled off a disguise of an old man walking into a convenience store and ending up taking the whole place into a robber's mess. That was the first crime he committed that made it to the news the next day. Apparently, he did not get busted for it, leaving the police scratching their heads when they arrived at the scene.

When his activities as a master burglar began to climb up to higher levels in terms of the amount of money at stake, which he called "proceeds," he realized that the job would already require him an extra pair of hands. He had one experience before when, as he was about to make his exit out of a house he had carefully and stealthily robbed of some proceeds, the housemaid had woken up to take a midnight piss and unfortunately seen him. He had just stepped out on the terrace of the second floor, prepared to climb down to his escape when that happened. The old woman was about to scream, but then he quickly pulled her and put a knife on her neck, telling her to keep quiet or else he would slit her throat. She did the former, but the latter would have helped him escape without raising an alarm. The only problem was that he was reluctant to kill, and always had not wanted to see himself shedding a spill of blood for his criminal activities. As much as possible, he wanted to do the job coming in tiptoes and coming out the same. But in that case, he might really have to leave with a bang on the door.

"Do as I tell you, old prick," he whispered to the woman's ear. "I'm gonna let you go and spare your life if you promise not to make a single sound. Not a single bit, do you understand?"

The woman nodded her head, nervously.

"Now I'm going to let go, and what you're going to do is you walk three steps forward, count to ten, quietly, and then run to your room as fast as you can. Nothing else, you hear? Just do what I say, and everything's going to be clear between us. Do you understand?"

The woman nodded her head again.

"Good." Slowly, Old Billy loosened her grip on the old woman and pulled the sharp blade away from her neck. As soon as she was out of her hands, she stepped thrice forward and then counted to ten, just as she was instructed. *One, two, . . . , nine, ten.* And then she heard a loud thump coming from a distance below. Instantly, thinking that the burglar had already jumped off, she turned around and ran to the edge of the terrace, seeing the burglar just about to stand up from the grassy soil below and apparently feeling some pain in his buttocks. She screamed at the top of her lungs, while the master burglar, who refused to get his hands dirty, sprinted like the police were already sprinting after him.

The burglary reached the TV the next day: broadcasted the escape he took by jumping out of the terrace and holding a terrified housemaid silent for ten seconds before she screamed her lungs out in emergency. Although the escape was deemed a success in his part, Old Billy looked at that one with alarm and a need for some ponderous consideration. Later he looked at it with a sense of urgency. He had to have someone who would do the dirty part for him—to bash someone out of consciousness, or maybe even to kill.

And so happened the entrance of Eddie, a small-timer he preferred to have out of some who presented with potential. Eddie was a teenager when they initially partnered, just one tick away from being a minor, and who lives without a family, knows too little to understand logical interlaces of plans—and thus clearly easy to control—and does not ask too much questions. Old Billy anticipated that someone of the latter's opposite would only become an annoyance instead of an efficient accomplice.

Old Billy and his sidekick Eddie had done countless burglaries in countless homes for years.

And the large house of billionaire Lincoln Fajardo had been the next in line.

As they carefully watched the target from their spot, in stealth and assurance that they were not drawing suspicion from anyone, the large front door of the house opened and out stalked a small boy, about five years old and less than four feet in height. Both Old Billy and Eddie were unfamiliar of him, as he had not come out of any of their searches when they did their research work about the family three days ago, upon the conception of the whole plan.

"Who's the boy?" Eddie finally spoke the question they both had in each of their minds.

"No idea. Never heard the man had a son."

"Could be one of the housemaids'?."

"That kid is too overdressed to be a housemaid's son. Anyway, a boy as small as that peanut would not be a concern, I'm sure. Let's get the hell out of here."

They had started to walk off when Old Billy inadvertently caught a glimpse of the little boy, now sitting by the steps across the door, glancing at him. A smile rose over the thin lips of the boy, and momentarily it sent an eerie feeling to him, like a thousand volts of electricity had passed through his body. For that brief moment, as they moved their paces forward, Old Billy remembered his late son.

The duo returned that night, behind the stealthy and quiet midnight hour when the whole place had been now reduced to a ghost town. They scaled the empty road toward the back of the house in what seemed like tiptoes. Carefully, they made sure to rid their actions of unnecessary noise, and they had done it so far so good, master burglars that they were. They stopped by a wall about three meters high and what parted one side of the house from the vacuous road they had walked.

Old Billy was a tall man, standing almost to six feet. Eddie however was a mere five and two inches, and weighed no more than a sack of feathers. Having spared some seconds to look around for unwanted observers, Old Billy went on planting himself by the base of the wall. He then bent his knees slightly and joined his hands together palms up to his torso level, making a step for Eddie so he could boost him up to the top of the wall.

Eddie was easily pushed up to the top, where he sat like a careful Humpty Dumpty for some seconds—thankful that the top of the wall was not lined up by peeking pieces of broken shards of glass—before helping Old Billy climb the top himself. His advantageous height fared him well on the climb. By the next minute they were already on the other side of the wall, stepping on the grassy backyard of the Fajardo's lot.

They tiptoed toward the nearest window and peered through the glass to see whatever was waiting for them inside. They hoped it would be silence, and a number of valuable stuff. The latter they could see, but the silence that echoed out through the window felt somehow different to them.

Eddie laid a palm on the glass and started to push it slowly to the side, hoping it wasn't locked. It gave way to an opening. A faint smile of triumph rose up in his lips as he slowly pushed the glass to an ample width. In his mind he began to picture the night closing out with another victory for the two masters of their art—again and again and again.

"You go first," Old Billy whispered to his partner.

Eddie climbed up the window, easily. In no less than a couple of seconds he had pulled up his sack of feathers over the window ledge and into the house. He landed on a couch below the window, where he sat for awhile, feeling the auspicious moment.

"Now help me up, Eddie," Old Billy whispered again from outside. Eddie leaped on his feet over the couch to get a better reach on his partner, but before he could act further, somewhere a telephone rang.

"Hide, kid," Old Billy said as he quickly brought himself down below the window outside. Eddie darted in quick tiptoes toward a short table beside the couch and stooped down. A long ceramic vase on top of the table, shaped like a Coke bottle, had helped him keep his face out of exposure, at least from afar the couch. The ringing commenced for some time, and when it stopped, the two burglars independently decided to spare some more time in silence. Nothing happened.

Eddie peered from his hiding place, and saw nothing had changed inside the house.

"Come on, Eddie," Old Billy said, his face peeking over the window ledge.

But as soon as Eddie had turned toward the window, the telephone rang again. Old Billy's face went into a daze and it signaled Eddie to get back down behind the table. He ducked to his own hiding position below the window outside. The telephone rang thrice before falling silent.

A switch being flicked sounded around the inside of the house, and it sent Eddie's heart climbing up his throat. It was still dark around him, so luckily it had not been the switch to the lamp above his head. But his nerves wasn't taking it for a relief.

The next sound that came was from some footsteps. He froze in his place behind the table. But he listened to the footsteps, intently, trying to make out where those feet were inside the house. It was getting nearer, and it sure did sound like footsteps coming down a stairs. *Someone was coming down the stairs!*

"Alright, but make sure to get home tonight," a voice said through the quiet. "I can't bear spending the night with the boy." And then, "Okay." Then, "Uh-huh." The voice was closing in on the distance.

Eddie glanced behind him and saw Old Billy peeking with one eye carefully from one corner of the window.

The voice stopped momentarily along with the footsteps. Eddie tried to steal a look from his hiding place, quite assured of himself that the surrounding darkness would yet conceal him. He slipped an eye forward enough for the slightest view he could have on the stairs, which he hunched was a dozen steps from the window.

"I'm downstairs getting some food. The boy's ravaging again." The voice was from a woman's. Eddie had only now made it clear to himself, when she had moved considerably closer. "Yes. Tight. Don't worry."

Eddie glanced again to the window and saw his partner pointing his finger to a spot inside the house, apparently toward the direction of where the woman was. He gave his partner a nod.

The voice started to move again.

"Hey," Old Billy whispered from the window. "Come on."

Eddie saw his partner beckoning him to get back outside. Quickly taking a look toward the stairs, he saw the woman no longer standing there. With a quick start, he ran back to the window and jumped out, clearing the broad, open space easily with his skinny frame.

"Where is she?" Eddie asked.

"I don't know," Old Billy replied. "She was no longer where she was when I looked again. Come on. Let's get out of here."

"We won't get this done with?"

"No. Didn't you hear her say someone was coming home tonight? Let's go. We'll do this some other night."

The duo started tiptoeing back toward the wall. With every step from the window and with the silence still about the place, both their agitation gradually abated. The silence was still as deafening as it had been since, and it still somehow put them in security and assurance that this current job would roll without a hitch, whether they could finish it or not.

Old Billy arrived by the wall first, where he immediately positioned himself for the hand-lift to boost his partner up on the wall. While this was being done, suddenly they noticed somebody nearby, quietly looking at them.

"Kuya."

They saw the boy they had seen last morning standing just a few steps behind them, hugging a small teddy bear.

They looked at each other inquiringly, both undecided what to do. When Old Billy glanced again at the boy—

"Come on, partner," Eddie said, watching Old Billy suddenly froze in his footing.

"No. The boy."

"What? Come on. Let's leave before he gets us into trouble."

"I don't think he'll get us into trouble. Look at him."

Eddie looked at him, and saw nothing more than a boy who had woken up in the middle of the night and startled a pair of burglars just about to abandon their plan.

"We must . . . we must not leave him here," Old Billy muttered.

"What are you talking about?"

"You heard what the woman had said about him on the phone? She doesn't sound like she was being good to this boy. She might have been mistreating him."

"What do you propose we do then? Take him? We can't take a boy-to-care-for with us, partner."

Old Billy looked at Eddie with eyes that were opposite of what he was—what they were and why they were here in the first place.

"Is that a plan, partner?" Eddie sounded rather cunning. "Yeah, I can read it in your eyes. You want us to take the boy?"

Old Billy appeared to nod, very slowly nonetheless.

"Alright," Eddie returned. He walked over toward the boy, carefully, hoping the little fellow wouldn't scream. Not even the least of sound came. The boy didn't do anything in fact but look up at Eddie with a somewhat tearful pair of eyes.

"Hey there, buddy," Eddie spoke, as charmingly as he could. "What are you doing out here at this hour? It's already late." A large rather phony smile beamed up in his face as he spoke.

The boy remained silent, his tears still held up in the corners of his eyes.

"Okay," resumed Eddie. "We're going on a midnight trip somewhere, buddy. It's some place I'm pretty sure you will love. There are toys in there, there are candies. How does that sound? You wanna come with us?"

Silence still, although a slight change of emotion could now seen on the boy's face.

"Come," he said as he gently pulled the boy toward him and lifted him on his arm. Right then he became quite sure he would finally hear a scream.

But the silence persisted.

An hour later, the three of them had come into a small dark room where the two burglars had decided to keep the boy. It was an extra room of the small house they had settled in since the onset of their criminal activities. The house was extremely isolated, standing in the middle of a wilderness and woods that only the two could possibly find a way through in and out. It proved absolutely perfect as a hiding place for two burglars. Now it proved way perfect as a hiding place for two kidnappers at work. Even if the boy would scream his lungs out for help, no one was ever going to hear him but them.

Surprisingly though, the boy was still zipped in silence, and his face had now turned from tearful to completely void of expression.

"Tell me what's your name, buddy," Eddie said as he laid the boy down on a bed.

The boy looked and locked eyes with him for a couple of seconds before Eddie took his own out of the stare. The boy was now starting to creep him out.

"My name is Junior, Kuya," the boy at last spoke.

"Were you hungry?" Old Billy asked, sitting beside the boy on the bed. "Why were you out at such late in the night?"

"No, Kuya. I go out of the house every night."

"Every night?" Old Billy returned, startlingly. "Why are you going out every night, son? Aren't you afraid? It's dangerous."

Eddie looked at his partner warily, seemingly taken aback by how he was suddenly showing concern for the boy, not even the least aware of the irony of what he had said last.

Junior fell into silence again. He bowed his head, stroke his teddy bear with a hand, and then lied down on the bed. A faint noise came in succession from him a little later, like he was singing a song. He was singing the bear to sleep, Eddie thought. Old Billy watched the boy, who had lied down with his back toward them, and the way he looked at him resembled a father watching over his son asleep. Eddie may have felt odd about it, but he was sure there was no need to worry.

"Will we call the Fajardo's now?" Eddie asked after a while.

"For what?" Old Billy answered, looking rather a little surprised with the question. But then, recovering from the careless slip, he spoke again, before Eddie could: "Oh, yes. No. I mean, I don't think we must call them now."

"You sure? They've probably noticed him gone by now."

"Yeah, I'm sure. There's no need to rush." Old Billy nodded his head slightly before he stood up from the bed. "Come on. Let the boy sleep."

The lone window inside the room was spanned with iron gratings and wooden jalousies, and when Eddie closed the latter, the room fell into darkness immediately. It had only been the moon outside that supplemented light in the room through the window. They lit an oil lamp afterward and placed it on a nearby table, where the two consequently discussed whether to keep it inside the room. After a short exchange of words, they decided to keep the lamp inside and further to keep it from the boy's reach. They moved the table far from the bed and chained the boy's foot to one of its legs.

"He might get up and burn us all in here," Eddie had quietly said.

When they had walked out of the room, Eddie put two locks on the door, wholly decided on not to take any chances.

Sleep came for the two immediately. Eddie, though having an odd feeling about Junior, decided to wander his mind on the probable amount of money they would get from the boy's parents. Tomorrow they would start dealing with them—a phone call and a little threat were what it would take. An easy job it seemed to become he wondered why they haven't thought of it before.

At around 3 A.M., Eddie was roused by some scratching sounds from the next room. Frightened, he was about to wake his partner up when a feline scream followed the dying out of those sounds, which afterward eased him. He went back to sleep, right after thinking about the chain and the two locks he had put on the door of the boy's room, letting it ease his mind completely.

He woke again at 6:30. Old Billy was still fast asleep and he decided not to wake him up for the moment. The call could wait. Who he expected to possibly could not wait for it were Junior's parents back in their large house. He was sure they had gone frantic by now.

When he stood up he felt a soft object under his left foot and immediately looked down to see what it was. He had stepped on a teddy bear stuffed toy—Junior's stuffed toy!

"What the—" he shouted.

Old Billy roused up from his sleep, leaping off of his bed in an instant.

"What's wrong with you?"

"You're shittin' on me, partner. What is this toy doing under my bed?" He pointed a finger angrily down at the stuffed toy near his feet.

"I don't know what you're talking about, Eddie. How did it get there?"

"You don't know? Well, I don't know too, partner. Maybe he—" He fired up his feet suddenly out of the room and toward the boy's. Old Billy followed him. When they were there the locks however were still on the door and appeared rather untouched throughout last night.

"He couldn't have gotten out of that room, Eddie," Old Billy said.

"I know. But how do we explain the bear already on our floor?" Eddie looked at his partner inquiringly, and then somewhat accusatory. Old Billy read it.

"No way I'm gonna do such thing," he said. "Why would I get in that room and take the child's toy and put it under your feet? I have no time for fucking pranks!" His voice was vehemently defensive.

"You must have seen how frightened . . . Well, alright, alright. Let's get in to see, and we better see him still in chains."

He took off the locks on the door, and when he had opened it, they saw Junior standing by the lone window of the room, his back toward them. The jalousies were now open, permitting the early morning light to pass through and illuminate the whole area inside. The light of the oil lamp was now extinguished. And what horrified Eddie the most was that there was no more of the chain clinging around the boy's foot. It hung empty from the side of the bed where Eddie had attached its other end last night.

"Hey, buddy?" Eddie said, fighting through the fright and walking forward in slow steps.

"What are you doing by the window, Junior?" Old Billy said.

"Hey, Junior," Eddie said as he got closer to the boy. He pulled his arm to make him face them, and when the boy did, both Eddie and Old Billy exclaimed in terror and surprise. Junior's face was splattered with blood all over. A huge part of it was under his nose, where apparently all the blood had come from. It was now dry on the other parts of his face.

Eddie contemplated the sight intensely. He had seen blood on faces, of course—even inflicted it himself. But he had never seen it on a child's face. He was too less of a criminal to bear the thought of children in pain. Anyway, he would only hurt if that was the only choice he had.

But Junior didn't look to be in pain at the slightest. He looked at them with blank eyes. Despite the mess around his face and the terrified reaction of the two men about it, the boy was still as expressionless now as he had been last night.

"Are you alright, son?" Old Billy said, dashing on his knees across the boy. "What happened to you?" But when he had put his face that close to Junior, it became the perfect distance for the boy to swing his fingers toward his face. A set of long parallel lines cut through the skin of his cheek instantly, and in a space of a second, blood started to flow from each of them. Old Billy looked at the boy confusedly.

"You son of a bitch!" Eddie screamed. "What the fuck did you just do?" He pulled both the thin arms of Junior and shook him forcefully.

"Stop, Eddie," Old Billy said. He put one hand over his wounds. "I'm alright. It's alright. Just clean up the boy's face and put him back to his bed."

"What are you talking about? Look at what this piece of shit has done to you."

"Eddie, just do what I just said. I'm fine. Now stop blabbering."

"You're unbelievable, partner." Eddie reluctantly moved to start with what Old Billy had told him to do. He glanced once more at his partner, who had begun wiping off the blood on his face. He almost could not fathom how he was able to let the assault pass without at least a single word of retaliation toward the boy.

"Can I at least chain his hands first?" he asked, looking at the bloody stains on Junior's fingers. All the nails were about half a centimeter long and were visibly cut to a point. "And can we do something about his claws as well?"

"Yes and yes, Eddie," his partner answered. "Start with it now."

He chained Junior's hands together, carefully and warily looking at any possible attack the boy could do to him while he was at it. He made sure to leave his hands loose should he need it to fend one off. Weird but better be safe than sorry, he thought. He led the boy to the bed afterward and made him sit, where he consequently cleaned the blood off from his face. The boy didn't give an assault, not even the littlest bit of a violent reaction throughout the whole process. Eddie felt relief. There was something wrong with the boy, and he was sure of it.

"I think we ought to rid of him now, partner," he told Old Billy, once the boy was already settled in his bed.

"Yes, we're calling his parents today," the other answered. He winced from the pain in his face. "These are getting unbearable by the minute. Do you think I need stitches for these?"

"I think you do, partner," Eddie said, after a careful look at Old Billy's wounds. "But that can wait, I hope. Let's settle this matter at hand first. I know you've noticed, but I am not feeling any comfort being around that boy. He freaks me out."

"Yeah. I know, I know." But his voice was apparently far from meaning it.

"I'll call the Fajardo's now."

Eddie took out a cell phone from his pocket along with a small piece of paper. Before the failed burglary last night, they had secured the Fajardo's telephone number, although they really had no concrete reason why they did so. Now they had one. The number was written on the piece of paper, and Eddie started dialing it. A moment of silence followed as the call was trying to reach the Fajardo's home. Through the silence the ringing on the other side was audible to Old Billy.

The ringing eventually stopped as someone answered the call from the other side.

Eddie decided not to speak and just waited for anyone of the Fajardo's to do so. Yet there was only silence that came from the other line. He knew the call was alive however from the moving display of the call time in the cell phone screen.

"Hello," Eddie finally spoke, after about a minute of silence. "Fajardo?"

What came back was a vague whisper, probably from someone speaking in the background. After a couple of seconds, Eddie hung up.

"Is this really their number?" he asked.

Old Billy nodded, quite in hesitation. "Try it again."

Eddie did so, and when the call was taken on the recipient's side, someone spoke, at last: "Bury it." The voice came like a whisper, strangely cold. After that, the line went dead.

"What happened?" Old Billy asked.

"I . . . I don't understand," Eddie answered.

"What? What did they say?"

"They—"

"Give me that!" Old Billy snatched the phone from the grip of Eddie's hand and redialed the number. It did not take long before the recorded operator's voice sweeped in: "The number you have dialed cannot be reached. Please try again—"

Old Billy pressed the end button and looked at Billy. "Cannot be reached. What the hell is wrong with them?"

"Maybe we're calling a wrong number."

"Someone could have at least let us known it if that's the case."

"What do we do now?"

Old Billy fell into silence, thinking. "We'll do the transaction by snail mail. I'll go to the Fajardo's house

119

and leave a note at their gate. You stay here and keep an eye on Junior. And keep dialing the number. Maybe we can reach it again some other time later, just like the operator said."

Eddie looked at his partner in a frightened countenance, probably saying with his eyes: *I'm not looking after that freak boy*. But he did eventually, while Old Billy walked his way to the Fajardo's residence.

The house of the Fajardo's was surprisingly serene, far from what Old Billy had anticipated it to be. He stood a few meters away from its gate and concealed enough by some cars parking on the side of the street. It was a hot day, and the wounds on his face were reveling with the heat.

I must get this thing done with as soon as possible, he thought.

He slipped the ransom letter through the mailing slot of the gate, and waited. He was yet in disbelief over the silence of the house despite the fact that a little boy from it had just gone missing. "I didn't know they were this heartless," he whispered to himself. "But they must pay up."

He was utterly sure they will. After a few more seconds, and still without any deviant noise from the house, he clicked the doorbell button on the gate and ran off before anyone would come out.

The silence remained as deafening.

And it contained him so wholly that the sudden ringing from his cell phone caught him completely with surprise. It was from Eddie.

When he held the speaker over his ear, a series of loud and screeching noises came along with the hysterical voice of Eddie whining completely indiscernible words.

"Hey, hey!" Old Billy muttered. "Calm down. What's happening over there?"

"You have to . . . you have to get . . . back here, partner," Eddie replied, obviously drawing out exasperated breaths. Loud banging sounds then came, as from someone knocking furiously on the door.

"What's the matter, Eddie?"

"Come back here!"

Old Billy hung up the phone and rushed immediately back to their house. From the door he heard the same noises he had heard over the phone, being distinct now. He barged in.

"What happened?" he asked, seeing Eddie standing by the door of Junior's room and wielding a small axe over his head.

"I'm gonna bust his head off if he gets out of that door there, partner! You bet I would!"

"What's going on inside?"

The forceful banging on the door seemed strong enough to shake the whole house. There was no way a small boy as Junior could pounce on the door with such tremendous force.

"Junior, stop it! Stop your banging now or I'll have no other choice but to get in there and—" The noises suddenly ceased before Old Billy could finish his statement. The ensuing silence was a complete void. Old Billy and Eddie exchanged glances with each other.

"Stay away from the door, Junior," Old Billy said, slowly placing his hand over the knob of the door. "Listen to me, you understand?" He turned the knob carefully until he made it to its full turn, and pushed the door open carefully as well. Eddie followed him warily, all braced up with his weapon and not minding if it was on a small boy he was going to swing it onto.

Old Billy had pushed the door to a sufficient width for them to see Junior. The boy lied on his bed, almost motionless save for the regular rising and falling of his chest. He was sleeping, soundly in fact. Old Billy wondered if he had really screamed a while ago, or if there really were those heavy beatings on the door. The boy slept like he had been asleep for a year.

"What the hell is going on here, partner?" Eddie asked, in a fearful tone. "Look, the boy's foot is still chained on the bed!"

"I don't know, Eddie. You heard it too, right?"

"Yeah, and the door's a kilometer away from the bed, partner. How in hell would it be possible for him to beat the shit out of that door while chained to this bed?" His voice went hysterical again.

"I don't know, Eddie. How would I know?"

The boy moved, waking up, facing them. His expressionless eyes stared right through both of theirs— not particularly at exactly one of them, but both of them. It was like looking at a still of someone's face and staring at the eyes, and then feeling like these eyes are staring back at them, and even if they move to a different spot, they could still see the eyes fixed on the stare and following them wherever they move.

"Hey, kid," Eddie said. "Whatever it is that's wrong with you, if you mess up with us, I'm assuring you that you're going to get what you're looking for." But the threat just went on deaf ears. The boy neither cringed nor changed a bit of his face. He went back to sleep instead.

"Have you sent them the ransom letter?" Eddie asked his partner after they had left Junior asleep in his room.

"Yes. I left it on their gate. And you know what I found out in there? The whole house was like a grave in a cemetery on a midyear. You can never hear a bit of a sound from around the place."

"Really? Oh, I'm not surprised. Weird children, weird parents."

"It wasn't what I was expecting. But I left the letter anyhow."

"This better be worth a whole lot of money, partner. The boy's made a mess of your face, if you look at yourself. By the way, I kept calling their number while you were out and I got the same result over and over again."

"I left a number in the letter for them to contact us. But if they're not calling us through the rest of the day today, I think I may have to go back there. Send them another warning, perhaps."

Eddie looked at him with a pallid and frightened face. "Maybe it would be a better idea if we'd switch places with that, partner. I think I'm never gonna live a second alone here with the boy."

Old Billy eventually nodded in compliance. From there his thoughts went back and fixed to Junior. Sure there was something mysterious about the boy. Something sinister and malevolent in fact. What could explain the strange consistent lack of expression on his face anyway? And the strange occurrences that had happened lately. It was perfectly understandable indeed why Eddie had grown afraid of the boy. He could hurt, he could possibly hurt other people—and it should be very urgent now that they get rid of him, take the ransom from his family, and then maybe stay away from these criminal activities for some length of time first. They might need that time off.

The day had worn off almost completely, yet the two had still not received any call from the Fajardo's. So they decided that Eddie should go back to the house to check on the ransom letter.

When Eddie had gone off to do his errand the next day, Old Billy decided to stay with Junior inside his room. The boy was sleeping, lying on his side with his back toward him. He sat on a chair a few feet away from the bed, looking at the boy fixedly. His eyes glanced alternately at the back of Junior's head and the chain that tethered his foot to the side of the bed.

Old Billy, though sure that there really was something about the boy strange and horrifying, wasn't afraid of him. Despite what the boy had done to his face, he even felt pity over him. His behavior might just be caused by the very lack of care and attention from his parents for him back in his home. They did not even apparently put on an effort in getting him back from them. He recalled how empty their house seemed to be when he went there, like they had already deserted the boy. There was no other reason he could think about that odd silence all over the house except that they had completely given up on looking for Junior.

Bury it. Suddenly came a whisper. He did not know where it came from, and neither did he know where to locate it. When he looked around him he found that he was now suddenly being enclosed in a white space. He became afraid he may have turned blind. Or have suffered some attack and lost consciousness. The space of time between the last glimpse he took of Junior lying chained on the bed and the realization of this whole empty backdrop around him seemed infinitesimally brief to decide. *Bury it. Bury it. Bury it*—

It went on in ellipsis, growing louder every moment. It was escalating gradually to a scream from an initial whisper. And then it stopped. He closed his eyes in a blink's rate and when he opened them, he saw Junior already across him—lying on the same bed and at the same distance. The white background around them was still on however. Slowly, Junior roused up and sat on his bed, now facing Old Billy. The boy's face had become wizened and his hair disheveled like a bird's nest. His look was rather contemptuous and the smile touching up his cracked lips was a malicious one. Junior did not look like a small boy anymore.

"Am I dreaming, Junior?" Old Billy asked. As if the boy was going to answer.

But he did.

"Yes."

"You're not real?"

Junior let out a sarcastic laugh. "Yes and no. Yes, I am real. And no, you're not going to wake up anymore."

Old Billy had just enough time to be taken aback by what the boy had said last—since he was in fact about to ask the question to that answer—when Junior rushed quickly toward him, raising both his hands like an attacking bear. The chain on his foot remained the sole chance for Old Billy to escape the incoming assault, but when the time came for it to stop the boy, it suddenly broke apart into pieces—half-expecting it yet happening much to his horror. He took the split of a second left to try to dodge the attack, but it was not enough. Junior's long fingernails, all ten of them, dug another set of lines on Old Billy's face. They almost would tear up his face completely. The pain was burning in his face.

"Stop it!" He was now down on the floor, looking up fearfully at the monster of a boy who was standing atop him. Junior prepared to launch another attack. "Stop it, Junior! Please!" Old Billy was sobbing now, his tears flowing down toward his ears and over several lines of his fresh wounds. They were like gasoline to the fiery pain. Now he could comprehend completely the nature of Eddie's fear toward the boy.

Someone shook him. And all of a sudden, when he opened his eyes, the infinite blank around him became the familiar surrounding of Junior's room again. He was lying on the cold floor, still trembling from fear. Down on his feet beside him was Eddie, waking him up from that terrible dream.

"What happened, partner?" Eddie asked.

"The boy," Old Billy answered, slowly rising up on his feet. The voice that came out of his mouth as he spoke was evident of the fear that was still in clasp of him. Eddie could not miss noticing it.

They both looked at the bed where Junior was supposed to be lying—and Old Billy hoped that the boy was still lying down on it. But . . .

The bed was there on the floor across them, seeming like the monster of the boy itself, and now sans the boy. They looked at each other's aghast faces, undecided what to do. And then apparently from the adjacent room, a loud noise of a door being forcefully shut came hastily through the air. A series of clattering sounds came next, drawing closer. They were both looking at the door of the room they were in now.

But the whole place fell into silence afterward. It went on for almost a minute, leaving the two fellows silent themselves and crept up by an utmost sense of fear. After that, the door suddenly started to open, going on slowly, terrorizing them by the minute.

"Partner, if that boy's doing all of this, I swear to God I'd be the one to pay his parents if they'd let me kill him myself," Eddie said, trying to pacify the fear inside him.

Old Billy did not answer.

After a couple of seconds more, the door had finally opened wide, and there he was—standing stiffly by the doorway, once more without an expression painted on his face. What was on it was blood. Covering almost the entire area of his face. Horror beyond horrors.

"What are you up to now, shithead!" screamed Eddie.

Junior turned his face toward them—and grinned. And instead of a set of white teeth showing up in his mouth, the boy showed them a set of rotting and disfigured teeth.

"I have to sleep." Blood flowed out of the boy's mouth as he spoke, and then he followed it with a laughter that shook Old Billy and Eddie toward more horror. They watched with their terrified eyes as Junior started to walk toward the bed, slowly and still laughing. One could not see any movement from them except for the slow sliding of their eyes. They were completely frozen on the ground.

"What do we do?" Eddie whispered to his partner's ear.

"Let's get out of here," Old Billy answered.

They blazed their feet altogether as Junior had lied down on the bed. And as they were nearing the door, Junior instantly spoke, in his diabolical voice: "Close the door, will you?"

"What do we do now, partner?" Eddie asked again. They had finally stopped after running for half an hour away from the house.

"I don't know, Eddie. But we really ought to do something about it. About that boy."

"Yeah. Really." Eddie's voice trembled in sync with the quick beatings of his heart, and suddenly he remembered something. From the pocket at the back of his pants he pulled a folded envelope. "I got this on the front gate of the Fajardo house. I think it was for us." When he unfolded the envelope, Old Billy saw Junior's name written on the flap.

"Give it." Old Billy took the envelope and opened it quickly. From inside he pulled the same ransom letter that he had slipped below the gate of the house, only there was something written on its back now. The letters were large and bold, inducing apparent emphasis.

BURY IT!

"What's the matter?" Eddie asked, seeing the terrified face of Old Billy as he looked over the paper. He gave it to Eddie and read what was written on the back. "Bury it? Bury what?" He gave it a thought, and yes, he remembered. "This was it. That time when we called their number, this was what the person on the other line said. *Bury it.* I just didn't understand what it meant. It makes no sense."

"It makes sense now. I think they want us to just kill the boy."

"Kill the boy? And bury him?"

"Probably. Bury it. *It.* They should know all about the boy, including all that shit we've gone through. I wouldn't protest if they'd prefer him dead."

"Shall we do it?"

"I think that's what we ought to do."

They eventually decided to go back to their house and finish off the boy, once and for all. They didn't care for the ransom anymore. Old Billy had completely turned his head around feeling concern for the boy. What they thought imperative at this moment was that they must get rid of *it*, and running away from *it* was apparently not enough.

It was no easy decision for anyone of them. Eddie was reluctant to go back to their house and see the boy again, in his very grisly form. That was just too much of a horror for his heart to take. Burgling houses does not pay me enough to face this kind of monster, he thought. For him, he'd prefer to run away from the house than go back and try their chance in killing the boy.

"Anything can happen, Eddie. As long as that boy is alive, there's always a chance that he'll trace us and do to us first what we ought to do to him now. And I'm telling you, he can find us, Eddie. Aside from his family, we're probably the only faces he has seen and recognized. And he has all reasons to look for us and kill us." Old Billy, although quite terrified himself, had weighed down their options and had drawn the conclusion. They themselves had all reasons to kill the boy too, anyway.

They first dug a large hole a few meters away from their house to where they'd throw the boy after. The house was quiet ahead, and the window of the room where Junior was kept showed to them the light inside was on. *I hope the bastard is still asleep*, Eddie thought as they gradually closed in on the distance. From the deep silence enveloping the house, it was highly likely that Junior was still asleep.

They found the door still open from when they had ran out of the house earlier.

"He's probably still asleep, partner," Eddie said. "Otherwise, he would've closed the door." Eddie took a breath of relief, and inside he was currently feeling better.

They headed straight to the room of Junior, carefully and quietly so, the master burglars that they were. The silence had run from outside all throughout the inside the house. There were no telltale movements, just from the two of them, at the moment at least. The door of the room was closed—this they had left so on the run earlier— and Eddie once more breathed relief by the thought that maybe Junior had not yet gotten up from the bed. By that he would be an easy kill.

"Slowly, partner," Eddie whispered, as he watched Old Billy start to push the door open. Slowly and gradually, the interior of the room appeared before them. Eddie's heart, who had somehow pacified a while ago, beat madly again now. And a flush of paranoia came into his mind. *What if the bastard is no longer there? What if he's already somewhere around the house, preparing to attack us?* His thoughts went wild.

The bed, they saw, was now empty. Immediately they were crept up by a feeling of utmost dread, something awfully powerful seeping into their senses. Both of them seemed to see darkness hastily encasing the whole house. And then the voice came.

"You came back!"

Old Billy and Eddie almost simultaneously turned their heads about and saw Junior standing just behind them. The small boy (barely a boy in appearance now) looked up at the drained faces of the two men. Blood came out of his mouth where an evil smile was currently drawn.

Eddie was able to shout his surprised fear before Junior buried four of his pointed fingers into his right leg. Blood immediately surrounded the wounds, and Eddie filled the whole house with screams of pain.

"Get back, you piece of shit!" Old Billy screamed, after which he kicked the boy's head with all the strength he could exert, sending the boy back a few paces from them and slumped face down on the floor. He did not move for some seconds.

The frantic screams of Eddie were all that prevailed around the house.

"You kick like a little girl," Junior suddenly spoke, and followed it with a maniacal laughter. As it rang around in fearful succession, he slowly rose up to his feet. "I'm tired of this game. I want to finish it now. Or play another one perhaps."

"What do you want, Junior?" Old Billy asked. "Do you wanna go home? We'll let you. We'll forget about the ransom."

"I have no home. For now, I just want to have fun. Killing is fun."

Eddie looked at him menacingly. Despite the enormous fear weighing down his mind, he had conclusively thought up that fearing Junior right now would bring no help to either him or his partner. That now was not the time to cringe back in terror and just allow the monster to have his fun at their expense. It was time to act like the criminals that they had long been.

Junior started to move toward them. Eddie braced himself, the ax tightly clasped in his hands. The wounds on his leg were screaming but he paid no attention to it. All of his focus now fell on the monster approaching them, and his eyes blazed with utter ire and an eluded fear.

Old Billy was himself preparing for the coming assault. It eventually got down into this, the worst that it could get. What both of them had never expected was having to go down to this—where they would have to fight for their lives in the hands of a diabolic entity. This would probably spell the end of everything for them.

"Hey, partner," Eddie whispered to Old Billy. "If we get through and actually kill this thing, I'm going to send his scalp back to his family. Will that be alright?"

Old Billy considered this and said, "Send back his whole head."

A brief smirk rose up on Eddie's lips, as if he was sure they could get through and actually kill the thing.

Junior was closing in, but before he could take another step closer, Eddie lunged swiftly toward him, raising the ax over his head for all the force he could swing it with. Yet Junior was quicker to dodge the attack. In only a split of a second, he was already behind Eddie, his hands with all the sharp fingernails in them raised above his head.

"Well, shit." Eddie heard something snap on his back. Shortly he felt a warm flow of something on it he was completely sure was his blood. He looked down to his chest, terrified upon the sight of fingernails that shouldn't be coming out of it.

"Eddie!" Old Billy had screamed, watching with dread the fingers that had gone through his partner's skinny body. He sprang into action immediately, dashing toward the *shithead*, but was quickly outstripped by the swing of the latter's grisly hand—the same one that had stabbed Eddie. A set of deep parallel gashes broke out of the skin in his forearm. The subsequent pain overwhelmed him in an instant and he almost forgot that Junior could very well go for another attack. The *shithead* swung his claw-like hand toward him once more, but this time he was able to back up a few steps and keep himself out of range, albeit a very infinitesimal allowance. That last swing almost slit his throat.

Junior's momentum brought him sprawling to the floor, and Old Billy took the chance to look at Eddie, lying completely still now. He'd no doubt his partner was already dead. Seeing Junior remained on the floor without further movement, he quickly grabbed the ax beside his fallen partner and drove it down onto the open back of the boy. The blade cut through the flesh, and the boy didn't move a muscle. He just hoped, with the littlest amount of it, that that finally did it. That perhaps all it took to end this monster was a single swing of an ax onto his back during a brief window of opportunity that the *shithead* had carelessly given. But he knew it didn't kill him. If a single blow could do it, it must be a blow to the head. So he picked up the ax, and aimed, and began to swing again—

The blade cut through the air in a matter of seconds until it was only an inch away from the back of Junior's head. But that short distance proved long enough for the boy to roll to his side and watch the blade hack the empty floor. "Nice try," he said, as he made his move toward Old Billy. The next moment found the man already pinned down under him. Old Billy raised his arms over his face to fend off the boy's attack. But Junior wasn't attacking yet. He carried on sitting over the man's chest, feeling its rising and falling from his rapid breaths. He began laughing mockingly, lording over his prey.

"Stop this, you son of a bitch!" Old Billy screamed.

Junior just went on laughing.

Old Billy spared a second to look at Eddie sprawled on the floor. Dead. He found himself crying, bringing his arms down on his side. Slowly he was letting go of his guard. The dreadful sense of hopelessness seeped into the situation. All of a sudden, he became completely decided of his doom.

"Go on, kill me!"

Junior let out a much louder laugh before he raised his claw-like hand again and swung it down toward Old Billy in one rapid move. And so this would be it. The man just closed his eyes and waited, certain now of his end. In the wilderness of the closed shutters of his eyes, he saw different scenes from his past that lie in a lengthy line for his mind to pick up. The line seemed to extend infinitely, and he watched each and every scene filled with a mixture of different and profound emotions. This must be what it's like during the last seconds of your life. In a brief span everything and every place you have ever been is bound to come back and fill your thoughts. And though it is fulfilling as it should be, it must also be the most lonesome point in your life. Old Billy compressed all these pictures in his head within the fleeting moment.

The next sounds that came resembled that of bones being snapped, and he expected it to be coming from his ribs being split open. Yet he felt no pain. Then he heard screams, and he knew it didn't come from him.

It came from Eddie. "Die you piece of shit! You lunatic sick shithead! Die! Die! Die!"

Old Billy opened his eyes and sat up on the floor. Junior had been no longer on top of him—he was lying face down on the floor now instead. And bloody. And still being bludgeoned to a sheet by his furious partner.

"Eddie?" As if he wasn't still sure it was Eddie.

The ax rose and dropped a countless times on to the head of Junior. And Old Billy managed to smile, relieved at the sight of the boy being reduced into nothing more than a lifeless and bloody doll. After about a dozen more strikes, Eddie stopped and dropped the ax beside him. He glanced at Old Billy and managed to smile himself, his teeth all hued by blood.

"You all right, partner?" he asked.

"I'm fine. You, you're hurt, Eddie." Old Billy pointed to the chest of his partner, which was puking blood to a stream. He stood up, helped Eddie on his feet, and ushered him to the bed nearby.

"I'm alright now. I have killed the shithead." He laughed, but immediately halted after feeling the pain it shot in his chest.

"Don't move, Eddie. I'm going to get help. We're gonna patch you up, and run the hell out of here."

"I wish I could get the hell out of here, partner. I really wish I could—" Tears started to fall out of his eyes. "I don't think I'll get through this chest problem. I wish I had quit smoking earlier." He laughed again and this time he made it through the pain. *Through the tears.* Eddie was left with just about a dozen of labored breaths before he finally stopped breathing. He died on his partner's arms.

All alone now, and after all these events he never would have imagined to happen, he somehow felt a sense of clarity. There had already been enough violence and terror for him to finally realize the need to shift gears. He had decided to bury this day into the deepest recesses of his memory.

And to bury the *shithead*, ending this once and for all.

He dug a hole in that very floor where it all happened. It was a deep hole, just as he wanted, and into it he threw Junior—what was left clinging to him, anyway—and buried him and every horrifying memory of him and of the past days. At the last bit of dirt finally covering the hole, he began to feel the most satisfying sense of relief he had ever felt in his life, probably the most he would ever feel. It was all over at last.

He buried his partner in the hole they had earlier dug outside, and constructed and erected a cross over his grave. Then finally, he prayed for his eternal peace, wherever the wear in his soul during his time on Earth would lead him in the afterlife.

Old Billy decided to travel toward a far-away province south of the city, where he remembered having a family of relatives he could temporarily ask for shelter. He didn't know what was waiting for him there and he wasn't sure if it was the right direction. He could maybe surrender himself to the authorities, he had also thought of that. But in the end, he felt there's a better life for him in a place somewhere no one would be judging him, and no one would lead him eventually back to the horror he had just freed himself from.

He spent the long hours of travel in the bus asleep, but he wasn't spared the nightmare. The house was at the end of the road he stood facing. Although he could see the sunlight forcing itself through the spaces of the foliage above his head, the whole place around him still appeared to be engulfed in total darkness. He continued moving toward the direction of the house. On the way, he saw the fresh mound of soil over the grave he had made for his late partner, but the cross was no longer planted on it. Then there burst a continuous scream from inside the house, instantly dragging him to a full speed toward the door. When he opened it, a terrible sight met him along with the gradual clarity of the words coming with the sound.

"Come back, partner! Come back! Help me!" Kneeling on the floor in the middle of the dark, Eddie stretched his arm in front of him, beckoning for his partner standing by the door. Tears streamed from his eyes. And in spite of the harrowing features showing on his face, he appeared very alive to Old Billy.

"Eddie?"

"Come back, partner! There has been a mistake."

"What are you talking about—" The bus suddenly came to a stop and Old Billy slipped out of the nightmare. Now there rose a sense of urgency in him—an urgency to get off the bus and the whole of this travel south altogether and return to the house. The nightmare had played in his head to imply something—Eddie was implying something through it.

An exchange of murmurs ensued inside the bus, and from what he managed to pick up, an old woman had requested to get off for a minute and take a much needed bathroom break. Old Billy then knew what to do. He followed the woman as she walked to step off the bus.

"Where are you going, sir?" the bus driver asked.

"I have to get off," Old Billy answered, without glancing at the driver.

"The next stop's just a short distance ahead, sir. Are you sure you're getting off now? This part of the highway here is quite deserted."

Old Billy suddenly sprang into action, grabbing the driver by the collar and pushing him toward the glass window behind him. The other passengers let out almost a unanimous gasp. "I'm getting off now, you understand?"

"Alright, alright. Go. You don't need to be such a—"

Old Billy quickly stepped down out of the bus and crossed to the other side of the highway. From there he began to trace the way back toward north and toward the house he had just hours ago decided to leave.

Several paces further, he got on another bus that was bound for the city, and in less than an hour he was back in the old house. The tranquil surroundings had been almost the same as in the dream, save for the darkness in the latter. But the air around similarly reeked of the same pang of terror A few steps ahead he saw the fresh mound of soil over his late partner's grave. The makeshift cross he made still stood over it, unlike the scene in his dream. He stopped by it and decided to spare a minute to pray again for Eddie.

The door of the house suddenly creaked, and Old Billy shot a glance toward it. Swayed steadily by some gentle breeze of air, the door had a large X mark at its center that looked to him to be drawn using blood. It took him aback, but he wasn't sure he ought to be afraid. He knew for a fact that all around this place, he was the only one alive. Little by little he himself began to doubt it.

He directed his feet back to the direction of the house. There had been something in the air now that helped him aim those feet into that direction, like something was going to happen anytime. Instantly the relief he had felt having killed and buried Junior vanished to the last bit and replaced by the terrorizing fear that held dominion over him during the past ordeal. But in spite of this, he unhesitatingly continued with his steps.

When he had gone just a step short, a brief but strong breeze went past him and onto the door, pushing it fully open and revealing the chaos of things inside the house. It had not been this way when he left it hours back. He was sure of it. Perhaps somebody may have raided the house earlier for valuables. Or the authorities may have already tracked them all the way here. Or maybe—

He walked inside and headed fast to Junior's room, where the *shithead* had been buried. What he found out shook him to his ground. The most horrifying scene he never wanted to see. The soil was now dug up and the grave, much to his horror, was sans of the boy he had buried it in. He looked to the bottom of the hole and saw a piece of paper—the ransom letter! And the words written on the back seemed to have been revised now.

BURY US?

Using blood to write them.

Whatever it meant, whatever it implied, Old Billy decided not to care anymore. He had scudded his way out of the house before he'd lose his sanity inside. And as he passed by Eddie's grave again, he saw that the soil had also been dug up—and whether the grave was empty or not, he did not slow down, for all the reason in the world, to check.

Up in the Air

I was maybe flying in the air for five seconds. But that would be silly. Less than two seconds I guess would be the most accurate count, but if you had been in my shoe, in my shirt, with a leather jacket over it—if yours had been the head in my full-face helmet, you'll know it actually seemed like years had passed while I was up there flying in the air. But let's say it was five seconds.

Riding gloves should be written in the bible of motorcycle riding. I almost always wore a pair. There were maybe two times I could remember when I didn't—the first had been that one time when I had to ride bare-handed because my gloves stank of dog piss and I had to wash and hang them up for days. James Corden, my dog, found them on the floor and, I don't know, maybe saw them like a fire hydrant. Fortunately, I was on a long vacation from work then, so I had no valid reasons to get out of the house and burn doughnuts on the roads, save for that one instance when my wife, whom I had been suspecting of being unfaithful to me with some douchebag at her office, screamed at me into submission, and I was left with no choice but to lift my ass and pick up our little daughter from school. But that had been the

140

only instance in that whole stretch of rest days I had. The rest, I let her go and pick Minnie up herself.

Not that I was a bad father. I love Minnie. I do. I care for her. I certainly don't want her to get home from school all by herself—she's only nine. But my wife, screaming at me like that, like it was the only obligation I have for little Minnie and implying that I can't even do it? I took offense from it then. It seemed it, it was what was in my head then, after I had brought my daughter home and had been left to ponder on it all—when I am left with my thoughts, that's when my head actually functions. And that was my conclusion—she can't scream at me like that. I am the father of the house, I provide for the both of them. I need to be respected, I need to be left alone when I am on my rest day—I can't ride my bike without my riding gloves!

The second time I rode my bike without donning a pair happened just a while ago. A second ago, in fact. Technically, I am no longer riding my bike if I am already afloat in the air at the moment. While I was thinking about that first time and what-not that I just related, a second had passed already since I started flying off of my motorcycle. I knew it would be a violent landing once this whole five-second trip was through. A couple of broken bones at least—more than a couple I'm sure. Spots where skin would be peeled off—particularly on my legs, what with me wearing just a pair of shorts. Bruises. Blood loss. Loss of consciousness, maybe. But at the least I could give myself an assurance that when later I'd land on the asphalted ground, there would not be a serious damage to my head, and the gray matter inside it. I had my helmet to save me from that. I had to trust it. It should do the job, with the ridiculous price tag it came along when I bought it, it should. It was the hip helmet, it was the bomb! If

141

you have it on while you drive the roads, you are the Ghost Rider incarnate. Yet now I had to spend the second second of my current trip thinking and thinking sure this expensive piece of shit could absorb all the momentum of the impact once I'd finally crash on the ground for the boom.

Then the succeeding second suddenly I spent on the thought of my wife. Before all the doubts, before all the suspicions of infidelity, before I looked at her and looked at her like she was less a living thing than James Corden, I used to look at her like she was the Crab Nebula. There was love at the sight of her. She had seemed to me the sun I would gladly agree to collide with and live out the rest of my mortal seconds in such beautiful disaster. When I married her, I knew I married a piece of classical music, a conglomeration of stardust just roaming around the universe for billions of years waiting until I was ready to love. She had been the comeliest little space traveler this side of paradise. I knew little about the chance of her stardust elegance fading away in time.

Now she seemed to me a stranger. The day unfortunately arrived when I found myself waking up and asking, "Who is this woman sleeping in my bed, eating on my table, watching my TV? Who is this alien slowly sucking me into her own vortex of strange components where I'm sure nothing goes along but despair and hatred?" I realized I was living with a foreign entity where no dog-piss-on-my-riding-gloves could make me want to stay at home forever.

She had been the reason why I was compelled to ride my bike today despite not having my riding gloves—this for the second time. The intel that involved a motel room and an hour or two of illicit fluid exchange, and the Ghost Rider was off along the trails, ready for the climax and denouement of this once magical fairy tale to be amalgamated into one seamless scenario. But make no mistake, I wouldn't be there to get my wife, I wouldn't be there to unleash whatever I was supposed to unleash with the supposed celestial pang of jealousy I was supposed to have in my heart. I wouldn't even be there to kill anybody. I would be there because I wanted to end things with her all while catching her red-handed, clothes-less in bed with another man. I pictured out a scene where every hateful word came only from me, because where would she ever pick the slightest right to talk her side of the story while she's wallowing in a fresh iteration of her sin?

But that was all out of the question now. The only room I'd be finding myself in after this journey aloft would be the emergency room. But I could accept it. I had no choice. Instead of the explosive scenario I planned to have in the motel room, I guess I would have to resort to a calmer approach. When she would be standing there beside me on the hospital bed, that'd be the time to tell her it's all over between us. I wouldn't be able to unleash any vehement tirade, or explanation. I knew that already. That moment would be a peaceful nova of what was once had been the only sol my earthly heart was orbiting.

Three seconds had passed, and now's the time I realized that while the helmet may prevent my skull from cracking open, there may still be the chance that I'd slip into some serious aftermath in my brain, perhaps some case of amnesia. I've seen movies with this kind of plot. And I worship movies enough to not dismiss the possibility— may it be majestically infinitesimal—that I would end up waking to a world where everything would seem new to me. I'd lost every memory I have from when I could stretch it all the farthest to these last five seconds before I hit the ground. I couldn't wander along with this chance and spend these last precious seconds of consciousness remembering things that are mired with misery and hate. If I should slip into the void of unconsciousness and open my eyes in a once-again uncharted world, I would rather take with me to the edge the memories from when I feel the most of Earthly joys.

Minnie. My little princess Minnie. She was all the brightest star left in this part of space since everything fell out with my wife. A nine-year old cosmic creation that shone the most beaming of light waves since she was born, since she was laid on my arms the first time, since the first solar flare that came out of her eyes astounded me and conjured in me a soul that was more than just riding gloves, motorcycles, and interstellar choice of words. Minnie was born a star and her gravity was more than I could bear. She pulled me into her own slice of the universe and kept me there revolving, rotating, and making my own place in the world the only place to be in.

As Minnie was growing up, she became even more adorable. And when the animosity between me and my wife started, I was able to focus all my care and endearing to her, and that had been when the realization that only Minnie could bring true happiness to me became entire. No one else came close to my heart than my daughter. My Minnie. My little Minnie. Only two days ago I bought her a new stroller bag, pink-colored, and when she first saw it, I could see solar flares bursting out of her eyes and her joy was a contagion I was wholly reduced to magical infection.

The last second. I never thought this to be the part where I'd reconsider every decision I had been planning to undertake, the one particularly with my wife. I knew the glimmer of her cosmic constitution had become dimmer and dimmer already, and becoming dimmer and dimmer still by the second, but she was still my little Minnie's mother. Every bit of stardust that made up my Minnie's picturesque existence came from the woman I married. And I don't want my little Minnie to grow up within the remnants of an apocalyptic cosmic system. I knew that despite all the hatred and all the ill wills that had slowly severed the orbit my wife and I once had of each other, everything could still be compressed into a singular chance at reconciliation. And in getting through this accident, after this five-second trip up in the air, we would turn things around for the better, for the sake of this share of celestial space we had borrowed from the universe.

And then a second of darkness. I had finally crashed.

I could hear sirens. I could hear people talking. I could hear someone, near, maybe stooping on the ground beside me—must be the emergency response team.

"Just keep still, sir. You've been in an accident. Help is coming. Keep still."

I could feel the heat of the asphalted ground where I had crashed. The visor of my helmet had been broken and detached, and I could see from about five meters away the motorcycle that I had made a diving board of. And despite the apparent intensity of the accident as a whole, I could feel no major or tremendous discomfort anywhere in my body—that maybe I had just made it through this entire tragedy unscathed. Maybe a few bruises and scratches but overall, I couldn't feel any searing pain or realize any part of my body that I can't poke the nerves of. It could be that the shock was overriding the pain—that was a possibility. But I tried to get on my feet, and somehow I managed it. All my bones were left intact, at least. I could hear the man talking me out of doing what I was planning to do, but I needed to know. I took off my helmet, trying to see better what I had just seen earlier when I was on the ground. I had seen a pink stroller bag, lying near the motorcycle.

It couldn't be. I had told her not to go home on her own. That I'd be picking her up today. My little Minnie, my dear little Minnie, she shouldn't be crossing the street on her own—she was only nine.

And my star, she was lying there, on the same asphalted ground where I had crashed into like a miserable meteorite, peaceful, bathed among the clouds of stardust that she had emitted. And it didn't make sense. It didn't make sense at all. (end)

December 29, 1896

The night whispered words he could not understand. *Or were they whispers at all?* It was dark. It was gloomy around the room. The serene tide was completely enveloping the whole world. Sitting by his desk, his dim face being danced on by the shadow of the swaying light of an oil lamp, Dr. Jose Rizal quietly wrote what would be his final literary piece, and which may as well serve as the final outburst of his welling mind. Right now, everything he would do would be a final one. After the sun would rise tomorrow and before it would set again, he would no longer be here.

There was too much to write, he thought. Perhaps the length of one evening would never be enough for him to pen down every crucial piece in his mind. The stream of words would come out eventually. Writing was something he could do anytime. The only question there was right now was how enough would the evening flow in length in accord with the things he would want to write down. *The final words they would hear of me.*

The prison room was poorly lit. Aside from the oil lamp on the table, the room was barely illuminated by a few faint rays from the moon passing through the metal grates that had spanned the length of the window beside where the table was. All the corners were dim. Void. The dance made by the tiny light of the oil lamp could not keep a steady eye on those corners, which in turn made the doctor put them as a background for the swarm of thoughts inside his head. Was he desperate? Was he grieving?

A while ago he had seen a man walk out of one of the corners' shadows. He knew the man very well. He might have been him actually. The man was just a mirror reflection of the very person that he was—it was him who created that man.

"What will happen now, doctor?" the stranger asked.

"The people will know what to do," the doctor answered, looking up eagerly at him. Or it was rather an expression of fright.

"Will they?"

"They will. Eventually. In time."

"You've worked all your life to open their eyes to the truth, doctor. I don't doubt they will know what to do, eventually and in time. But what I wanted to know is what will happen now?"

"I've had my share of the sorrows, my friend. What will happen is that they're going to kill me—I will no longer be here before the next day would pass. I will be going back to my Creator, and it's up to the people left to keep on with the struggle."

"What you gave to the people is freedom through peaceful means, doctor. What the country needs is a revolution."

"They will know."

"You killed me. You threw the lamp into the water and left the hope dangling."

The doctor looked through the eyes of the figure with his own fierce eyes. "What do you want, Ibarra?"

"You will know, doctor," Crisostomo Ibarra replied before he turned his back slowly and walked his way into the shadows again. And just as the figure vanished among the empty dark, another voice rolled around the room, a voice he remembered very well.

"Pepe."

"Inang?"

Walking from the shadows of another corner of the room, his old mother was carrying a small bundle of blankets over her arms. But it was not just a bundle of blankets. It was a newborn wrapped completely by layers of cloth soiled with mud in many places. He felt a nerve twitch painfully inside his heart when he saw it. That was exactly how he had wrapped his dead son before he buried it under his hut back in Dapitan.

He stood up immediately and moved toward his mother and the dead boy. Teodora Alonzo was crying, her tears visibly falling on the corpse she cradled on her arms.

"Inang—"

"What's going to happen, Pepe?" his mother asked the same question, now coming to him tearfully. "Who will die? How many more will die?"

The doctor looked at the woman with heavy eyes, aiming to seize the time to speak, but could not get another word to push out of his mouth. Beamed by the scanty light of the moon, the dead infant's face looked like some molded Plasticine that had apparently started to decay. He looked at it with some reticent bliss, thinking it would not be long now before he was going to see him again in the place after this life. *My son, my son.* The feeling of relief somehow washed away the desperation heightened up in his head filled with rambling thoughts. He averted his eyes toward the face of his mother, and she looked at him now as if she was going to smile, in contrast to the outburst she showed a moment ago.

"Everything will be alright, Inang," the doctor at last spoke. "Everything will be alright. My death will spark a hope among the people, and they will know what to do. The time is coming."

"The people will look up to you, Pepe."

"And it's a shame to die at the height of it all, sir." Suddenly another voice stole the current scene of the prison room, grabbing the attention of the doctor and made It go into a complete turn. A figure gradually emerged from behind the one of his mother. It moved toward him, passing through the woman and leaving her as a thin perturbed smoke which then slowly disappeared as it did inside the head of Dr. Rizal. His attention rested now on the newcomer, a figure that did not belong in any of the current swarm of thoughts inside his head.

"Who are you?" he asked.

The man did not look like a Spaniard or a Filipino. He was clad in a neat set of dark coat and tie, almost invisible in camouflage with the dark corner behind him. He spoke a smooth tone of English which readily made the doctor associate with an American. He was actually one.

"My name is Gary Morris, doctor," the man answered, offering his hand for a shake. "It will be a pleasure to meet and finally speak to you."

"I'm Jose Rizal," the doctor returned, slightly hesitating.

"Yes, I know you. I have been watching your whereabouts for the past few years."

"The past few years?" Dr. Rizal stared at him in surprise.

"Yes, doctor. I know all about your travels. I know all about your ideals. And I find you interesting."

This time the face of the doctor turned sour. "Were you following me? Who really are you? Are you a spy of the Spanish government?"

"No, I'm not, doctor. And I'm not here to cause you any trouble or harm. I looked up to you and your abilities, and maybe I could in fact be of help."

"What are you talking about? I am not getting any of what you are saying anymore. Why are you here?"

"I'm here to offer you a choice, doctor. It is a choice that may help you in your cause. And most of all I'm here to tell you a truth that had been kept a secret and a mystery throughout the ages. It's kept reduced merely as a myth, a bedtime story for children. Something many of us don't believe, which I will no doubt find you on the similar side."

"I don't understand you, sir. I have a lot to write about tonight. Tomorrow they're going to execute me and I can't afford to pass this night without composing my final thoughts to leave to the people. If you're just a fabrication of my mind, then I'm telling you I have to quell you right now. I don't know how I got to mend something like you inside my head, but I really don't need you this time. Especially this time."

"You can try washing me off your head, doctor. Go try."

The doctor threw himself back on his seat by the table and quickly grabbed his pen. He moved his hand over the stack of papers on one side of the table and resumed writing. His head bowed down and eyes adhered to the paper, he wrote in his usual swift strokes, thinking that the stranger was no longer in the room with him. But he was wrong. His eyes moved up with his head still bowed down, trying to catch a glimpse of the man, at least his shadow on the floor before him, and expecting to see nothing of it this time. Gary Morris still stood there however.

"I'm sorry to upset you, doctor," Gary spoke.

"You're supposed to be gone by now."

"Again, my apologies that I may only upset you, doctor. But pushing me out of your mind, just like what you said, is simply impossible. I'm not a figment of your imagination."

The doctor gave out a short sarcastic laugh. "You're starting to get funny, sir."

"Gary, doctor."

"Yes, Gary. It is I who may upset you, actually. In a short time, in five seconds, you'll vanish like a popped bubble. In five, four, three, two—"

Nothing happened. Gary still stood before him.

"Doctor? I'm still here."

"Let's count again. Five, four . . ."

"No, doctor. I'm afraid you'll disappoint yourself again. You see, I'm real. I'm not a fabrication of your rather expansive mind."

"What do you want from me, Gary?"

"I want to give you a chance to pursue what you have started, doctor."

A series of silent seconds followed after that statement. Dr. Rizal could not look at the stranger before him with anything other than a touch of surprise in his face. His thoughts had gone in a haze, out of control, reduced to a state of complete chaos.

Gary walked toward the sealed window beside the table and took a couple of seconds looking up at the sky outside. Tranquil and still, the moon beamed its rays all over his face and his complexion shone as bright as the moonlight that bounced over it. The doctor was seeing this in aghast. The mystery of this strange man had become more and more suggested as seconds went along.

"As a child, have you been sent to bed by your mother at night with stories about strange creatures roaming the land and bringing a frightful scare to you, doctor? Have you been scared by the supernatural tales told of you during those times?"

"What are you talking about? What's that to do with our current situation?"

"Do you believe in ghosts, doctor? Witches? Lycanthropes?" Gary paused for a split of a second, wanting to draw some height on the next word he was going to say: "Vampires?"

"This isn't making any sense, sir."

"It will." From the moon outside the window, Gary shifted the direction of his eyes toward the doctor and showed him a wide grin—a terrifying, wide grin. Two sharp canines sprouted from either side of his smile and made his overall countenance a picture of grimacing terror. The doctor watched in utter disbelief, all color in his skin seemingly drained from fear. The air passing in between them suddenly became very cold for the doctor. He felt frozen solid from what he was witnessing.

Gary erased the smile he put out from his face. His teeth now hidden from view, the doctor was then subsequently able to gather himself, as if seeing that monstrous indication was like putting him under a spell.

"Stay back, sir!" he exclaimed, stumbling a few steps backward.

"I suggest you keep your voice low, doctor. Catching a few more set of ears won't do us any good here right now. Calm down."

"God help us!"

"Relax, doctor. You don't have any reason to fear me. I would suggest that you calm yourself down, return on the chair, and listen to me. This is very important."

"And you expect me to do such things? You're a . . . you're a vampire? For God's sake, don't you dare get near me!"

"Yes, a vampire in the same room with you. A vampire who wants to talk things with you. Please, doctor, if you would just listen to me."

The doctor drew a series of heavy breaths while he stared frightfully at the vampire. The moonlight reflecting on Gary's face turning it more sinister, and all the while his pale lips mumbling and asking for trust.

Lend me your ears, doctor. Let me tell you a story about a hideous vampire—

"Here, sit down." Gary pushed the chair a little distance toward the doctor. Slowly, cautiously, Dr. Rizal moved to take the chair. His eyes were still locked on Gary nevertheless. "That's it. That's it."

"This is a dream, you know. A product my mind has made out of sheer desperation."

"It may be a dismay to know it isn't true, doctor. I am real."

Dr. Rizal had sat down.

As the silence passed between them, Gary slipped his hand inside his coat and fumbled something inside his pocket. From it he drew a booklet out and thrust it forward on the table, looking intently at the yet stirred doctor.

"This is part of the diary of a good friend of mine," he spoke. "Like myself, he's also a vampire."

Dr. Rizal picked the diary up and started opening the pages. He skimmed over them, not really finding interest. Not even reading a single word from any of the pages. He was however curious whose diary it was.

"A man named Abraham Lincoln," Gary said.

The doctor caught the name with surprise, and immediately returned to the diary, skimming again over the pages with an intent to read now. From random pages his eyes caught the words "President," "Office," "Gettysburg," "Vampires." He stopped abruptly on the last word. *Lincoln mentioning vampires in his diary?*

"I would have wanted the two of you to meet, doctor," Gary spoke, noticing the look of doubt and surprise on the face of Dr. Rizal. "But the president has become busy these past few months with his duties in the Circle."

"The Circle?"

"A group of vampires, doctor. Our group. With the most recent members being Abraham Lincoln and Edgar Allan Poe."

Dr. Rizal nodded briefly, with still a trace of doubt mingled with the gesture. Doubt had been consistently existent in the doctor's thoughts since Gary had appeared. But who could blame him? It is not every day that someone barges into your room—your prison cell, no less—and tells you he is a vampire, and that the great Abraham Lincoln and Edgar Allan Poe are vampires as well.

"This group of yours," the doctor spoke, "what are you aiming for? What are your objectives in forming such a group?"

"We are a group of vampires who support the betterment of the majority, doctor. We are consisted of members who have ideals and a rather rational outlook of the world. We aren't just the stereotyped vampires the myths have smeared our name with."

"I think that needs further elaboration for my sake, Gary."

"I understand so, doctor. I also see the need of it. And there are some things you have to know too."

The doctor put aside the diary of Lincoln and heaved a sigh. The look on his face was one of deep contemplation, apparently reaching for his wit's end to imbibe everything into his system completely. The night drawing nearer to its death, Gary suggested that they proceed at once with their impending discourse.

"There have been vampires over the course of time, doctor. Countless of them have roamed around the world, existing side by side with the living, oftentimes feasting on them. Atrocities relating to vampires are more rampant than those that aren't—those done by the very evil of humans."

"You know these vampires?"

"Some of them I do. Many names have endured throughout the centuries, some of them you may have known. Elizabeth Bathory. Vlad the Impaler. Ring a bell?"

"And they are still walking the Earth up to this day?"

Gary nodded.

"They are part of the Circle?"

"No, no, no. Of course not."

"All this time I thought the world could no longer be more perilous."

"We already have a constant eye on Bathory. The Impaler we are still tracking down. Currently he has been the most hunted vampire outside the Circle."

"He could strike anytime then."

"Anytime, you say. In fact, the latest cases we attributed to him just happened within the last decade."

Dr. Rizal looked at him questioningly.

"1888. You know him as the Ripper."

"Jack the Ripper?"

"Yes, he is, doctor."

"That's unbelievable. Almost."

Gary was pleased with the nascent progress of the doctor's interaction with him, and he felt it was the right time to get to the core of the matters at hand.

"But the Ripper is not the concern we have right now, doctor. I'm here because I wanted to offer you a chance to see your life's works' progress, nevertheless as an undead. If you're willing, then you can have the opportunity of pursuing your cause for the Filipinos."

"I can't see how a vampire could pursue his patriotism, but I will not deny that I am up for a bit of consideration on the offer."

"Well I doubt if there's a better chance you'll have in pursuing your patriotism in the coming years if you won't be in a form of a vampire, doctor."

"What do you mean?"

"One is what is bound to happen to you tomorrow, and two is because they are coming here."

"Vampires?"

"Yes. The ones outside the Circle."

"Why are they coming here?"

"Abraham Lincoln has wiped them off in the United States. The Civil War not only quelled the forces in

157

support behind them, but has also hurt them where they could feel pain the most—their stomachs."

"The Civil War victory of the Union crushed the Confederacy, and abolished slavery in the States."

"Exactly. Turns out that the slavery has been an ulterior option for vampires outside the Circle to simply acquire their meals legally."

Dr. Rizal's face brightened with horror.

"I and the other members of the Circle fought alongside Lincoln in the Civil War. All just to end the bitter trade of slaves and the fatal abuses of the vampires behind the South."

The web of information about the war in the States, Abraham Lincoln, and the vampires mapped the hazy thoughts of the doctor for the next couple of minutes. After his years of struggle to win the rights of his fellow Filipinos from the colonizers, he never thought that there had been a crisis in the United States that was far more sinister than what he had known. The logical sequence of events in the history seemed very much reasonable to not surpass any doubt. He had tried being suspicious a while ago, but it proved to be bootless. The truth was already laid here in front of him, where he could not bat a blind eye.

How would a war between supernatural forces proceed? How could one win such war? And Gary said that they were coming here. Obviously to feed off from the Filipinos who could no way resist them. Patriotism after all would take more than wits to possess.

"They shall not lay their hands on my fellow countrymen," the doctor declared.

"You know better than I do about that spirit, doctor. What I wanted to know now is either your consent or your refusal to my offer."

Dr. Rizal fell back into another round of deep thought. Weighing sides on each of his hands, he first considered the possible effect of it on his physical body assuming it would no longer be of a human being. Vampires had been a myth for him ever since, and wondering how it would feel like to be one had never crossed his mind before.

I'm a doctor. I know a whole lot about the human body. And being a blood-sucking, pale creature was out of the question, much more being answerable by any branch of Science.

On the other hand was the fact that if he refused it now, then this would be the end of it for him. All he could ever hope was that the people would eventually find the courage to stand up for their rights after his execution. During such time, he would already be but a soul walking absent of the subsequent outcomes of his hopes. What a way to end his constant struggles! There were a lot of people out there hoping and looking up to him, possibly seeing his impending death as a tragic event on their search for individuality in this country.

"Will I be engaging in an armed revolution if I give you my consent?" the doctor asked, at length.

"There will always be a need for arms, doctor," Gary answered. "These people, they have seized you using the power of arms. They oppressed your people. You try hard to search for your place in the society they put you in, but you are still nothing but a country of oppressed people. You know better than I do on that. I have read your novels."

Dr. Rizal gazed at the man carefully through the swaying flicker of the oil lamp. He studied every emotion in his face. *A blood-sucking hideous creature himself in fact.*

"You are not the first one I approached, doctor," Gary spoke again. "Although you were the one I have considered approaching first."

The doctor uttered no reply, just an inquiring look at him.

"There's a brave young man I knew. By the fire he has in his heart and the courage he possesses, I can see a good potential in him carrying out my offer. Andres Bonifacio."

"I know him, certainly."

"And he does know you too. In fact he admires you. When I came to him, he was holding this book, your novel I found out afterward, and has required everyone in his group to read and understand it. He is hoping you could help him in his cause to win your independence. He has seen hope in your words, doctor."

"But he's doing it through violent means. What the country needs is Spain's recognition of us as part of her. To have the same set of rights as her people have."

"I know what you believe in, doctor. Pen is mightier than the sword. But for how long?"

"Gary—"

"How long would a pen serve you? Do you have enough ink for you to reach what you aimed for? How many lives, how much more blood should be spilled for nothing?"

"By spilling more blood?"

"By showing them that you can outfight them. Even to death."

Silence ensued, and the only noise audible was the heavy breathing of the doctor.

"What happened with your meeting with Andres?" the doctor asked.

"He refused. I expected it, nevertheless. Being an undead would deplete the very reason he is fighting. Of course, he is fighting for the lives of the people. And he's doing it alive."

"And you think I would do otherwise?"

"Don't think I do. I have much more expected the same thing from you than from Andres."

"Why are you offering it to me now?"

"He told me to try. He thinks you would be bound to consider this more now that you have been sentenced to die. He says there might be a chance that you would not let an opportunity to continue the fight for freedom slip."

"He thinks I am desperate."

"He thinks you are wiser."

The night was slowly falling deeper and deeper. Time was running out for the doctor.

"I have seen some of the Confederate vampires communicating with the Spaniards in this country. They are slowly leeching their way in the situation. Doctor, they are bringing the slave trade here, using your people."

"That cannot be!"

"They're starving. And they're looking to acquire their food at the expense of your people."

Dr. Rizal fell into another ponderous state. His face had turned gravely serious this time, and Gary hoped this was finally the time he had wanted to have. They both were silent for a very long time. Gary had walked over to the window again, looking straight into the bright moon. Blinking no eye. The doctor watched the swaying light of the lamp, and recalled the story his mother had once told him.

The moth flew around the flame, mesmerized by the beauty of it. Its mother warned it not to fly any closer. But it insisted. It wanted to touch the flame. And as the distance gradually thinned out, the flame caught its wing, and the moth vanished, burned out.

Tell me what to do, Inang.

And in his mind he thought he could see her. Smiling. *You know what to do, Pepe.*

I know what to do.

Dr. Rizal woke up at 4 AM. A guard stood by the door of his cell, looking straight ahead. Slowly, he sat on his bed, feeling a little dizzy. And then he remembered what happened. *Or what he thought had happened.*

Was it all a dream?

Starting from Abraham Lincoln, to Edgar Allan Poe, to Gary, to Elizabeth Bathory, to Vlad the Impaler, to Andres Bonifacio. *Puñeta! Of course, it's all a dream!*

"Silly. Perhaps that's a desperate measure my subconscious took to ease me on my deathbed," he whispered to himself. He laughed quietly, but the guard had heard it however and looked at him, confusion traced in his eyes.

In English, the doctor said to him, "Can you compose my last words?"

But the guard just ignored it.

The doctor stood up finally and walked to the window, feeling the kind and cold breeze of the early dawn. He looked for the sun, and deep down in his mind, he thought, *Will I burn in the sunlight?* Then suddenly, a sharp pain rose up to his right arm. He twisted it for a check and found something in his wrist. Two pairs of small dots, almost the same distance apart for each one, were found in both the front and the back. The pain was escalating slowly.

He touched that part with his other hand, trying to calm the nerves inside. But he felt nothing—what nerves would he calm when there seemed to be not a nerve there at all? He searched for the throb, the sign of life in that part of a human body. And one discovery led to another: No nerve, no pulse, not a human body anymore.

APPETIT

At the end of the street stood a quaint, little funeral parlor. For more than a decade, it had been one of the few landmarks of this street, in actuality one so stand-out it seemed a larger locale than the street itself. A Mr. Adrian Yu owned it—an old stingy fellow who looked way deader than any of the bodies his funeral parlor had had taken in.

Business had been good through the years. Mr. Yu had amassed quite a value of fortune from it, and it still seemed sturdy enough to probably continue operations for a lot more years.

He currently had two workers under his employ: a middle-aged man Ronnie, and his teenage son, Marcus. The former had been working for Mr. Yu for the better part of a decade, succeeding a number of previous workers who had either died while still employed or was fired because of erratic, outrageous behavior, not to mention that some of them had been purportedly necrophilic. Marcus started working in there three months ago, after the latest one with Ronnie accidentally drank a whole glassful of embalming fluid, mistaking it for a glass of water, and died almost instantly.

Business went about its usual routine one morning when a shabby homeless man came upon the door. His haggard countenance suggested the many days he had wandered off the streets, skipping nights of sleep, and days and days of meals. He had had on a set of tattered soiled-to-the-earth clothing, and though it seemed like the shirt was not large, it hung loosely from his body you could still fit an elephant in the remaining space inside.

Marcus found him already leaning on the glass door of the establishment's receiving office. His face lay adhered against the glass, and the friction between it and the man's face distorted its skin it made his gaunt eyes flash at Marcus with an appearance of bloodshot horror and dread. Hastily Marcus leaped up and scudded out to accost the stranger. The latter pulled his face away from the door so Marcus could push it full before him. The pungent smell of the homeless man coursed immediately through the space of the door opened, drawing a wincing face out of Marcus's as if he had just been hit by a punch on the face. A hand up on his nose, he looked at the stranger with a sharp, contemptuous stare.

"What the hell, man? You smell worse than a man died a hundred years ago!"

"Pardon me being so filthy, mister," the homeless man said, "but I actually haven't had taken a bath for years. I am so sorry."

"Stand up."

The stranger stood up to his full height, to only about an inch shy of five feet. Marcus, who stood almost six feet tall, looked down literally at him, nose still concealed by the palm of his hand. He could see the top of the stranger's head, its disheveled and very thick hair, a bird's nest by appearance.

Soon a sound of footsteps came pouncing down as from a staircase and coming nearer toward them. Mr.

Adrian Yu appeared by the door and instantly pulled himself back as the stench also came to hit him with a gaseous invisible jab. His feet recoiled a few steps backward and he muttered in almost a yell, "My God— Marcus, what's that foul odor about?"

"From this man here, sir," Marcus answered, a finger pointed to the homeless man.

Mr. Yu moved to push the glass door back to a close, but the stranger immediately blocked it with his hand.

"Please, sir. I haven't eaten for a long time. I've been wandering around for years."

"No, no. I'm running a business here, not an institution for the destitute. Go away now. My business is going to be in bad luck with you around here. Go!"

"Please. I will do anything you say. I'm willing to work for you. You don't have to pay me. Just a place to stay and something to eat."

Mr. Yu stopped short, his attention clearly caught by the statement. Something in it rang like a bell inside his ears. He could faintly hear within him the sound of paper bills shuffled slowly, teasing him—his greed rapidly creeping up. His servitude for money is as concrete as his belief in business bad lucks, and business bad lucks are facts of life to him.

The proposal of the homeless stranger to work in the funeral parlor without pay sounded very agreeable to him. In fact he would bite on some such proposals any time any day.

He cast a rather deceptive look at the stranger. The stench that had a while ago assaulted his nose had been thrown off of their gathering now. There was only him, and Marcus, and the filthy stranger, the glass door halfway between them—the foul smell was no more.

"What is your name?" Mr. Yu at length spoke. He pushed the glass door to a full open.

"My name is Onil Batayo."

"Well, Onil, I'm Adrian Yu. I am not much a picky employer when it comes to getting workers, as you know my business deals with people who can't anymore mind at all what hands are touching them. You are obviously in dire deficiency of sanitation. But that won't matter. I only have two able men working for me currently, and I shall be gratified to have an extra pair of hands."

A bright smile touched Onil's face.

"Are you taking me in, sir?" he asked.

"Yes. But let's be clear first, that you are going to work for me without wage. Are we clear with that?"

"Yes, sir. I will work for you for free."

"Okay, that's understood. I will provide you with a place to sleep and food. Marcus here and his father will teach you the work you will be doing in the morgue. We keep a busy environment around here, Onil. So I expect that you get your hands actively working every time. I loathe lazy workers."

"I understand everything. I do."

"Good. And one thing, take a damn bath or you'll wake the hell out of those dead bodies inside."

And with the job offer, Mr. Yu took Onil in to work in his funeral business. First and foremost was throwing the newbie on a long, badly needed bath. It proved no easy endeavor unsurprisingly. He stayed under the shower for almost an hour and by the end used up three boxes of soap and a dozen sachets of shampoo. Yet even after the exhaustive wash-over, Mr. Yu still felt a slight brush from the air of traces of the stench that managed to still cling to Onil. He spoke no word about it, nevertheless.

Afterward, he provided him a set of clothes to put on aside from the shirt he was to wear for work. Onil put the clothes on and reappeared before his employer. He stood apparently oblivious that his body was still releasing a putrid smell, and Mr. Yu, furtively keeping his reaction to the stench, decided he might just get used to it, thinking that it had already been natural for Onil to smell so awfully bad given that he had been homeless and lacking of hygiene for a very long time.

Onil looked at his master with his gaunt, heavy eyes.

"I will let you reside here," Mr. Yu spoke. "In return, you will work for me and respect me and give me your loyalty. We have agreed that you will take no wages for your service, right? Also, I'll provide you with meals."

Onil nodded to every word that his employer said, and upon hearing the last one, his eyes abruptly widened and they looked at Mr. Yu with a glow.

"I am so sorry, Mr. Yu, but I am really so starved out right now," he said.

"Ah, I can see. I know. My wife is currently in the kitchen cooking for dinner. You can join—" Mr. Yu stopped short as a thought quietly struck him— the incessant stench of Onil, in particular—before he resumed, "—you will have a share of that."

Onil grinned excitedly, thanking Mr. Yu with fervent intent. It had been a long time since somebody was ever kind to him. This deed was rare. Nobody wanted to dine with him before. Well, whoever would, with the stench?

When the meal was prepared, Mr. Yu told Onil furtively that his wife wasn't used to having strangers around the dining table with them, and she might become uneasy if he joined. Onil took this lightly and agreed to eat on his own in the kitchen. At the moment the only thing that mattered to him was filling himself up. He had been starving to death.

The meal consisted of a plate of fried chicken, mixed vegetables, and a cup of rice. The chicken was about the size of his fist, the vegetables were only about three spoonfuls, and the rice didn't really look so intimidating. He ate them all generously nonetheless, and with speed suggestive of the meals he had skipped over the span of his wandering years. Now he could see for himself why it was a good thing after all that he ate separately from Mr. Yu's dining table. He ate with his bare hand, carelessly and improperly. Some morsels of food fell down on the floor, and he ate them anyway, without a tiny bit of hesitation. He seemed more like a starving wild beast than a human. Within five minutes, he scooped the plate empty, spic and span—even consuming the chicken bones. Then he went to the refrigerator nearby and drank a whole pitcher of water.

For a moment he felt full. In a plural number of years that he had nearly nothing in his stomach, he felt full after a single meal. Briefly, he felt that what he had just consumed turned in sufficient on filling the years he carried an empty stomach. But that moment faded instantly. He realized that he was still, and even more, famished than ever. The years of starvation he endured proved too mammoth to be overcome by a single scanty meal. The craving became even more intense now.

He stood up and wandered slowly across the room. His instinct turned into a hunter out in search for food. He opened the refrigerator and found a good amount of edible items in there, but he thought better of it. He must not make such early impression to Mr. Yu, who had just taken him in his residence and employ in but less than a day. He closed the refrigerator and wandered his eyes around the rest of the kitchen.

When he at last realized that there was nothing in the kitchen he could eat aside from the refrigerator food he already ruled out, he quietly slipped out of the house and into the adjacent garden.

He walked around there warily. Around was a teeming scatter of vegetation. There were flowers blooming in the current moonlight, passing beauty around despite the dark. But Onil had no inclination to receive the pass. He walked around mad for something to devour. He passed by a small shrub with green leaves sticking out of its slender stem, and stopped to glance at it. He stooped down upon it, and there was fragrance, and there was enticement swiftly conjured. And just as swiftly he snatched it from the soil it sprouted from and shoved it, leaves and all, into his mouth. The plant went cruising down his stomach, where the latter would do its biological process. But that didn't do near enough to fill up his appetite for the night. For the next several minutes he circled the garden and ate every growing plant there was, nevertheless careful not to make a stormy aftermath out of the scene with every plant he picked.

He was in the middle of this binge when he heard Mr. Yu call his name from the house, and he got back in the kitchen as fast as he got out.

"I went out, Mr. Yu," Onil said. "To get some air."

"Okay. Follow me, I'll show you where you'll be sleeping."

Mr. Yu ushered Onil into a small room which was situated beside the morgue. It had a little window on one wall, which overlooked the wall fencing Mr. Yu's premises from the neighbor's on that side. This wall was aptly high for sunlight and occasional breeze to pass through the window. A bed, a drawer, and a small desk fan atop populated the room.

"I have some clothes inside the drawer I am not using anymore," Mr. Yu said, looking at it. "You can have them."

Onil nodded. Well, actually, his mind was wandering off somewhere at the moment. He wondered if—

Mr. Yu stepped out of the room after some additional words, which Onil had not paid attention to. He only kept nodding his head. He lied on the bed deep in thoughts, still hungry.

Onil's employment in the mortuary officially started the following day. Mr. Yu woke him up at five in the early morning, telling him he was sorry for forgetting to inform him about the work schedule the day before. Onil agreed to it, while he really had no choice, but quickly inquired about breakfast, wondering if he would have one.

"Yes, we'll eat at once," Mr. Yu answered.

Onil got up from bed and ran his way out, ahead of his boss, but stopped upon reaching the door. He remembered he was no longer a vagrant out in the world where his behavior wouldn't be appropriate for this new role of his.

The breakfast consisted of an egg, a piece of sausage, a cup of coffee and a cup of rice. Onil took a look at the meal and doubted if it would even reach his stomach, but again he confonted himself with the choice he didn't have. So, he ate his meal as he could, left alone to himself, and got up hastily afterward. When he brought himself back before his boss, Mr. Yu told him the first line of business was the garden, specifically cleaning of the garden. The newbie was quicker to cater to it than his boss expected. But to him, it was a chance to eliminate any telltale signs of last night.

He was a little disappointed, he wouldn't deny. But from the long years he had wandered off, this sense of disappointment was no more a novel thing to him. After all, with a bottomless appetite too rare for plural mentions across history books, it was a mystery in itself what measure it would take to fill that abyss.

He was out in the garden later, sweeping some dried leaves, when he heard a rustling noise nearby. It came from behind a row of flower pots. It would eventually stop, but would come again after a moment. Upon looking more intently, he caught a glimpse of two furry hind legs, slender and dark. The cat purred, as if acknowledging the observation. It lied on a small area between two of the pots.

This somehow rang with a sound of delight in his head. His stomach joined in with a grumble. He moved toward the pots, careful and quiet, and saw the feline reposing and unmindful of him closing every inch between them. As his shadow dimmed over the cat, he looked warily around if anyone was looking, and after seeing no darted eyes toward him, he picked up a rock nearby half the size of the animal and smashed the brains out of it. It went with a fleeting feline cry and then was still, for a moment then for good. The cat now lied dead on his hands. He made another turn of his eyes around to see if someone had peeked at the murder, and still found no witness. He put the dead animal behind the pots, completely concealing it from view.

Two bodies were taken in that day.

When night came, Onil sat on his bed in disappointment again. The dinner of a piece of fish and a cup of rice a while ago did not even seem to make it to his stomach. He was starving to death as the disappointment was pressing down on him.

His stomach grumbled and remembered something. Off his feet he leapt and scurried out of the room. As he passed by the morgue entrance he was suddenly crossed by a fragrance suggestive of some food. There was meat in there, he knew there was.

But he eluded the redolence, at least for the moment, and went on walking all the way out of the house. Behind the pots the dead cat he had hidden earlier that day was still there, pestered now with flies. The blood that had oozed out of its head had congealed where most of the flies were crowding. Off they flew chaotically when he stretched his arm toward the cadaver to pick it up. It was their food, anyway. But oh Onil, it was his!

He held the dead animal over his arms and carried it back toward his room. He moved his feet in tiptoes, lest he might cause some noise and wake his boss up. But as he moved forth on the return to his room, with meal on his arms, he heard some faint noises coming from the morgue. There were footsteps and scratching sounds at first, but later, a string of short almost inaudible moans started to mingle with the steady air, which terrified him in an instant. His mind went to overdrive and thought about probable paranormal roots of the sounds. Being in a funeral house made it more likely in his horrified mind. His heart palpitated more rapidly and sweat fell from his forehead in huge lumps. His blood ran cold inside his veins.

A picture of a corpse inside the morgue coming back to life, standing up, opening its bloodshot eyes, walking limply out of there and toward him ran in his mind. Its pale hands would be like claws and it would aim them to him, and then it would eat him, drink off his blood, and leave him a mess of himself. It was a terror to comprehend.

Quickly he ran to his room like a dog chased, leaving the door locked behind him. He crouched on the corner of his bed, allowed seconds to pass staring at the door, and no sooner began to feel safe. Just as soon as his nerves settled down, he went on with his feline meal.

And somehow, the cat was able to hush his stomach.

Marcus owned the animal and the next day he went looking for it. Every morning, he would take a chair out into the garden and sit there to eat his breakfast, where he'd then drop morsels of his food to the cat waiting by his feet.

Marcus had sat on his chair and had beckoned the cat with a whistle, but it hadn't appeared like usual. Maybe it just wandered off, he thought. It'll show up later.

But the cat was never going to show up again.

In the days that followed Onil had gradually become mad from his constant insatiable hunger. He was starving every minute. He wanted to eat the world if that was what it would take. His hunger saw no end.

Days rolled by. It had become a habit of Onil to hunt for rats down the ditch at the back of the funeral house. Rats were abundant, but sometimes he would be lucky, at times when some stray cats waltzing by the house wouldn't be. He would kill these poor animals, hide them in someplace somewhere temporarily during the day, and savor them at night before going to sleep, just as the first time with Marcus's cat. This he had done for days so carefully clandestine. Nobody had the slightest idea that there was a sick fuckwad that had come to town.

Despite that, he had worked diligently for Mr. Yu. He learned every detail of the job at a rapid rate, which greatly satisfied his boss. Throughout the training, he also showed so much enthusiasm and delight, as if embalming the dead had been his true calling all along. Something ulterior a motive however had been in play behind this showing of positive attitude, which in fact was most evident the first time he touched a corpse. In a disturbing, albeit unsurprising turn of events, he derived a strong eagerness to put one in a dish.

He began fancying a way of procuring the parts he could replace the cats and rodents with. It wasn't too far different from the animals, after all, except that the ones in the morgue didn't need to be killed anymore. And obviously he had to do everything at night. It wouldn't be just as simple as the hide-behind-the-pots scheme.

So he tried his luck. On the very night the plan sprouted in his head, he decided to sneak inside the morgue. The somnolent evening had gone deeper, and he had stayed up late for the plan. After making sure that the place was already clear and quiet, he made his first step out of his little room toward the morgue. He tiptoed at the next step and then stopped to relay his senses further about. No one was watching him, he perceived. He took another tiptoe and stopped, and then went on until he was but one more step from the entrance of the mortuary.

"I'm good," he said to himself, and took the last step. But as he did so, the faint noises coming from inside the morgue, the same ones that had scared him once a few nights back, whiffled into the air again. It withheld him from stepping in even further, because the noises scared him again this time. He ran quickly back to his room and dived on the bed. Immediately he lost sense of his starving stomach and catered instead the fear that rapidly circled his mind.

"Sleep. Sleep. Sleep—" He murmured, straight on to a thousand times, but the noises just seemed to continue terrorizing his head. He covered himself with a blanket and started singing himself a lullaby, all the while inserting repetitions of the word "sleep" in between verses.

The noises coming from inside the morgue kept his ears captive despite his attempts to distract himself. They were persistent, and they seemed to grow even louder in time. But soon the noises started to deviate. Drifting distant from the terrifying ones that had scared his wits, the current noises now fed him a sense of curiosity instead of fear.

The noises were no longer faint, as if real. There even seemed to be some words along them now, completely putting Onil in a curious haze. His hunger and want of sleep obscured, he now managed to step down from his bed, thinking of going back to the morgue and making it inside. Fear begets monotone, and only the curious has something to find.

His steps had led him out of the room now. From there the words began to construct some sense. He stayed still and silent, trying to make it out.

Moans. *Hot. Inside. Still.* Moans.

Doesn't make sense, he thought. He tried concentrating again.

You're still hot inside, damn it.

Onil was mystified, surprised, and appalled. The sense he made out with the words was nothing like he expected it to be, not a whisper close to being of paranormal sorts even. His feet moved bravely forward on to the path leading to the morgue.

The words right there by the door, as he stopped and stood, became even clearer, and became clear enough for him to determine whose voice it was. Noticing the door ajar, he slowly pushed it to a width enough where he could slip half of his face to peer inside and to prove his hunch of whoever was bringing it on in there. There was no doubt in his mind who it was, and he assured himself he wasn't wrong. And he was not.

Standing by one side of what looked like a hospital bed was Mr. Yu, his back toward the door, where Onil stood quietly peering in. Mr. Yu had no shirt on and his dark trousers and underwear were off below his hip, clinging to the middle of his knees. His bare ass was out for all the world to see, and at the moment still in action. Somebody had to be lying on the bed. His wife perhaps—

But why the hell would they do it inside this room? The cold wind around nudged the cheeks of Onil, and he could not help but shiver. Inadvertently, the uncontrollable motion of his body, his arm in contact with the door in particular, slightly pushed it an inch inside and stretched the opening. This sequence of seemingly trifle events had the situation for worse when the door consequently made a noise that caught Mr. Yu's attention. You cannot imagine his face when he glanced to see Onil by the door.

"Onil, what are—" He had quickly snatched his lower garments and pulled it back up to his waist.

"What are you doing?" Onil said, stepping inside the room now. "What—what are you doing here with—" He tried to look past Mr. Yu at whoever was lying on the bed behind him. Mr. Yu in turn attempted to block his view of it. Now, you cannot imagine Onil's face when he found out who was lying there, or rather what was lying there. *You're still hot inside, damn it.*

"No, it's not what you think it is, Onil."

"What? What? That's a dead girl! You're doing it with a dead girl? You're putting your thing inside a decomposing—" He paused, wanting to add more, but the surprise was simply extreme for him to speak straight.

"Lower down your voice, Onil. You'll wake up my wife."

"And then you're putting it inside your wife!"

"Shut . . . alright, alright. Just shut up already, Onil." A split of a second pause. "Don't you dare tell her or anyone else about this."

Onil was still gathering himself from the queer shock, but that last one his master said felt like something out of place. With this disturbing discovery, he felt undeserved to be on the other end of such a threat. He was not letting it through.

"You can't tell me what to do."

"What? Hey, don't forget that you're working for me, Onil. I saved you from being a scavenger in the streets."

"I could return to being a scavenger in the streets anytime, Mr. Yu. I could live without your employment, your scanty, cold meals, this shit of a house. How about you? Can you live with the shame if they find out about this here? I don't think you can, Mr. Yu."

Mr. Yu could only look at him with fierce eyes.

"You cannot threaten me with anything now," Onil said.

The emotion in Mr. Yu's face turned calm, reconsidering. "Alright. I'm sure we can settle this out. Just don't tell anyone about this." Pause. "Is there anything you want?"

The lungs were the tastiest part, although he would not settle for a favorite. Every day since the night of the big discovery, Onil had been served with an uncommon mass of dead meat by the cornered Mr. Yu. The subsequent days became days of feast for him. He ate vociferously, never leaving a trace of everything given to him, and also did he never show any ill retraction from the terrifyingly ration of meals.

The blackmailing job he did on Mr. Yu proved to be very effective. He had latched very well his gluttonous stomach around the old man and had controlled him to the point that he soon was reduced to narrow down his choices to just giving Onil an entire body.

Mr. Yu had stopped with his nocturnal activities eventually. Perhaps because he had found at last a more disgusting act to make him realize himself how sickeningly disgusting his own was. In the passing days he had nursed somewhat a phobia of being even remotely near a cadaver. No meal had passed without him losing his appetite in an instant by thoughts of Onil and his insatiable hunger. He spent the consequent days battling disgust, loathing, and nausea.

The phobia obviously took a toll on his business, as well as on his own physical health. After another string of days, he started to lose interest in running the funeral parlor. He began refusing to take in bodies, he terminated Ronnie and Marcus without much explanation, and in final act of desperation, he consented Onil to take all the unclaimed corpses left in the mortuary for his consumption.

Then he got ill. The mingling of all the mental stress and the loss of his appetite had rapidly deteriorated his body, and consequently his world became compressed into his bed. The closure of his business went on the bed with him, as well as the fortune he had amassed. It did not take long before his wife finalized her decision to pack up her things and leave, although he had been gracious enough to continue sparing the woman all of the repugnant truth. After all, his money had been everything that kept the two together. Now every bit of it was gone, so was she.

What also did not take long was Onil's supply of food in the morgue. Corpses were dwindling where nothing comes in anymore. Onil had everyone inside his stomach like Hermione Granger's bag, and still he felt no utter satisfaction.

Mr. Yu drowned himself in the darkness of his room. The fluorescent lamp was off and the windows were shut down. He lied on his bed as usual, covered in a sea of blankets, denying himself any instance of getting up. Nothing new ever came in this room for the past weeks. The picture had always been the same.

Even the string of nightmares he had for a succession of nights didn't deviate. They were always the same— the grisly eating regimen of his boy Friday, his eventual realization of his own disgusting activities, and the collapse of his business and his family. He would spend countless hours wide awake so he could elude those nightmares. But sleep was the only choice he had had left to suppress the depression currently dominating his mind and to keep him from probably losing it.

He had no care left of the world anymore.

The silence inside his room was at a depth he could hear the time ticking past him. And every instance of it only reared his seeming desire to kill himself. He thought that perhaps any minute now, the ticking would finally stop and he could then kiss his bedridden ass goodbye. He had already contemplated it, but he seemed to be too coward to summon death on his own.

At the moment he was halfway between being asleep and awake. He kept his eyes shut nonetheless, but he had been sure he wasn't asleep. Later a force pulled his eyelids apart. There even came some force, the same as the first one perhaps, pushing him out of the bed—to confront it, was the most probable cause there was. Maybe it was death, finally.

A brief sound of someone burping came into his ears and immediately roused him up from the bed. He shoved the blankets off his face and looked to where the sound came from. It brought a sense of uncommon fear into him.

The door slowly opened, and the scant light from the outside filled into the room, but not enough to overwhelm the dimness inside from obscuring the image of the someone now standing by the doorway. The sound had come from it. A hand pushed out of the shadow and reached for the side of the door, searching for the light switch. A click of the switch and the room was instantly filled with light. Onil walked from the doorway toward Mr. Yu on the bed.

His appearance startled the bedridden man. It seemed that despite the tremendous amount of meat he had consumed over the past weeks, his eventual figure still resembled a cadaverous, starved-out man. He was even perceptibly thinner than before. The eyes buried deep inside their sockets were bloodshot and hollow—eyes of utter horror out of an utter nightmarish movie.

He stared at his boss balefully and with such strange weight that Mr. Yu felt pushed even deeper into the abyss that was his bed. Nevertheless, he assured himself that despite being ill and bedridden for a long time, he knew he was still physically more able than the lanky spectre approaching him now. When push comes to shove, he knew who's going to pin down who.

Onil was about two or three steps short from reaching the bed when he suddenly stopped.

"I am so hungry, Mr. Yu," he said. Then out from behind him he pulled a long knife slicing through the hollow air in between them.

"What are you doing?" The alarm ringing off in Mr. Yu's head took over him in an instant. He leaped out of the bed as it did so.

"You cannot imagine how it is to be in this stupid body, Mr. Yu. It's a cursed mess."

"Stay away from me, Onil."

"I'm sorry, Mr. Yu. I am just so hungry." With a maniacal laugh, Onil jumped over the bed in a blazing speed and dropped a swing of the knife toward Mr. Yu. The sound of the blade whizzing through the air whiffed audibly around the room. Contary to how he looked and to Mr. Yu's judgment, he seemed stronger than expected and the speed he took with the jump left Mr. Yu in a trance. But the latter's instinct fortunately kicked in albeit at the last minute, leaving him a very tiny fabric of time to be able to escape the swing.

The knife stabbed its way through the air and into the wall behind Mr. Yu. At the briefest of time he was allowed, the sick man managed to dodge the assault and the eventual split on his skull. Onil's momentum brought him falling down on the floor, while the knife remained stuck solidly on the wooden wall.

Mr. Yu allowed a second to pass glaring at Onil, his face yet showing utter disbelief. Then relief washed over him. Onil remained motionless on the floor for a couple of minutes. By that time, Mr. Yu had already gathered himself and had run speedily out of the room. He had stopped by the door to look back at Onil, but from that side the bed had wholly concealed the madman face down on the floor. He looked around and saw no trace of him, and luckily had the sense not to dismiss everything as another nightmare.

He knew he had to think of something to escape this madness of Onil, or better yet to stop it. He had to think of something before Onil gets up. He ran all the way downstairs, intending not to look back anymore. It didn't take long before the telling sounds from his room came indicating the madman was now up on his feet.

He reached the main door of the house in an instant, having been fired up by a height of urgency. But amid the ensuing throng of different forceful feelings within him, he spared a good amount of seconds to look around what had become of his house during the times when he had gone bedridden. It looked as if a tremendous storm had rounded up that floor of the house. The furniture were scattered randomly around, and in many places, things that were not supposed to be there were there, scattered randomly all the same. And what set the exclamation point of the repugnant situation in there was the presence of several rotting human body parts. The door of the morgue, which was some distance from the house's main door where he now stood, suddenly flapped open, seemingly beckoning him with a voice coming straight from a horror movie monster—or was instead a voice of someone from a deep hole.

Step in here, Mr. Yu. Step in.

But he wasn't one to be brushed off of his rationality easily. The road to safety was behind this other door. That morgue had given him wealth, had given him life for years, had given him heat during a lot of times when he was cold, but it had also given him horror, had given him a monster, and it might now give him death. A slip of his reason and it might not be long from now.

Who was calling him from the morgue? And why was there some compulsive strength in it that seemed making him consider stepping in? The beckoning grew stronger by the minute. And the time continued to run thin. He could now hear the dragging footsteps of Onil coming toward the top of the stairs.

What is inside the morgue!

The sounds of the footsteps were drawing near. He looked up at the top of the staircase, expecting to see Onil by now.

"Stop this already, Onil!" he screamed.

Then Onil appeared, looking back at him with dead seat eyes and clutching the knife in his right hand. Blood was scattered all over his clothes and skin, an enormous mass of which was collected on his left hand. *But there was really no left hand anymore!* His left arm dangled limply from his shoulder and ended short at the wrist. Below that were just bits and mess of what remained from his severed hand.

"Can't help it, Mr. Yu," Onil said, sounding as if he was going to burst into a fit of tears. He sounded as if he was beseeching Mr. Yu for some sympathy. He seemed to be chewing some flesh out of his severed hand. All over his mouth down to his chin was blood.

Mr. Yu looked at him with horror and disgust, and with other mixture of feelings circling around his stomach like a bunch of drugged rats running restlessly all about. Obviously there never would be a chance for him to show Onil the sympathy his voice had demanded. He began to move. But, heaven may only know why, he instead ran toward the morgue—toward the morgue!

For some reason, he felt a sense of relief running on the way to the open door of the morgue, like he knew there would be safety waiting for him inside. No other thing came into his view but the doorway. That run may seem a tremendous mistake, but he suddenly felt sure he was rather running toward his freedom from all this horror.

He immediately shut the door behind him to a lock when he had gone inside. Before he could take a gander around whatever mess had been left in there, he best made sure he had securely locked himself in. Keeping the thing upstairs out was the priority, even if—

Even if Onil was also there inside the morgue with him!

The discovery left him dumbfounded. Onil was there, seated on a chair beside one of the gurneys, where a corpse lie cold and torn in many places. The scavenger was eating it, bit by bit, piece by piece. When sooner he noticed Mr. Yu's presence, he glanced at him and smiled, the most monstrous of smiles he had ever seen.

"Ah, Mr. Yu, what are you doing here?" Onil asked.

Mr. Yu stared at him in disbelief. Oh, he would never be looking at him anymore for the rest of his life with anything but disbelief. The ensuing silence went on long and insane. Mr. Yu didn't speak. It had been so much of a nightmare for him to be able to speak.

"What's the matter, Mr. Yu? You're very pale. Are you alright?"

There still was nothing he could force out of his mouth. Just the same picture of horror in his eyes—so much horror.

Onil shrugged it off and went on with his meal. The same long and insane silence followed, broken at times by the noises inside Onil's mouth as he chewed fat and muscle like a dish of raw steak.

At last, Mr. Yu managed to slightly compose himself, moving his hand slowly over the door handle behind him. As the lock was about to turn loose, Onil glanced again at him, and his face was one in a deep concern this time.

"By the way, I've got something to tell you, Mr. Yu," he said. "This is actually the last body in here. I might need some more to eat, you know."

There was only bloodshot horror seen in Mr. Yu's eyes.

The Elevator Man

My life is a life full of running. In all directions. But that's the thing: you are always reduced into a constant race with time. Some people just sit and wait in a corner, and some people run and live the race. As for me, I run because running is what makes my life still.

Now, here's the picture: two men—one was a young teenager, on the left side and facing the door, and the other was an old man, on the right side and much nearer on his side of the wall than the young one—stood inside a claustrophobic room, quietly, at least for some time. The young man was embracing a brown leather bag in his arms, and the old man had his arms free, save for his right hand pressed easily on the buttons on the side of the door before them. As time went by inside that elevator, the young one was feeling an increase in discomfort within him. I should know—that young man was none other than me.

"Are you alright, boy?" the old man, a so-called elevator man, asked. "You don't seem alright, if I may say. You're awfully very pale."

The young man looked slowly toward the other one's direction, mistrustful, I'd say.

"You don't look fine at all," the old man said.

"Just a . . ." the young man began. "Just . . . a little dizzy, I guess."

"Do you have a thing against closed rooms? Do you get all panicky when you're inside one?"

The young man had returned his eyes back on the closed door in front of them, and seemed to have not heard the questions the old man had asked.

"Alright, I'd tell you now," the old man said. "You're running away from something, am I not right?"

The young man glanced back at him, his attention utterly taken. A whole lot of sweat threatened on the folds of his forehead, and if he could only see the look of his face at that very moment, he'd laugh his ass off surely and forget in himself that that elevator ride was just the first one of the rides he had planned to take in but another escape attempt of his dear young life.

"What did you say?" he asked, as if he did not hear what the old man had just said.

"How many times have you run from something, Randy?"

"How did you know my name?" The panic had risen considerably up to his throat now. "Who are you?"

"An elevator guy," the old man said. Randy, the young man's name, had taken a few steps back away from him, instinctively. "Or, if you would allow me, I can be someone who can help you out on this novel escape of yours."

"Help?"

"That's right. I can offer you a hand."

Randy looked ponderously at the old man for a string of seconds. "Who are you, mister?"

"My name is Danny." The old man offered his hand for a shake, which Randy took reluctantly. "And I am going to tell you that I am not just any of your old, anonymous elevator men. I know a way out of everything."

"What are you trying to tell me, mister?" Randy asked.

"Please, call me Danny," the old man said. He moved his hand over to the floor buttons and pushed the one for the eighth floor. Currently, they were just cruising past the fourth floor and going down.

"What are you doing?" Randy protested.

"Relax," Danny said. After he had pushed the "8" button, the elevator seemed to have come to a stop. The noise coming basically from the gliding of the elevator had turned into an eerie silence. Slowly, the numbers embossed on the other buttons started to disappear, leaving only the eighth floor button with a number. A few seconds after though, the number 8 slowly rotated counter-clockwise and stopped on a "lying" position, making it look like infinity symbol.

"What's happening?" Randy asked, frantically.

"I'm showing you a way out of the trouble you've put yourself into, Randy. I'm offering you a hand, a friendly hand, that is."

Randy clutched his bag strongly closer to him, although he wasn't at all conscious of it. The mystery enshrouding the old man, and the, let's say, supernatural turnaround of things inside the elevator had caused him to absently lose hold of himself. Consequently, as cliché would suggest it, he thought he was just submerged in a very deep dream, and sometime later he would just wake up from all of it.

But this isn't no dream, Randy. Yes, it's me, Danny, the elevator guy. Welcome to the place called "the past."

The elevator door opened to a blinding flow of light. Randy battled it off his eyes with his arms and inadvertently dropped the leather bag that he was holding by them. Gradually, the light dissipated and showed to him what was outside the elevator as they had stood inside it at the minute. A hallway, basically, the eighth floor hallway. But he remembered he had just been welcomed by the old man into a new place, apparently, which he called "the past."

Randy opened his eyes carefully, not knowing that the light had just been fainting out. When his vision had cleared out at last, he saw that it was not the eighth floor hallway that waited outside the elevator. He had somehow expected to see this different place, anyway. And he was also still clinging on the notion that what was happening was merely a dream.

The open elevator door lead out into another room—someone's bedroom. The ambiance implicit around it concurred with the nomenclature provided by the old man. It did look like a room inside a house inside an era of the past.

"Take a step out, Randy," the old man said. "I'll follow you shortly."

Randy asked no further question. He stepped out of the elevator into the surreal room that looked sepia all over, and was quite unconscious of his steps. When out, he finally saw the entirety of the room. Danny followed him behind.

"What is this place?" Randy asked.

"The past," Danny said. "To be exact, this is a room straight from sixty-seven years ago."

Randy's eyes stretched in utter disbelief. "You mean to tell me that I have time-traveled sixty-seven fucking years into the past?"

"Yes, you did."

"What are we doing here? This is your proposed way out for me?"

Danny walked toward one side of the room, to a wall where a number of framed pictures were hanging, and stood specifically beside a large black-and-white photograph of a man staring dead-on seemingly toward every direction.

"His name is Don Teofilo Villon," he said. "He's a doctor. And I'm sure you don't know him."

"Who is he?" Randy asked.

"Well, let me tell you his story. There was once a young Spanish adventurer many years ago who had joined the crew of a large Spanish ship named the Voyager. This adventurer's name is Lopez. The Voyager was set on an expedition toward the Philippine islands, unbeknownst to them all that that would eventually be its last trip. So they sailed on for a month when somewhere they encountered a small canoe in the middle of the ocean which was just floating aimlessly. In that canoe was a famished, almost dying man who refused to talk who he was or what fate had beset him prior to his current predicament. The ship's crew took the man in and provided him with much comfort, since they had expected that he would no sooner die. Lopez was the last man to see to him before he died; and without the knowledge of the other sailors, the dying man had told Lopez, before his last breath, about a large diamond he had swallowed during the mutiny of the ship's crew he had last sailed with. The diamond was worth a fortune beyond all fortunes. He told Lopez that if he dies, and he's sure it won't be long then, he told him to slit a part of his stomach open and take the diamond. He did just as what he had been told.

"When the others had heard of the man's death and seen the wound in his stomach, they immediately thought Lopez had killed him, contrary to letting the man die a natural death, which was what they intended. Lopez was sentenced to a walk the plank for his alleged crime. But before that, after he had taken the treasure from the dead man's body, he had also swallowed the diamond himself, lest the others would find it. He plunged the cold waters of the ocean and was left by the ship to his fate. Fortunately, another boat passed by the area after the first ship had gone a considerable distance away. He was taken in on the boat, which was in fact also on a journey toward the Philippines.

"At the time of their arrival, Lopez went about looking for a surgeon to take the diamond out of his body. That was how and when his path and Don Villon's path eventually crossed. The doctor agreed to operate on him, after Lopez promised to give him a large part of the fortune that precious stone was worth. Unbeknownst to Lopez, Don Villon was secretly planning to kill him and take the treasure all to himself."

Danny paused speaking when suddenly a movement was seen from the other side of the room. There was a bed on that side where somebody lied beneath a couple of layers of blankets. Randy instantly had a strong guess as to who that somebody was.

"Shouldn't we go now?" he asked.

"No," Danny said. "If you're concerned about the man finding us here inside his room, then I'm telling you, that concern of yours is pointless. At the moment, we are but an inexistent pair of visitors in relation to their timeframe. They cannot see us, they cannot feel our presence."

The door of the room located few steps away from the bed suddenly opened, permitting the entrance of a young woman. Her face had been drenched in tears, and she slowly walked toward the man lying on the bed.

"Who is she?" Randy asked.

"She is Don Villon's daughter," Danny answered. "Mary."

"Why is she crying?"

"That is because, Randy," Danny turned to look at the young man, "Don Villon is dying."

Randy observed the following sequence of events inside the room, and discovered another incredulous property of this peephole they had been looking through. Don Villon's daughter, who was sitting on the floor beside his father's bed, could be seen clearly mumbling some words. Randy could see her lips move. But in wonder of all wonders, not even a faint sound was audible from her. It had been like watching a moving picture in a TV set in mute.

"We can only see, Randy," Danny said, noticing the look of wonder on Randy's face. "This part here has no audio yet."

"What is she saying?" Randy asked.

"I don't honestly have an idea. But what I do know is that Don Villon has to have someone to pass the diamond to now before he finally dies away. As you can see, he has to do it the soonest as possible. Mary is a woman of pure heart, but she is too inclined to so many things other than their family fortune for the old man to entrust with her such a precious object. And thus what has happened. That diamond is no longer in the family line in the current time."

And Randy was struck with the quick understanding of everything before him.

"I know who you're running from, Randy," the old man said. "I was just looking for a chance to confront you with this once in a lifetime chance to relieve you of all your troubles. This is your chance to change this part of history and turn it into your favor."

"Who really are you? Don't tell me this isn't all just a dream."

"There are people pursuing you, dangerous people whom you owed a large amount of money. This is your chance, Randy."

"I am dreaming," Randy said, wandering about his place in complete daze.

"Don Villon has lost that diamond to history. Now, I'm giving you this precious opportunity to change the its course and make your own fate. Imagine the wealth that lost gem can promise you, Randy. It's a vastness of richness beyond measure."

Randy looked straight into the eyes of Danny, reading their depth.

"Time is no more a luxury in your position," Danny said. "You have to think about this now."

"No, I still have time," Randy said. "I need time to think about this. I will get back here tomorrow. And by then you will have my decision. I need the treasure, I can fathom its promised fate for me should I obtain it from Don Villon, but I still have to think this over. Until now, these things haven't settled in the bottom of my mind yet."

Danny let out a brief sigh. "Alright. I'll be just right here tomorrow. I shall expect you and your final decision. Be wise, Randy. Be wise."

Randy then quietly turned his back to the open door of the elevator. It looked very much a different world than the room of Don Villon. It was the world that he had lived for years. Turning his back on it to face another one hopefully to pry him out of all his present troubles would surely be a matter needing of a heavy thought. Deep within him, he was torn by two sides way much parted from each other.

He got inside the elevator, waiting for Danny to move his way back in also. As soon as the old man had gone inside, Randy said to him, "You have to tell me everything I need to know about this dimension and this travel itself if I would ever comply to your offer, Danny."

"Of course," Danny said, fetching a smile on his lips.

Randy needed the time to think, but at that very moment he had already been fixed on a final, irrevocable decision—Don Villon's diamond, of course. Perhaps, he just needed the time to prove to himself that everything was not inside a dream.

After managing to find a way through the people in his tracks, he once again found his way inside the elevator the next day, standing alone with Danny. The old man initiated that second meeting in a thought that Randy would be hesitant to talk first. And, as is usual, every time-travel should start with a smile.

"So, is it a yes?" he asked.

"Tell me the dos and don'ts," Randy said.

"Perfect!" The old man faced Randy and thrust his hand to the eighth floor button beside the elevator door. "Strap your safety belt for this incredible journey, Randy."

"First, you've got to tell me if there's a chance that I could return in the present time."

Danny seemed to have been taken aback, but he quickly regained himself. "Well, there is this one important rule we have to consider for this travel, quite connected to what you've just asked. You see, once a person has gone back in time through this elevator, all his memories of the present time will disappear from his mind. But no worries, since you would have the knowledge of a typical man of that era once you get there. You won't be starting back learning everything like you're an infant inside an adult's body. That's what I'm trying to say."

"You say I won't remember anything from the present?"

"Yes. I should've told you yesterday, but I thought it would not be a thing of concern to you anyway, given the past whereabouts that you are trying to run away from here."

Randy heaved a deep sigh. At first, his only reason in asking the question was to at least know a way out of the past if ever he should find himself in the middle of trouble again in there. Knowing a way out of something is always a rule. The news of the consequent total amnesia once in there was a bit of a surprise.

But what was going to be a matter for consideration following that vanishing of his memories, anyway? He started thinking about the life he had led, the nineteen years he had spent in this fabric of time. There had been not a bright year, it seemed. He had no family, he had no friends, and hell! he couldn't even find a point in his past that was worth keeping in memory. So maybe it would just be fine, losing his memory.

But, "How can I get back here, in case?" He let out the question nevertheless.

Danny looked at him in quiet awe. "How can you get back here?" was the first thing he could say after spending a couple of seconds in silence.

"Yeah, in case," Randy said.

"Perhaps we can do something about that," Danny said, hesitantly so. "But you won't be remembering anything, anyway. You won't be aware that you came here in the first place."

"Just in case, Danny," Randy said, almost in a whisper.

"Alright." Danny sighed. "I know it's an odd thing to suddenly live in a life that is not yours firstly. We have enough secrets in this world to try and come up with another one. I know you won't be comfortable, in any way, concealed behind the fact that you're living in a completely foreign world, much more a completely foreign era.

"So here's what I'm thinking you should do. Once you get out of this elevator and into the past, inside Don Villon's room, you will take the diamond from him, and find your way back to these doors." (He pointed toward the ones of the elevator.) "Of course, it won't be visible anymore from where you'll be inside the past, but I will you show the trick of it. And of course, I will tell you where the diamond is hidden."

Randy's face seemed to beam with excitement, though he actually tried to keep it from the old man.

Danny took out a piece of paper and a pen from his pocket, wrote something for several seconds, and continued, "Bring this. Hold on to this so that you could read it at once."

On the paper was written: "I HAVE TRAVELED BACK IN TIME. I SHOULD ASK NO QUESTIONS. I SHOULD GO OUT OF THIS ROOM AND INTO THE ROOM DIRECTLY ACROSS IT. THEN I SHOULD GO TO THE CABINET BESIDE THE BED OPEN THE DRAWER AND GET THE BOX INSIDE. THE DIAMOND I HAVE COME HERE FOR IS IN THERE. THEN I SHOULD GO BACK TO THE FIRST ROOM AND STAND BY THE WINDOW WHERE I HAVE COME FROM. I SHOULD CLOSE MY EYES AND THINK ABOUT THE YEAR 2014. JUST THINK OF THE NUMBER. REMEMBER NO QUESTIONS!"

Randy looked dubiously at the old man after he had read what was on the paper.

"Just focus, Randy," Danny said. "This is the only, and might just be the perfect way, for you not to get stuck in the past."

"Okay," Randy said. The situation called for him to stay silent, as he tried to make a final pondering about what he was about to do. But the game had been fixed in his mind. He folded the paper into a lengthwise strip and put it between his two fingers. He looked at Danny, now with a seeming gratitude, and said, "Thank you."

"Always be happy to help," Danny said.

The door of the elevator finally opened, and the gloomy interior of Don Villon's room appeared before them like a sick old man on a hospital bed appeared before you—as gloomy as the room itself, it had seemed. Randy glanced for the last time at Danny, smiled a little, and then took his first step out of the elevator. Officially, if it would be a great deal (as it apparently would), he was now standing in two time eras at the same time.

The elevator door closed behind him in a slow, thrilling fashion, and for a thousandth time in his furthest memory, he felt alone. But then he thought, there is no need to worry about the breadth of my memory anymore—I'm going to lose it in a second now . . .

In a second now.

He looked around the room, curiously. He recalled the first time he got in here and he hadn't been this curious as to look around the things inside. The bed was there on the far wall, sheets bulging and taking the shape of the old man lying beneath them. A continual rising and falling of them indicated the pace of the man's breathing. And then he remembered he was actually at the last moments of his life now. And he remembered . . .

Remembered?

Wait a sec.

I cannot possibly remember anything. And *I*, yes I. It all goes back to me now. The Randy who's been running and running from almost everything.

This can't be right! I look around the room faster now, and I feel the paper slipped between the fingers of my hand. Danny's note.

I HAVE TRAVELED BACK IN TIME. I SHOULD ASK NO QUESTIONS.

But then I am filled with them now. I read the next lines and feel odd about it than ever. I have decided to follow it. I run out of the room as fast as my feet could, finding the said room across this first one. And then at that point, all memories suddenly have come back to me. Every memory I have of this room, and of this house, and of this era, apparently. I am starting to remember. But understanding is still out of the question.

The room before me now, I know it. Yes, I know whose it is. The vague thoughts following the sight of it—cloudy thoughts of the past.

Past?

Which past?

By then, I have remembered: For years, I have actually been putting the future into my past.

But I am referring to another past this time. I cannot make my mind to concur with it, but apparently, there seems to be two fabrics of the past that I have lived through. The one which introduced me to Danny, the elevator man, and the past I have with this house.

And then it starts to become clear. The rule. The important rule of this time-travel. All your memories of the present time will be lost in your mind—and the reason why the memories I have before I took the elevator ride aren't lost right now is because that time is not my present time. I have not belonged to that era!

The door across me suddenly opens, and behind it stands a young woman—a familiar young woman. Her cloudy eyes stretch to a width when she sees me, like she hasn't seen me for eternity. And eternity, it may have actually been.

"Randy?" she says, in her broken voice.

"Mary?"

"I thought I wouldn't see you anymore!" She breaks down into more tears as she throws herself to me, embracing me with a grip that is a clear implication of how badly she has yearned for it. "I know you wouldn't leave me. I know you didn't mean what you said."

"Mary." And I cannot bring myself to add more words to that. The very memory of what and why Mary has clasped me as she has starts to seep into my mind now—a memory involving her, an unexpected news, my want to escape from it, Don Villon's threat, and a mad scientist. *Sixty-seven years into the future*, the latter has said.

I have entered the time machine to escape her, and her father's will to kill me for deciding to elude my responsibility. And who says the old man is dying? And who says anything about a precious diamond? The old man is already old, but he can still shove that fake diamond story, or a whole elevator, down my throat!

"Please don't leave us, Randy," Mary says, amidst the chaos inside my head. "We need you. Little Danny needs you."

Danny?

And my mind shuts off at that instant like a movie cuts to black.

The Ultimate Survivor

Ron Blanco didn't get the sense of why he hangs out with George Devanteer. But maybe it was by default that they became friends, founded by the fact that the two of them had been the last two men vying for the title of Ultimate Survivor when they joined the *artista*-search TV show "Starstruck" three years ago. Ron, though, was steering this friendship against the current because, for one, he couldn't even understand half—or almost three quarters—of what George would talk about whenever he talks to him. George spoke in straight English, and Ron was just an all-looks and all-Bisaya kind of boy (and, well, of course, a manageable accented Tagalog). The former became his ticket in landing the spot he landed on the TV show, and the latter became his baggage whenever a role of, say, a rich teenager opens up anywhere in the local showbiz world. On the occasional instances that he would find work, his roles had been almost always in the narrow neighborhood ranging from a naïve sidekick to a flustered comedian, to a gullible promdi who can't even figure out how to get anywhere in an elevator.

He was a promdi, in real life, and he hadn't been home in the whole three years since he had come to Manila, which meant that for three years he hadn't been able to see so much as a glimpse of the old province again when he left them all behind to start the pursuit of his dream of becoming an actor—if it should all pan out as he pictured it to be. He just wanted to experience life out of the sleepy grasp of the old province.

Now, he had lived three years in the big city, and lived under the shining canopy of his celebrity status. City boys are not to be tied down by the monotony of, say, a provincial way of life. City boys—celebrity boys—spend nights in parties.

A flick of a finger pulled Ron out of his trance, then a voice followed.

"Hey, man," George spoke. "You space out or something?"

"Ha?" Ron said, not quite certain who was speaking at this point. When he realized it was George, he gathered himself and spoke again, "I'm okay."

George followed the direction of his eyes. "Ah, you're checking out Melissa. Nice tight buns, I should say. Up top, man!"

Ron raised his hand rather reluctantly to high-five George's, but he had really felt embarrassed to be deduced of what he had been keeping himself busy with the past few minutes. *Nice tight buns.* That was a way to put it. He wanted to deny it to George, that he was really looking particularly at nothing. Just looking straight and deep in thought. Some thought. Not checking out Melissa's ass. But he had already high-fived George—too late to deny it now. Somehow, at least, he felt relief that the whole place was doused with music and perhaps nobody else had heard George.

Now he just wanted to be out of this place and be back in his apartment. He didn't want to be here in the first place. He wasn't given any part in the earlier concluded awards night, not even a spot to read some bullshit intro to some nominated movie. He only came at the invitation of George, and George was a somebody tonight—a big somebody. He just won the Best Actor award, back-to-back with his last year's win.

"You alright, Ron?" George spoke again.

"I'm okay." Ron looked around for a second, before resuming, "I have to go now."

"What? The party's just started, man."

"I'm not feeling okay."

"I thought you were okay?" George chuckled, and saw partly the haziness of Ron's thoughts at the moment, apparently scrambling for a more solid excuse to bail out. "Okay, man. If you have to go, you got to go. Thanks for coming, alright?" George held up a fist in between them.

"Congrats again, George." Ron connected the fist bump as he stood up and began to walk his way home.

When he got home, he was mired with thoughts about the party. One that worried him first was that George catching him on his "sightseeing," and the way he had confronted him about it. It was much more dubious how he had not apprehended him, maybe even cross him with the fist instead of the innocuous bump. Had the situation gone to blows instead, at least he was entirely certain he did have messed up in the party and he wouldn't have to reduce himself to paranoia over thinking whatever George had regarded him right now. And right now that was what kept him caged in deep pondering. *Maybe George thinks I'm a pervert, a young man above most of everybody and a dirty, disgraceful pervert at the same time. Maybe he thinks I'm a disgusting pest within the acting world and I don't deserve my place in it. Maybe he'd just dismissed what he'd seen in the party as a casual act, a boys-will-be-boys act. But I know he doesn't really think that. He thinks I am sexually harassing Melissa. And he will dismiss me as a pervert. A sick pervert. A disgrace to actors, to city boys, to men in general. Maybe he would tell Melissa about it. Oh my, God!*

But really, that Melissa. He had been infatuating about Melissa since he had seen her on the first day on set. They have been taping episodes for a *teleserye*, where Melissa was cast as the leading lady to George Devanteer's leading man role. George again! Ron never had the chance to star in his own *teleserye*. Everything had to go to George. As per usual, his role in this one was a supporting—a little more than an extra, it had seemed. Yet he thought it was alright, as long as he had every chance to see Melissa.

But, all this attraction, all the butterflies in his stomach when Melissa was around, this was not for a sort of romantic inclination, or love. All he saw of Melissa was her voluptuous racks and her tight buns. Maybe he was a pervert indeed, maybe he could attest to that. But he could only be one if anybody else could call him as such. And so far, he had kept himself in check and had prevented any telltale indications of his deep-seated sick true color. Except that one in the party, but that was yet to be weighed.

Everyday on the set, he would steal glimpses at the nymph—his nymph, in her natural habitat—waiting for a disaster, some wardrobe malfunction perhaps. But she had always dressed carefully, and there had been no saboteur as far to miss a button, or loosen a stitch, or decrement a tiny inch to her garments for a disaster to take place. All the same, Melissa—in her heedful get-up and Venus de

Milo figure—always excited him even without plunging into that disaster.

At home after tapings, he'd replay every scene he had had saved up in his mind-drive and visualized them in sync with the strokes of his self-massage.

He stepped into the shower, all thought dwelling on Melissa, and her tight buns held together to lecherous grandeur by her tight blue dress. *Yes, I checked them out, George. And there's nothing you can do about it. You can kiss, you can cuddle all day, all throughout the damn teleserye. But Melissa's wonderland is mine, George, you foreign-tongue swine!* He repeated these, versions of them repetition after passionate repetition. And Melissa never fails him, never even makes him last longer than a couple of minutes. Washed away by the waterfalls above his head were the halves of a million would-have-been Ron Jr. He stood motionless for the subsequent minutes, his eyes closed and thinking. This time was the time he would feel a little guilt, and a little concern. He knew this was inappropriate, downright disgusting even, and it should remain top secret no matter what. But every time the urge beckons him, he would feel powerless by it. It had grown into some kind of a compulsion. He knew he had to stop at some point. Perhaps win a woman he could answer it with just like normal people do. Not particularly Melissa, he was sure of that.

Yet he'd resort to leaving the guilt afloat, out of his reach. Let the future Ron to deal with it. For now, maybe there was no hurt to enjoy the sweetness of a clandestine affair with lustful imageries. The important thing was to keep the clandestine part in place.

He sat at the sofa staring straight at the TV screen. It wasn't on. On the dim LCD he could see his darkened reflection. He'd think of him again. Popoy. He'd think about the incident that happened many years ago in the old province, back when he was around ten years old. He had been what he was now even before.

They had some neighbors then, a family whom a beautiful woman, in her mid-twenties at that time, had belonged. This beautiful next-door nymph had made it a routine to take a bath every middle of the night, and young perverted Ron had known about it just a couple of times into the start of that routine. Ron sucked at being a child then more than he sucked at being a grown-ass man now. And so, knowing about the routine that the woman wouldn't make a mistake breaking, Ron in an instant turned into Tom, with the designation of "Peeping" bestowed to him along with it. He would climb the roof of the outdoor bathhouse of the neighbor family and had punctured a small aperture on the GI sheet enough for his eye to gander over the panoramic action going on every midnight inside. And voila! Ron feasted his eyes with a view that made every night lose him rung after rung of the ladder up toward an innocent boy he would never be.

But all "good" things must come to an end. One night, Popoy had seen him, while he was up on the roof and peeping through the hole. Popoy the villain, now and then. And Popoy never let it go, even though he didn't really let the whole province know about it. He kept mum, but he had tortured poor Ron since then over episodes of teasing and mocking intimidation. Every time they'd meet on the street, Popoy would tease him with the same question, with a jeering grin, "*Gaunsa ka sa atop, Ron?*" And he'd keep silent, wondering when the tormenting would ever cease. Young as he was then, he had already realized that maybe he just had to kill Popoy to get it all over with. He never did, and now cities away he was from the old province, Popoy had stopped being a problem.

And sometimes he would use the past memories of that beautiful neighbor in his present nights.

He turned the TV on, and the first image that burst out of the screen was the face of George Devanteer, speaking in an interview. As the camera zoomed out there could be seen the host of the show sitting behind a desk beside him, and on his other side sat another young man. He was introduced as George's cousin, whom he had grown up with back in the States, now here in a brief country visit. They were talking about a lot of things, and Ron had listened attentively. When the cousin talked about the time when a nine-year old George once walked around their neighborhood naked, all of them in the studio laughed. It was a funny story—innocent young George, now a two-time best actor, had once walked around his childhood neighborhood in his birthday suit. And it was funny then, it was still funny now, it seemed, listening to the unanimous laughter around the whole set. But Ron couldn't find the humor in all of it. He sat there gravely watching the goings-on of the interview, and he was actually cringing with anxiety.

Why would I make light of something like that in my past? If I had been there in George's place, I would have knocked the front teeth of that stupid cousin! Shit like that is embarrassing, even if it had happened many years ago. How many years ago don't matter! Stupid things like that should stay in the past! I've made a name for myself and I'd rather not let an embarrassing moment from years ago spill out in front of a goddamn live camera in exchange for a few seconds of laugh.

George's cousin is a leech, trying to take a ray of George's spotlight for himself. And at the expense of George. Just because he had seen one thing from his cousin's past that is maybe worth sharing to everyone now that his cousin had become a glorious somebody doesn't give him a privilege to do so. When you've become a success, everyone is apt to take a slice of you for themselves, even if it means embarrassing you live on TV and then dismissing it something that everybody should be laughing at. That's why I have severed every ties I had with my old home province. I'm quite sure now that everyone in there wants to have something of me for their own twisted pleasure. I won't be surprised if Popoy one day emerges out of that sleepy province and into the city to share that—

Well, shit.

Ron suddenly delved into panic. Somehow he hadn't thought of it. Through the past three years since he had left the province, he had always thought that he finally broke free from the torment of Popoy's one secret about him. Popoy had been a walking time bomb homed in eventual detonation only around him, and when he left he thought it had been enough to defuse it. Popoy was still a ticking threat, and with his turn as an actor here in the big city, only time would tell when Popoy was going to show up and take his fifteen-minute spot in an interview about his childhood experiences with Ron Blanco back in the old, old home province. And catching a future celebrity peeping through a hole into some beautiful neighbor's bathroom was, Ron was sure, to them a humorous piece of trivia everyone should hear.

Ron wouldn't take any of it. He had to defuse the bomb. He had to silence Popoy's ticking capacity to destruct everything he had acquired as an ultimate

Survivor. He had dreamed, he had believed, he had to survive some more.

Ron left early for his trip homeward the next day. It would be a ship then a bus travel, and now he was aboard the bus. His phone had been vibrating like crazy in his pocket, but he had no intention to answer any of his manager's calls. The text messages that accompanied the missed calls screamed out to him: where the hell he was, and did he have any intention to show up on set for his scenes? The taping was the last thing in his mind right now. Somewhere in the home province was a business much more needing of his attention. From his seat in the bus he could even perceive the ticking of the time bomb that he would be suppressing today, come hell or high water.

He thought he could sleep at last after the calls and text messages stopped coming in, but the thoughts of finally going back home and the urgent task he had at hand there kept him out of slumber's door. He realized he actually hadn't hatched a plan of how he would carry out the said task. He looked out the window beside him and deduced they were more or less half an hour before reaching the province's bus stop. He needed more time to think of a plan.

"*Oi, si* Ron Blanco *man diay ni*!"

He looked up and saw the bus conductor standing on the aisle and looking at him.

"*Atay! Ikao jud lage! Katong artista*!" The bus conductor was short of jumping up for joy at the sight of Ron. The other passengers started to glance at his direction, and he knew he could not divert himself away from their eyes anymore. "*Pa*-picture *ko bai ha*?" the bus conductor spoke again.

Ron managed a reluctant smile and said "*Sige*" almost in a whisper. The bus conductor produced a cell phone out of his pocket and stooped to get his face side by side with Ron's, stretching out an arm with the hand holding his gadget to snap the selfie of him and the province's very own, Ron Blanco. When the other passengers began to clamor around for their turn for a selfie with him, he quickly stood up and asked to be unloaded from the bus, to which the whole passenger populace returned with a frustrated gasp in unison. But Ron didn't give a damn about all of them. He got off the bus immediately after it pulled over. Then he stood in the middle of a rustic highway, edged on both sides by an almost endless rice fields.

He decided he'd just walk the rest of the way and use the stretched time in coming up with the plan. Fans sometimes annoyed him—most of the time, almost. So the way the road ahead had been de-peopled made his impulsive decision of getting off the bus all the more agreeable. He walked on, and placed himself in a depth of thoughts at the same time. It would be hard, for certain, and for certain he was aware of that. After all, he was just a pervert, not a psychopath. Yet he really needed to do something about Popoy. He had already walked a considerable distance from where he had started, but no concrete plan had taken form in his mind as yet.

Up ahead the road he began to see a figure silhouetted against the morning sun. He walked slower, trying step after step to discern what the figure was. A few paces more and he could see that it was of a man, and the first thing that popped into his head was the probable scenario of him being recognized and the other being star-struck by the sight of him. As he walked on, the stranger's countenance gradually became vivid. And then he saw clearly the tattered shirt, the dusty face, the barefoot ends of a pair of legs covered by a hanging *maong* shorts that might have been a pair of jeans ages ago before being altered by natural causes, and the disheveled bird's nest of a hair.

Ron looked at the man without reservation anymore, assured by himself that such filth on feet wouldn't be able to recognize him, or know who he was, or even know which planet he was in. Only a meter parted the two men now, and at that distance Ron could finally ascertain what he had been thinking about since he saw the stranger's face. What had three years done to Popoy!

Popoy began to move, gesturing his arms as if he was beckoning something on the empty road. Ron thought he looked like he was directing traffic—imaginary traffic, at least.

"Popoy?" he said.

Popoy didn't speak, didn't even look at him.

"Popoy, *ako ni*," he continued. *"Aysa, kaila ka nako?"*

Popoy still didn't answer nor glance at him, and instead went on with what he was doing.

Ron thought in silence for a minute. If there was a place and time where and when he should carry out his plan—or the idea of the plan—here and now should be it. There was no one around the place but the empty road and the vast rice fields. The only hitch about this nascent plan was that all of those in the bus could readily link him to Popoy if he just left his remains lying around in view. Thence, he thought, there shouldn't be anything of Popoy to be left in view anywhere around. He had all the ground his eyes could reach to keep him out of view. And he was quite sure that by Popoy's current state of appearance, at this point no one probably had been missing him back in the old neighborhood.

Perhaps he had been already deemed dead back there—

"Hope?" Popoy spoke, all of a sudden, looking at Ron. "*Ha?*"

"Hope. Hope. Hope." Popoy was making a gesture with his fingers to his lips, and Ron could see he was mimicking someone smoking a cigarette—he was asking for a Hope cigarette.

"*Wala ra ba ko'y sigarilyo ngari.* Sorry."

Popoy giggled, like how an insane man should giggle, and Ron suddenly realized Popoy was no longer the Popoy he knew back then. Gone had been the days when this insane transient was a ticking threat to him. The secret he had feared would be spilled had already dissolved together with the dissolution of his sanity. And he realized it was all the more repugnant to kill him now. It would be like shooting an already dead person, he thought. After all, he was just a pervert, not a psychopath.

Popoy should be harmless now. Gradually he became ready to let this all go. He stood through the giggling of Popoy, before he spoke, "*Naa'y sigarilyo ngadto bai ay. 'Kaw.*" He pointed a finger toward the direction of his old home province—the old home province of them both. He decided this should be the end of the journey back home for him, even if he hadn't really made it home. A bus from the province bound for the pier should pass this road any moment now.

Popoy had turned around and started walking toward home and his Hope cigarettes. He was giggling again on the way, and speaking in between giggles, enough for Ron to hear, *"Gaunsa ka sa atop, Ron?"* Three times of it into the sequence and Ron had made another decision.

On Writting

Black Shell whispered to the wind: "And the darkness will set off and all will be gone." The hideous monster of the night took a leap from the belfry of the church and landed feet first, extraordinarily, and without noise on the ground below. The sound of the night was the music of his ears, and what a melody it was for this stranger.

He walked into the woods. The whistle of the evening air gently caressed the mass of trees, and further in their depth another sound began to register in Black Shell's ears. A hum. A song of some sort. For him, it was a cloud of blood in the water where he was the shark from afar. His paces accelerated and directed toward it.

Forward into the much deeper part of the woods, a man was walking slowly through the dark. The moon had shone very bright and the light allowed him to move easily, nonetheless slow. An hour ago, he had been in a friend's house, where a number of topics and a dozen bottles of beer had been exhausted. Now on his way home, in the dead of the night, he trudged the woods alone, a little inebriated, and numbed of the supposed fear induced to him by the dark. He breathed a soft music to while away the walk.

Black Shell made his way toward the unwary man, to that unwary victim, and he whispered between his gritted teeth: All will be . . .

   . . . gone.

The professor heard the whisper and along with a gust of wind that swept across his face, he started to feel afraid. The dark and cold evening gradually became a realization to him. And the woods became a strange place in a sudden.

"The darkness will set off," the voice turned again.

The professor saw a silhouette ahead slowly moving out of the shadows behind it. There was fog all over. It just came suddenly from nowhere. The figure moved closer and was gradually taking some form of a face. And the face had been hideous.

"Look at my bloodshot eyes," Black Shell spoke, in a voice that seemed to come from a deep hole. And the face that he wore looked to come from the same deep hole too. His eyes were blazing and his skin was burnt red. The teeth were more like claws and his forehead was sharp with fiery creases and without brows. The coat he wore resembled the empty spaces of the night. Out of the fog he appeared, and the terror he bestowed to the frozen professor was a terror out of a thousand streaks of nightmares.

"Who are you?" the professor asked.

Black Shell smirked at him and answered him with the same question: "Who are you?"

The professor did not speak. He fixed his terrified eyes on the hideous face that seemed burning from where he stood.

Black Shell spoke again: "Why are you speaking to the world of my creation?"

"What are you talking about?"

"Of course you know what I am talking about, professor."

"Who are you?" The professor had raised his voice now.

Black Shell gave out a loud, sarcastic laugh. And the trees swayed to a different gale of wind. There were influences of horror in the way the wind blew around them. It was as if his laughter was orchestrating the main performance of the gloomy evening. The professor was stuck frightened at all of this. He hadn't thought of running away, to elude the abominable presence of this monster. His feet had been frozen adhered to the ground.

"What are you going to do to me?"

"All will be gone."

The professor woke up, sweat streaming like waterfalls on his temple. He looked around him and sooner felt relief to find out where he was. Not in the woods, not in that nightmare of a place anymore. A sharp scream of thunder went past the sky outside. He sat up and closed his eyes. Silently he said a short prayer. *Thank God it was just a dream.* Again.

Many had been the nights now where he'd find himself in the woods. Always the same. The same stranger, the same scene, the same depth of the night on when it took place. This was a nightmare he had to battle every single night since the past two weeks.

He picked up half of his body and sat on the bed. The room was lit by a small lampshade on the nearby table. From beside it he picked up his glasses and put it on right over his wizened nose. He moved feebly. His age had caught up with him already, since about a score of decades ago. A circular wall clock hung against the wall across his bed and he read from it quarter to one of the early morning. He had just turned seventy and three quarters of an hour old.

What a dream to wake you up on your birthday, he thought. But that dream had already had the habit of waking him up at the same unlikely hour, for two weeks.

That dream, the pieces constituting it, was a familiar scene for the professor. He created it in his mind, putting it in a medium he had mastered. It was a scene from the latest book he had written and published, "The Black Shell." It was only published two weeks ago, the same time the nightmare started its nightly visits.

It felt as tantamount a horror as the first time the plot began construction in his mind almost a year ago. The darkness of it came to him out of the blue, suddenly after so many years he was reduced to a quiet life and career. He had been plagued with the writer's block for God knows how long.

His mind was weary, yes it was. And he knew what brought that weariness in it. He thought of retiring from his writing career, and that he maybe had already ran out of anything to write. He was not oblivious of it. He could not write a single line, much more a complete publishable work. And that had been for a single reason. A reason so concrete inside his mind: his wife, and her demise, and the sadness it had brought to him.

She had died in his arms, died helplessly. He could not do anything then as she was slowly letting go of her will. He saw with his own eyes the fading of hope in her face. And there was nothing he could do to save her.

Nothing. It was a nightmare with his eyes wide awake, and it became a nightmare of a lifetime to him.

Her death cost him his own gradual loss of hope in the consequent days. He felt dying himself. The days were mad and lonely. The solitary life that was laid out in front of him was a life that seemed to be a stirrer of his already chaotic mind, lost and hopeless, broken and frail. Unsurprisingly, a point came in that weary life when he turned into a suicidal lunatic. But something in him just refused to die. Something.

He tried to look for that reason, that something that persisted to exist in this world. Years went by, and slowly the reason began to take form. It had been his hand. His hand wanted to work again. There were pictures in his mind eager to burst out, however blurry and vague they had been from his raw perception. He tried willfully to understand, but then the plague made its round on him.

The tempest took the writing touch of his hands entirely. His mind was void of any imaginings he could write about, and if there was any scratch narrative that it could manage to form, any crude plot that perhaps could trigger it to do the usual rate of writing he wanted to revive, he could not supply them with words. Not a single line there was to free the ideas. Frustration had thus become his friend.

He slept and woke for days that were unsure.

But the time did come at last. The idea popped out of his mind in a sudden, first thing when he woke up on that awaited day. The idea was so promising that he at first feared that he might forget a word of it if he would not act fast. So hastily the professor found his way across his writing desk to start to write the early draft of the nascent idea. It was such a jewel that he thought he was willing to give up anything in a struggle with Fate to spare it from slipping away from him. And he was spared. He had kept himself far from such misfortune.

Thus happened the creation of "Black Shell." He wrote the 30,000-word novella in a span of two months, in seclusion for that whole interval. He shied away from the public, worked tediously on the idea, and aimed to complete it to utter perfection. At the end of that span, after the manuscript was written, rewritten, edited and all, he felt the kind of satisfaction he had so long been looking for. He starved for such feeling for a very long time.

After a week following the book's release, he had regained his forgotten reputation as a writer. None of the possible emotions he could feel proved to be more satisfactory to him than the feeling he felt when he was again carried up to his former pedestal. Out of the oblivion, out of the dim world suffocating him.

But the luminance of the nascent success had a dark twin born along with it. Those nightmares of the character he himself created became a thief of his nights. He felt as though Black Shell was ironically a stranger to his very mind. The character his own creative genius had crafted became a strange and haunting identity to its creator.

So these nights persisted, and he let them be. Clearly, he had not a way to stop them.

The professor woke up, sweat streaming like waterfalls on his temple. He looked around him and sooner felt relief to find out where he was. Not in the woods, not in that nightmare of a place anymore. A sharp scream of thunder went past the sky outside. He sat up and closed his eyes. Silently he said a short prayer. *Thank God it was just a dream.* Once more.

When he had opened his eyes his ears picked up some whispers. Along them was a gust of cold wind slapping against his face. His heart had been beating very fast and the nervousness he felt remained on a height. The dimness of his room contributed to that feeling, and so he stood up to turn the lights on.

He looked around him. The whispers still ran around in his ears. He did not know where they came from, nor did he know what it was telling him. The strange stream was cold and creepy, like whispers in horror films when you know something bad and horrifying was going to happen. Then a shadow appeared by the empty wall at the far end of the room. He traced the figure from head to foot aiming to see where it came from and whose it was. There was no source, it seemed. Just the shadow against the wall.

"Professor," the voice came, and this time it was perceptible. It came from the shadow.

"Tell me I am dreaming," the professor said.

"You are. From the start, you have been, professor."

"Who are you? What do you want from me?"

"I am in no want of anything from you, professor. You. You wanted something from me."

"I . . . I have no idea what you are talking about. Tell me who you are!"

"You know me very well, professor. Believe me, you know me very well." Slowly, the shadow took up another form, a tangible body out of the void close to the wall. The feet, the upper torso, the neck, and then the face. When the latter gradually formed itself, the professor recognized the familiarity of the countenance of the figure.

"Who are you?"

"How are you, professor?"

The professor didn't speak.

"You can't talk now, professor? Have not even a single word to say? After stealing thousands from me?" the apparition resumed speaking. The volume of his voice began to turn up. "Answer me, professor!"

"No, you're not real. Please, leave me alone." The professor tried to walk toward the door, his steps stuttering and out of fear, and it seemed like the door was a million miles away.

"You're not answering my question, old runt!"

"You're not real!"

"I am as real as anything real could be!"

The professor struggled on to the door. He was but a few paces from it now, but it appeared as though a universe separated them.

"I am both your worst reality and nightmare, professor!" the specter screamed, after which he burst into a thunderous sarcastic laughter that echoed all across the room. The light was blinking on and off.

The professor stopped and almost fell down. He placed a hand to his chest, out of breath, and knees bending from the gradual loss of strength. It was only a matter of seconds now before he would lose his consciousness. The sarcastic laughter still sounded from about him.

"I am Black Shell of the real world, professor, and I am out to get you!"

That had been the last line he heard before the light stopped shooting waves into his eyes.

*****

Morel Gimola started to get interested in writing when he was ten, after reading a Poe story in a College literature textbook. He found the book stocked in the attic of his house. After reading the narrative and finding it so compelling, he suddenly sensed a force wanting him to wander further into this new world he had stumbled on. Eventually it led him to answer what had been the calling of his heart: to write and share stories out from his own creative strength.

He enrolled himself to a Creative Writing program in College. There he was able to showcase what talent he had so long nurtured in his earlier years. He became a contributor to many papers and many of his professors admired his amateur works. Many of them saw a bright future in the field for Gimola. There barely were no criticisms for every prose work he had written. All but one professor, as was an exception to all Creative Writing majors in the school's history: the meticulous Professor Gonzales.

Professor Julian Gonzales was known to be a very feared mentor, and his notoriety had been a cause for intimidation to his students for eternity. A middle-aged man, he was a writer himself, having published a lot of stories in countless papers and had secured a seat for himself in the pedestal of great writers at the time. When he took the teaching post in the university, he eventually raised the standards of the writing quality from the students and graduates alike.

Gimola studied under Professor Gonzales's one subject in his fourth year. He took it upon himself as a challenge even prior to the start of classes, hearing the circulating whisper that the professor had never once rode the wagon hauled by the popularity of his writing. That the talent he had was a mere natural capability of anyone who can write. This had apparently caused friction in the gears of

Gimola's creative mind and his perception of Professor Gonzales. He hungered to prove himself to him.

The semester went on, and Professor Gonzales instilled a very strict environment around his class, in particular to Morel Gimola. The professor had seemed to put the closest eye on him. When he gives them a writing project, he would spend a whole night checking and double-checking Gimola's work. It would be such a ponderous scrutiny that when Gimola gets his work back, it would be filled with red lines and circles and paragraphs of comments and criticisms. He'd take them lightly at first, knowing the professor's notorious meticulousness. But soon when the succeeding works he submitted seemed to be nowhere better than the last one, and the red taints were only getting more strokes in his papers, he began to regard such checkings as a personal assault to his talent.

For the next months he would refuse to submit any assignment and would only write during classes instead of listening to the professor's lectures. The professor would constantly bash him for being too proud of his well reputation in the school that he no longer respects him nor his academic responsibilities.

The professor eventually decided to leave him be for the remainder of the semester, but he swore, in clandestine, that Gimola would never pass that subject so long as he holds it.

The semester was almost slipping away. The professor, as a final requirement from his students, required them to write a novella, about 20,000-50,000 words, in a span of a month. The pressure rose immediately across the whole class. No more meetings were held during that month. Every day would be devoted in writing the final requirement.

*****

The professor opened his eyes, wandered them around, and found himself back in his bed, which made him readily think that the previous happening had been just another nightmare. Always a nightmare, always something to haunt him. Just as he rose up, he saw a shadow on the wall at the far end of the room, oddly similar to the one in his dream.

"I am growing sick of you!" he said, but there was no answer, not a word from the shadow or from any phantom source. Then the cold wind blew through the open window of the room and slapped him on the cheek. It brought him a sense of fear, some sign that the nightmare was about to happen once again. He braced himself.

The shadow started to move toward the door. Like a breeze it opened wide upon the shadow's passing, where on the doorway some kind of mist gradually arose. It slowly turned its gaseous traces into a shape of a human, its spectral hand beckoning the professor. It started to move away, and the old man stood up hastily to follow it.

The mist moved through the long hallway of the professor's house and up the stairs toward the attic. It somehow dissolved into the darkness in there. The old man climbed up the stairs, seemingly fired up by curiosity, and there switched the lights on. He saw the mist again when the light had burned and saw it slipping through the thin slits of the lid of a box quietly deposited near the attic window.

The professor felt a sudden surge of memories revolve chaotically around his head when he saw the box. It was the only object inside that attic room, and it was the only one his eyes were willing to look.

He walked toward it, pacing like a hunter approaching his unwary prey. It looked nothing more than an ordinary box, but the mist that seeped into it made it extremely curious to him. Perhaps the mist was a telltale indication of something extraordinary inside. He began to lift the cover, all of a sudden expecting something to just spring out toward him—*maybe the mist had materialized into a solid entity inside, maybe even malevolent.* But his eagerness won him over and he continued to open the box, and afterward inside he saw nothing of whatever he had anticipated to startle him. He didn't even see the mist. The box contained books, notebooks, and several envelopes that had bloated from the many papers slipped inside each of them. Now he understood the sudden nostalgic feeling that swept over him. He moved his hands on the books, found that they were his collection since his childhood, and then shifted his attention to the notebooks. He remembered the many drafts that he had written on them, comprising the earliest works he had done for the craft. He had preferred writing by hand than using a typewriter. Later he moved his hands over the envelopes and found one that immediately caught his attention. It was an old, brown envelope, whose color had now faded in various spots. On its flap was written something, a familiar name: Black Shell.

He took it out of the box. Somehow he remembered it from before, although the reminiscence was still vague. He opened it and found sheets of paper inside it, and he took them out carefully, recognizing the seeming brittleness of the papers they had apparently acquired through the years. He read a few lines from them, turning random pages after another. It was a manuscript titled "Black Shell," written on the first page above the first paragraph. But below the title was another name: Morel Gimola.

The room seemed to become lost into a vortex and all around it turned dark. And then the memories crowded back into his mind, vividly, erasing every doubt he had. Right from when he started his profession, his acceptance of the teaching post in the only university he had taught, to the reputation he kept during his tenure, to his classes, to the faces he had forgotten whose—and then there was Morel Gimola, the only one he recognized, only one he remembered. It had come back now. In a snap he began to realize why he had been plagued by the same nightmare every night. All along the time since he was able to turn the tide of his fate, he had been celebrating a success that was stolen from a forgotten memory. Gimola had been haunting him with that message.

He heard a voice drifting across the room, a voice he recognized as his own, and it sounded like it came from him in a soliloquy. He tried to make out the words, realizing later that the voice was reciting lines from the novella that his former student, Morel Gimola, had submitted for his subject's final requirement.

The professor spent the whole night on Gimola's work, as usual, the day it was submitted to him, and by the end of the night, he became very sure he had read the greatest literary work out of all the literary works he had ever read. "Black Shell" completely caught him off guard. It had been so sudden, so unexpected, how quickly his perception of Gimola's talent made a complete turn. Something he had never thought he'd let happen. He became wholly certain that Gimola was a literary master in the making, and that "Black Shell" would end up as an undisputed masterpiece.

But a couple of years had passed, and not one of those ever came to happen. The story of Black Shell died along with his expectations. He never heard of the young man again, not once in the subsequent years. Soon, he himself forgot all about the story, and every bit of admiration he had for the raw talent of the boy all went down the drain.

The professor's mind was back in the attic, with Gimola's manuscript in his hand, and everything was finally clear to him.

Professor Julian Gonzales wanted nothing more now but to end the nightmare streaks. With the realization that he had just wallowed on a success that should have not been really his, he wanted to put things straight early. He was a professor, a man of repute, a man who had an honest career throughout his life. He was on the verge of it now anyway, waiting only for the final push off the cliff, so all he wanted now was to leave behind an untainted legacy.

The nightmares had been a message, not perhaps from Gimola himself, however he'd done it, but from the depths of his own subconscious. He had to find his former student to explain everything, before anything gets out of hand. With the critical attention the book had received, there was a fair chance that Gimola had already acquired a copy and realized the complete replication. He had to tell him it was an accident, and give credit where credit was due.

He was able to secure Gimola's address from the records in the old university. It had been provided a long time ago and it was probable that Gimola was no longer living in that address, but it would be a reasonable starting point in tracing his current whereabouts if ever so. He just had to hope he was still there.

Gimola's residence was a small one-storey house, old but quite kept neat, or at least from the outside view. It relieved him a little, knowing someone was residing there and in his mind must still be the Gimola's He parked his old car right across the doorway, and on looking at the window beside it, saw the curtain brushed aside enough for someone inside to peer out at him. He had a sharp, instant feeling that it was his former student.

The curtain swayed back sealing the window, and after a few seconds the door opened. Morel Gimola stood on the doorway, looking at him with a trace of surprise in his face.

"Gimola," the professor said, as he stepped out of the car.

"Professor Gonzales?" Morel asked.

"How are you? It's been a long time."

"Yes. Come inside, professor."

Morel ushered his old professor inside and offered him a seat at the kitchen table. None of them spoke for some time, and Morel left the professor to fetch something. When he came back he sat across him and laid a book on his side of the table.

"I heard about your latest work," Morel said.

The professor looked at the copy of "Black Shell" before him. "That is why I'm here, Morel. I want to explain everything—"

"You had the nightmares too?"

A brief astonishment caught the professor, and his voice came out in irregular flow when he resumed speaking, "Yes, I have been having nightmares about

Black Shell. The character. It's been haunting me since this got published. I just found out about my mistake."

"I didn't write it."

"What do you mean? You submitted it to me before."

"It wasn't me who wrote it, professor."

"Who then?"

"Markie. My late twin brother." Morel drew out a small black notebook from his pocket and handed it to the professor. "I had nightmares about the story too. And my brother. I thought he was trying to tell me something, and then I found out about your book. That notebook was my brother's. He had everything about Black Shell written in there. He had kept it since we were young. It had kind of grown into a sort of obsession to him."

Professor Gonzales held the notebook with a slight repulsion, as if it was hot to the touch. He flipped to the first page and saw this line written: All will be gone. Fear rose up in his senses, and even more as he went along the next pages, turning each one with a dawning sense of terror. There was something sinister in the very mind that produced all that was written in there. There's more than obsession discernible from it. There was darkness, absolute darkness.

"How did it start, Morel?" the professor asked.

"I'm not exactly sure, professor, but the first time I saw that notebook was the time he got sick. He was bedridden for a month."

"How did he get sick?"

"We don't even know. No doctor can tell us what it was. We didn't even expect him to recover." Morel paused and looked at his professor worriedly, before resuming, "One night when we were about to sleep, I smelled something burning around the house. But I could not see any trace of smoke anywhere. So I followed the smell, and it led me to Markie's room. He was asleep when I came in, and inside I became very sure that the smell had come from in there, although I couldn't see specifically where the source was. Suddenly Markie went screaming. He was shaking in his bed uncontrollably. I was startled. I didn't know what to do. I tried to restrain my brother. I called out for my mother, and we struggled to hold his hands and feet. I was thinking he was having a very bad dream. We held onto him for a minute before he finally sank back on the bed, weak as ever. His eyes were wide open, and it was a frightful sight.

"'All will be gone.' He said that. And then he closed his eyes and seemingly went back to sleep."

"Did you rush him to the hospital?"

"No, professor. After a minute he opened his eyes again and rose up from the bed. And I tell you, all the weakness had apparently been drained out of his body, not even a trace of anything suggestive of him being ever sick. He looked to both of me and our mother, and said he was feeling alright. I asked him whether he was aware of what had just happened. And then he spoke about the dream, the one I was referring to, the bad dream."

"What was the dream about?"

"The same ones we had, professor."

"Oh, my God."

"But he wasn't frightened by the masked figure, unlike us. He had rather grown a liking of it. Soon, obsession was all I could see of him toward those nightmares, and that dark figure. Black Shell became his one and only obsession."

"When did he start writing about Black Shell?"

"That very night. He wrote and wrote incessantly throughout the rest of the night."

"What progress did he make by then?"

"Unexpectedly, professor, he finished nothing. At first I was surprised by his productivity, writing endless narrative on a lot of pages, when all of a sudden he began to tear all of them and threw them away. I asked him what the matter was, and he told me what he had written was not good enough. That those paragraphs were trash, unworthy of the very subject that was Black Shell. He told me he must start all over again. He was completely overwhelmed by that character of his nightmare. He said it was Black Shell who saved his life and it was just proper and fair that he devote all his life to telling its story."

The professor fell silent, thinking ponderously. "When you submitted the story to me in class, was he aware of that? I mean, did he not at least consider that he was showing his work to others to somebody else's credit?"

"He was aware, professor. But he looked at it as a chance to finally tell the story of his personal hero, and I regretted all of it."

"What happened then?"

"He made a complete turn of his mind after that. He took the story from me, he was very angry, and then he burned it all completely. He ran away from home, and didn't ever come back. For so many years we didn't hear anything from him. Every search we took of his whereabouts all ended up in vain. It took countless of years before we knew. In a sad turn of events, my brother got arrested for arson. He burned three large libraries in one night."

"Three libraries!"

"Yes, professor. He did it all in one night, burning each of the three to ashes."

"Why would he do that?"

"He was thinking someone had stolen his story of Black Shell. He cried it out during the trial. Out of irrational desperation, he decided to just burn all libraries and bookstores there was. And had he not been caught that night, I'm sure he would have taken down more."

The color flushed out from the professor's face hearing this, feeling some kind of invisible jab to his chest. It was a blow coming from his guilt over publishing the story of what he thought was his own original character.

"It was also with fire that he ended his life with," Morel resumed. "He burned himself alive in his prison cell, screaming Black Shell's name as he was engulfed by the fire. It was never known how he started it."

After all of these were told, a loud explosion erupted outside the house, pulling the two out of the table and into the doorway. Outside they saw the professor's car gone off to flames. People had gathered around the curiosity. In a matter of minutes the fire had turned the once well-polished car into a charred piece of mess, while the professor was kept still by extreme incredulity. In his jumbled thoughts he instantly connected all the dots from the nightmare to his retrieved reputation to the story behind the story to the arsonist and to the flames growing and growing in front of him now.

As he stood there, the fear of Morel's twin brother about to come back to him from the dead grabbed him by the throat, ready to strangle the life out of him. He felt a sudden surge of temperature within his body.

It took long before some men from the gathering onlookers gathered the sense to extinguish the fire.

"Is he coming after me?" the professor spoke at last, in almost a whisper.

Morel glanced at him, eyes turning wide.

"Professor!" he screamed. "Your shoulder!"

The professor pulled himself out of his distracted mind and found that smoke was seeping out of his shoulder. He clapped his hand over it, feeling a sharp burning pain from within. Soon more smoke came out from other parts of his body. And the burning pain had scattered to these places as well. In a matter of seconds, it happened. The retribution from beyond the grave, from beyond the realms of reality. Screams of pain, howling through the thick conflagration, came out from the burning old professor. People threw pails of water at him, but the fire just kept on growing. And on the last bit of consciousness he had, the professor heard a sharp whisper, coming from a long, long way out of this world: *All will be gone.*

The Road Home

The steady gale brushing against the foliage of the trees outside was the only sound I could hear tonight. I put the last piece of my clothing inside my bag and winced from a sudden sharp pain, and that became the last straw. My hand seemed like a cartographic picture with all the bruises and blood congealing just underneath its thin skin. A mass of tears started to crowd the corners of my eyes. Tonight I would end this misery, this excruciating pain, this fear. Tonight I had finally built all bravery to go home.

My name is Barbara, Barbara Perez. Seventeen years old. A housemaid of the Torremis family. For a moment then I had felt tremendous bliss to have been named with such a beautiful appellation, but stepping in this Torremis home just about wiped that feeling completely off. They called me *Barang*.

I came here in Cebu from Leyte in hopes of finding a suitable job to help my family. Back home my family was very poor, a congregation of seven illiterate people trying to live our lives inside a can of sardines that we could barely call a house. Every day in that home prior to my travel had been like leafing the calendar of my life bearing all the hopelessness of this world. Poverty is a brutal company, and it's a trying-hard-best-friend too, trying to comfort you by making you lose all hope and never leaving you alone.

Well, everyday I spat at this best friend of mine. I tried several measures to get rid of it, and finally decided to leave home to find my luck in some greener pasture someplace else.

I regretted the day I left.

Because on this dim evening when I had finally thought of going home against what might come along the way, all the thoughts of what had happened to me for the past year were pouncing on me vehemently, harsh like a ravaging tempest, mad and agonizing. It was the longest year of my life. Everything I ever knew all boiled down to fear, and pain, and hopelessness. All throughout the year until now, when I finally knew courage again. A sense of courage that I hope I could wield at the best as I would take the steps out of this hell of a house, away from the claws of those monsters, of that deranged family I served with all dedication and hard work, and yet gave me a brutal company worse than poverty back home. Now I only wish to run, and run, and run, back to the home that I knew.

I closed the zipper of my bag and took a glimpse at the cuts on my fingers. I was at the kitchen last morning then, cooking breakfast for the monsters, when their ten-year old child suddenly snatched my hand and started to scribble lines on my fingers using a razor blade. The little imp laughed maniacally as I screamed like a mad woman trying to draw my hand out of him. But I was afraid I would hurt him if I acted it willfully, so I was left with no choice but to just let him make an Etch a Sketch out of my poor hand. And to cry, at least. That was my only outlet.

A pair of glowing eyes appeared by the kitchen door. When the child saw them he immediately scudded out of the room and left me a sound of sarcastic laughter that did not seem to come from a ten-year old little boy. The eyes stared at me like I was an abominable animal. And that had been it. They just stared at me and disappeared a minute after. Like nothing happened. I was left with a bloody hand, and a soul a little more battered than it was before.

My careful actions went on according to the plan I had laid in my mind. It was time to carry the bag over my shoulder. I tried to feel the weight over my limp hand and draw out an estimate of its number. I surmised it weighed around two or three kilograms, and, thinking of the bruises on my shoulders and back concealed under my shirt, I decided the estimate was quite manageable.

I had a battered back, acquired during the course of my time being a housemaid of this Torremis family. They are a bunch of ruthless people with heavy hands and cold hearts. One time, about three months ago, I was bringing a cup of coffee to Mr. Torremis. I swear I was very, very careful then as I walked the steps toward him. He saw by his desk, signing papers or whatsoever. When I was only a bare two steps away from his desk, my foot suddenly took an off-course step and got entangled with the other. I lost my balance and started to fall toward the desk, with the cup of coffee on my hand. I knew I was only a split of a second away from the dungeon again. The coffee splattered kindly all over the papers.

"Oh my God, Barang!" Mr. Torremis screamed, moving back in a quick impulse.

The cup eventually fell to the floor and broke into smaller loathsome pieces.

"I am sorry, sir. I am so sorry." I swiftly got to my feet and tried to take the papers off the desk, to which my master heatedly admonished. His eyes turned into fiery balls of cornea and lens. His look was deadly, strangling. I lurched forward instead and stooped down to pick up the pieces of broken ceramic on the floor. From there, with only the feet of Mr. Torremis registered in my vision, I could still feel the weight of the murky anger possessing him. Oh, why did those pieces have to be so hard to pick?

The feet moved but I paid no much attention as I was busy picking the broken pieces of the cup. His strides were heavy. They stopped a little sooner and what happened next happened so instantly. A wooden stool was hammered onto my back and caused me to drop hard on the floor. I could hear the dismantled pieces of the stool dropping behind me. I had my face lunged on the broken pieces of the cup and some of them pierced into my skin. But I thought to myself, they didn't hurt, they didn't, for the love of God, they didn't hurt me. I let all these relentless lies stick up in my mind.

Mr. Torremis kept pushing the weight of his contempt onto my back. I squirmed carefully from the pain but when he screamed for me to stand up, I got up on my feet in a second, as if nothing had just happened. Because it just did not hurt me at all.

"That should teach you some lesson of keeping your presence of mind at all times, you fool," he said between his gritted teeth. And then he set me off at once to get him another cup of coffee, and this time to make no mistake of throwing it before him.

Lies, lies, and lies.

The year under this cave had been filled with lies for me. Five months ago, I told Mr. Torremis that I planned to go home to my family, and in reply he said, "Oh, yes you would. Definitely. Because you are a useless pain in the ass in here, *Barang*." But home never happened to me after that. They kept me, and hurt me, and taught me to accept the truth that I'd never be going to anyplace else anymore. It did not hurt, it just, it just—

But the malignant sounds of all those months were about to go away now, I'm sure. I am walking out of this hellhole and breathe good-natured air again, and be free again, and be at truth again. To where? Home, certainly. Home is where your heart is and it wasn't with me presently.

I resumed my steps toward the door. My pace was considerably slow, as the pain creeping inside my body had reduced my motion into considering my broken pieces too. And my sight, my right eye specifically. My eye had not been gradually failing me for the past few months. I reduced myself to thinking it was because of the frequent stream of tears flowing from them. But why would I lie to myself? It was a couple of months ago when it happened.

I was ironing the school uniform of Bethany, the six-year old daughter of Mr. Torremis. I was making sure to be very careful with the chore. I love the girl because she reminded me of my little sister back home. She was about her age, and they were alike in most ways. The shape of their faces were so much in resemblance, the round cheeks, the shiny foreheads, their lips, and when they smile, the similarity only becomes very apparent. My Mary, I missed her so much. I missed seeing her smiles, but in a way I am comforted by looking at Bethany when she does too. Alike in most ways but one. Bethany also had the effect of the wicked upbringing from her monster parents.

So there I was, a couple of months ago, ironing her school uniform, when all of a sudden she got behind me and thrust a pair of scissors onto my hand. The thing didn't slice one of my fingers off but it wounded it enough for a streamlet of blood to begin oozing out from under the skin and on the clothing laid out in front of me, which happened to be her school uniform. The blood created a small blot of stain on the cloth. With a quick thinking I immediately held the uniform and put it on the nearby table before I brought my attention back to my wound. I didn't notice the startled face of Bethany looking at the stain on her uniform. Of course, it was a surprise

Then I heard Bethany's lungs give out a scream that shook me off my ground: "Papa!"

The glowing marbles appeared by the doorway again. In a second fear completely wrapped me, and looking at those eyes seemed like looking at the Devil itself. It was fatal. It was draining.

"What is it, my baby?"

Bethany cried as she answered, "Barang ruined my uniform." She pointed a finger at the small blood stain on the school uniform.

Then Mr. Torremis glanced at me, put an enormous weight on me with the stare he had thrown. He walked in heavy paces toward me and when he had reached the ample distance, he pushed my head sidewards onto the table where I could see the stained uniform. He screamed a succession of indiscernible words, but I was sure that he was hurling curses. And then he picked up the electric iron that was still plugged and pushed its hot surface on my right eye. I closed them both instantly. God only knows how excruciating the pain was! For the love of God! There were tears welling up in my eyes, but the heat would immediately turn them into steam inside. The hot surface had touched my eye for about three seconds, but for me it felt like years. I screamed at first but retracted it in an instant, and thought, it didn't hurt at all, for the love of God, it didn't hurt me a bit.

I leaped up and pushed my feet a few steps backward. My eyes were closed shut but I could see them in the blind. I could see them because they are people of the dark. They are imps of the Devil.

"Learned your lesson now, Barang? Huh?"

"Y-y-yes, s-s-sir." Afterward the sound of their steps began to drift away like coming out of a tunnel, myself left inside.

Of course, I had pretended before him that it didn't hurt. But that night before I slept, I cried on my bed. Cried endlessly.

The incident took away the sight of my right eye, and I had to work using my left one entirely, which was clearly not an easy thing to do. But it all boiled down to getting used to.

That had been my life for a year. Everyday there would be beatings, with reasons ranging from irrational ones to those out of sheer entertainment for them. They didn't know. He didn't know. He must not. I need to let him see that they didn't hurt me at all. I thought somehow sooner I would reach a level of immunity where my pretensions would become states of reality. Somehow. Someday perhaps.

I reached for the doorknob. It was a toil reaching for it, and turning it open proved even more. My body seemed to hurt in all places. I thought of reaching into my underwear, but eventually thought it would be a bad idea. I proceeded to open the door very carefully, at the least sound I could muster out of it. When the door was finally swung open to an apt width, I thrust my body out, feebly, and looked around with my left eye opened wide. It was dim, but I could see enough. There was an absolute silence around. I walked a little more.

My room was in the basement of the house, connected to the kitchen above by a short flight of stairs; and I could now see it from where I stood. For a moment I had a thought that one of its steps would later betray me—break itself into halves as I mount it, drop me to the floor, and I would scream the loudest of my life. Then the glowing marbles would appear, and—oh home! why do you have to be so far away!

I broke my thoughts hastily and proceeded to walk forward. The stairs I reached at once and took the first step with ease. No sound, not too much pain from my body. I was praying now, praying, please, please, please . . . Oh, God, don't let these stairs fail me. When I got to the last step, I felt a relief that had to be the most comforting feeling since I stepped into this hellhole. I reached for the doorknob, turned it, and bam!

The glowing marbles were there glimmering before me. Horrifying! I felt my body lost its color and what remained of my strength drained. I had not the slightest idea how my body reacted to the sudden shift of my emotions. I stared at the glowing eyes, feeling every bit of terror I was capable of feeling. One word and I would fall.

"Where to, Barang?"

I fell down the short flight of steps with my eyes still locked on his.

"Escaping are you? Why? Do you think you could? Really?"

"Please, sir."

"Where to, I repeat, Barang?"

"Please, sir. Please."

"Where!"

"H-h-home, sir. I want to go home."

"Ah! Home, you say. Why, do you have another home aside from this one?" He was gesturing his hands around, indicating the house we were currently in.

"Back home, sir. With my mother—"

"Shut up!"

And then he ran down toward me and grabbed the lifeless strands of my hair. With this as a grip he dragged me back into my room. I held onto his hand desperately to somehow break the strength he exerted against my scalp. I screamed and screamed, at the top of my lungs, but then he suddenly stopped and threw a hard slap on my face.

"If you don't shut that filthy mouth, I'd make sure to put a bullet into it. You understand, Barang?"

I answered with a weak nod. He brushed his long hair backwards and smiled at me. It was an evil grin. "Now, you behave here and remember what I just said. I will kill you if you scream again, and will make sure to kill every kin you have back home. You understand?"

I nodded. And then he closed the door before me. There were motions audible from outside that followed and later it sounded like he was putting up a lock on the door. It brought another gloomy feeling inside of me. *Now what? Now what, Barbara? You are locked up now! How else can you ever go home from a locked up rat hole inside a bigger one?* I was even sure that Mr. Torremis swallowed the key, to keep me here forever.

I lied down and tried to lull myself to sleep. I relied on the limpness of my body to give me a chance to slip out of this reality and be in a different world in my dreams. But it betrayed me. I could not sleep at all. My mind was crowded with enormous thoughts—thoughts of going home, thoughts of my parents, my brothers and sisters back home, who were relying on me to lift them out of their miserable condition. I cried because it was clear now that I was far more miserable than they were.

Looking at the wall now, and trying to come up with conversations in my head, I silently wished I could somehow slip into visual hallucinations. Be it senseless or out of this world, I didn't care. All I needed was something to quell the monotone of my poor room, lest it would not take long before I would lose my sanity.

My room was a rat hole, literally. There was nothing inside when I first occupied it save for one woven mat for me to sleep on. There was not even a cabinet here to store my things. The place was also a frequent rendezvous of rats. There had been many times that I had woken up by a rat crawling up my legs, or running across my face. And to add more to those, the room also becomes almost a catch basin for floodwater every time there is a heavy rainfall. Luckily, there had only been about a dozen instances when I had to sleep late from washing water out of the room.

This room had been a witness to all my melancholies. This is where I had poured out all the rats inside my heart that they feed me with their abuses on the days that passed. This is where my tears had flooded out of my own broken spirit. This is where I had part with reality to somehow escape its cruelties. This room had been my afterlife.

I fell asleep, at last.

When I woke up, I felt my back was soaked wet. It had rained very hard last night and the floodwater had gone down into my room. I jumped on my feet quickly, or how quickly it seemed my weak body had managed. There was a group of squeaking rats in the corner of the room, in revelry perhaps. I walked to the door and thought of calling for Mr. Torremis. But I consequently considered it a bad idea. I carried my bag up over my shoulders to save them from getting soaked in the water. And then I just stood there. I just stared pensively at the rats, wishing I was one of them, so that I could slip myself out of this room, out of this house, and be free. I was on the verge of tears.

I looked for the hole where the rat had come through and swept the water with my feet towards it. Somehow I managed to later wash away some of the water and made the rats run back into the hole.

That night I felt very weak. Perhaps it was from hunger and thirst. I didn't eat the whole day, expecting that Mr. Torremis would send down something to eat for me. But there had been none, and calling out for him still proved to be a bad idea.

A rat crawled out of the hole and traipsed lazily on the corner. It's a squid. It's a squid, I was sure. I was looking intently at it and the permission of that hallucination was the only consequent act my mind could make out at the moment. I moved slowly toward the rat, and with a sudden motion I snatched it and bit off its belly. Blood squirted onto my hands and I felt the rat squirming between them. I ate the whole of it except for the head and the tail. I pondered over it and had a minute's thinking but undeniably it was the most delicious meal I had ever taken.

I fell asleep a minute afterward, and woke up from what was a dreamless sleep to a sound of a sarcastic laughter. Beside where I lied sat a clown, and when I cast an eye on him, he giggled in such a manner as if he wasn't going to stop. I rose up immediately and pushed my steps back away from him. I had always been so afraid of clowns ever since I was a child.

"Hello there, Barbie."

I didn't answer him, but rather stared at him through a terrified pair of eyes.

"My name is Ken." And then he laughed so boisterously I was afraid Mr. Torremis would hear him from here.

"Please, don't do that. My master, he—"

"What, Barbie? What about him? He's not going to hear me. He's going to hear you."

I began to sob, all while still fixing my eyes on him.

"Shush, my Barbie, dear. Tell me. Tell me what you want. What do you want, Barbie?"

I was reluctant to speak, but I said eventually, "Home, sir. I want to go home."

"As what I expected. Home is very far, Barbie. Can you go the distance? And look . . . look at you, my dear. You don't seem to be capable of walking even out of this room."

I answered with heavier sobs.

"Hush now, my dear. Well, we all are going to get home eventually, is that right?" He laughed again, and the sarcasm in it so deeply pierced my heart. He resumed speaking, "What about a magic trick?"

I paid no attention to the mad stranger, but when I heard the cracking sound of the door opening, I looked up at him at once. He was holding the knob and opening the door slightly. The smile he wore had emptiness in it as he watched me look up at him in disbelief.

"Tada! Tell me what you think, Barbie."

"Who are you really?"

"I am your savior, can't you see?" He drew another sarcastic laugh, but I barely paid attention to it because all I could see was the door and the newfound chance for me to escape this macabre room. I slowly walked toward him without letting my vision stay out of the door. He didn't part with his smile either, and as I got nearer I could clearly see the stains on his teeth. "Come, Barbie. Come."

When I was only a step away, he suddenly shoved the door to a full open. He burst into a more tempestuous laughter and pressed it on my startled face. The opened door showed nothing but a wall and a huge painted word on it that read, "Boo!"

The infinite laughter of the clown persisted through my sobs as I brought myself down to the floor, and the desperate tears fell like rain from my eyes, piercing my cheeks, scraping my face. I pulled myself no longer out of this nightmare. I was slowly imbibing it, feeling it as the truth. There was no more chance. They won. They are always winning.

As the sounds around me died, so was the soul inside me.

I looked into the blank and cried like a baby. Now what? All my hopes and chances of going back home had obviously gone into dissolution. All I had now was a room that had its hands clasping my neck. I was crept up by a sense of claustrophobia. Everything looked like a swirl of black and white. I was sure, I was sure I was going to faint.

Then I fell asleep. A blanket of stars surrounded the realms of my dream, and the stellar picture was such a sight to perceive! I looked around me and found myself floating, like I was swimming under the sea. I moved through the space like a fish and aimed my path toward a star. This dream was so vivid.

When I reached a little closer from my destination, I saw a familiar figure ahead. A short stout woman who wore shabby clothes and whose face was wrinkled all over. She smiled at me. I moved closer to her and saw the calm face of my mother. I burst into tears and tried to swim faster toward her. She was smiling still, and she was mouthing the words, "I love you, Barbara."

"Mama! Mama!" I screamed. But then she disappeared suddenly. The stars disappeared. Every bit of what had been suddenly disappeared. Where was the beauty of the world when I needed it? Oh, what misery! I let my tears fall like I had never cried before. I wish to see my mother again, my brothers and sisters I left back home. I wish to be with them again. I want to go home. I want to go home so bad.

In the dark, there are dreams unspoken.

I woke up and then I saw nothing. There was an endless void around me. I moved my arms around and felt fear rising in my veins. Oh God, please no. Not my other eye. But then I spotted a thin ray of illumination. I was washed over by relief. Mr. Torremis had cut the wire connecting to the only light bulb inside the room. The small ray of light I saw came from a tiny hole in the ceiling.

At that point I lost all hope of going home. I prayed. God, if this would be my final resting place, then so be it. Please take me now. I believe in lives without a purpose, such as my own. I believe in people living merely for living's sake. Such as I have lived mine. Thy kingdom come, Thy will be done . . . Amen.

And then I cried a little more. That would be the last one, I swore to myself. There would always come a point in time where dying becomes the greatest favor you can give to yourself.

I took out a paper and a pen and wrote what would be my last words, for not one of them here would be able to hear it from Heaven. I started scrawling. I wrote about what was in the medicines that Mr. Torremis had been giving me every day. I wrote about the times when he would even give them to the children. Save them, save them from this monster, before it's too late!

And at the last stroke of the pen—*Take me home*—I fell into another sleep, and that would be the final one.

BLINDS

The ringing in my ears began two days ago. The day before that, one of my friends was shot point blank on the back of the head while watching a basketball game. Now, when I think about it, he wasn't really one of my friends. I just knew him on a game of basketball one time. The ringing in my ears has become annoying by the minute. I hope they catch the shooter already.

I stayed all day yesterday inside my room. Nothing particular as to why. I wasn't sick. I wasn't avoiding work. I just wanted to lie on my bed all day, without thinking of anything. Not even the ringing inside my ears. Well, I hope so at least. It's been pestering me. Anyway, I kept the light shut and the windows closed all throughout the day, hoping maybe that the sharp noise around my head would be drowned in the atmosphere of darkness together with me lying still on my bed.

Let me tell you about my room.

Well, my room is a small, one-thousand-peso per month room I have inhabited since last year. A year and a half now, I guess. It's a small room. It has a door, and a window. And a small fluorescent lamp. And my bed, of course. This room I rented is one of the ten rooms for rent spread in two floors of Mrs. Annie Luboc's boarding house.

Mrs. Annie Luboc is an intellectual, but she can be a pain sometimes. She hits solid points on a lot of things and does some dignified work, but on her free time she loves flipping off people who aren't swaying with her in her merry-go-round. But I'm getting ahead of myself.

My God, it's getting louder.

I hope they catch the shooter already.

The door of my room leads out to a hallway where four other doors of four other rooms for rent swing and stand like knights around a round table. All of the other four rooms have renters, and every last one of them is one I cannot stand. But the less I care, the less I have to deal with them. As long as they don't one day bang on my walls or knock on the door, I don't think I will be bothered to kill. I'm kidding, of course.

My room is in the second floor, and through the lone window out I can see the street where a lot of people don't seem to want to pass anymore. Not since three weeks ago when a College student was robbed at gunpoint there just across the boarding house. And then a week after another mugging took place, and then a couple of days afterward there occurred the same. Last night was when the worst of the beads in the string happened . . . But I feel we ought to talk more about the shooting in the basketball court. The ringing has been lately gaining volume. I hope they catch the shooter already.

Yesterday I heard Mrs. Annie screaming outside, but I already have half my care reserved to the door and half to the window to care for whatever she was screaming about. I think she's a frustrated something, whatever she is an intellectual of. But who cares, really?

I heard about the fateful shooting in the basketball court when I came home from work. I had to know about it in the evening news, half a day after the incident, because no one really in my distant neighborhood has the care to let me know of anything. I guess if ever the hallway gets on fire I would have to know it in the evening news. Well, that friend of mine—acquaintance, in actuality—was just minding his own business and busy watching the game afoot, when they said somebody just shadowed from behind him and went on and put two bullets through his cranium, everybody watching him drop like a rag doll. Panic swayed around the basketball court immediately, and if you believe everything the media says, it was the same old case of drug-related extra-judicial killing. I hope they catch the shooter already. He didn't even have the time to wrap my dead acquaintance with a packaging tape and pin the usual placard.

He was a good man, that friend of mine. I knew he was using drugs, but I didn't know he was pushing them. Well, he really had a lot of time to do anything there is to do in this neighborhood: watch basketball, play basketball, use drugs . . . The ringing in my ears is really pissing me off . . . I must confess—that one game I played with my deceased friend wasn't really the only instance that I got to hang out with him. I don't like people much, but Jason—his name was—became the lone bright spot all across the neighborhood to me. Me and Jason have played a lot of basketball games together, me and Jason have spent a lot of free times just sitting at courtside watching a lot of games. I have been in Jason's little, dingy shack. Jason has been in my comfortable room. So it makes it odd a little that I had to hear about his shooting first during the evening news. Where every breaking headline is about killings here and there, bodies wrapped in tape, placards put on every last one of them. Jason had used drugs in my room. Jason was using drugs. That's why he got shot, well, if you believe everything the media says. And sometimes we share the rock. Sometimes. More than one time, I guess. Well, now that I think about it—my God, what am I blabbering about? That man's no friend of mine! We only met on a game of basketball that one time. But I hope they catch the shooter already.

I think it's raining outside. Last night, when I peeped out through the window, I saw a motorcycle parked outside right in front of the apartment building. There's a waiting shed in there, almost useless now that no one really wants to stay long anywhere on that street. It was one of those motorcycles with pipes that will make your ears pop right out of your head when they start bellowing exhaust. It should be no different. And it pissed me off. I should have heard the sound of it before it got there parking. I should have known somebody, or more than one somebody, was coming. I must have been asleep then, but I haven't slept a wink since the shooting.

I closed the jalousies and I was once again dipped in the dark. I tiptoed toward the door. Oh my God did I need to be completely quiet! I opened the door slightly, and looked out to the hallway with only one eye. Why did the y have to bathe the hallway with light? So I saw somebody, but it was just one of the other renters, trying to open the door of his room with one hand. On his other hand he carried a bag of groceries. I could see the old man was struggling. He dropped his key, and he cursed, and he put down the bag of groceries on the floor to pick it up, and he noticed me. "A little help?" he had said. I swung the door a little wider, my two eyes now out to the hallway, and glared at him and closed the door. The old prick. For all I know he was the shooter.

That was the time I heard the motorcycle, and I was right. It was so loud it's unbelievable I didn't hear it earlier. I ran to the window to look, and I saw the somebody, two of them in fact. One's on the motorcycle already, revving the engine, while the other stood nearby, talking on his cell phone. I knew it! The ringing in my ears is on it again . . . The fuckers moved oh so casually!

It is raining now. I can see it. There's a lamp post on the side of the building whose lamp is just a palm's length away from my window. Through the light of that lamp I can tell how hard or soft the rain is falling. Neat little trick. But of course it works well with an evening backdrop. And that lamp sure beams with its glorious glow right through the jalousies straight into my room every single night, like clockwork. If I look out at night, I am a sitting tin can to any Django out there, the motorcycle men, for example. Last night, before any of them could glance up toward my window, I shut the jalousies with full fervor, and racing heartbeat, and hid under my bed, and sleep didn't ever come to me that night, once again.

This morning I bought myself a gun. Well, you can never be careless these days. One minute you're watching a basketball game, the next you're sprawled lifeless on the ground with bits of your brain scattered all around you. I practiced handling it, just to check if I can maneuver it from my window, through the horizontal bars that are the jalousies, without difficulty. I don't want to have to stick it out to make moving it easier. I tried aiming it to one bystander standing exactly where the motorcycle was parked last night, and I thought there wouldn't be a problem. I didn't pull the trigger, of course. This time anybody out there is a tin can to a Django in my room that is me. Ha ha.

Huh. I didn't notice the ringing in my ears. Some good sign. I think I'll catch the shooter by myself. The rain's getting stronger. I checked by the lamp. But, wait, I think I hear the sound of the motorcycle again. Through the window, opening the jalousies ever so slightly, I can see it has stopped by the waiting shed. Only one motorcycle man this time. It won't matter. He hops out of the motorcycle and gets underneath the waiting shed, out of the rain. Stupid fool, sets schedules when it's raining.

I wonder how it feels to die when you didn't expect it. Like being shot. I don't want to be shot. I don't want to die that way. Maybe I can get to a hundred years. Maybe I'd die in my sleep many years from now, in the middle of a happy dream. Maybe then I wouldn't notice that I would never wake up anymore, and I'll be trapped in that happy dream town without ever feeling lost. People getting shot to death and not knowing they're going to get shot may not notice they're never waking up anymore as well. But the place they shall be trapped in is certainly no happy dream town.

But people are getting shot these days. Eventually everyone will be. Would I wait for my turn? The old man neighbor I saw last night will soon be shot. Mrs. Annie Luboc will soon be shot. I will soon be shot. Oh, the ringing in my ears is getting started again . . .

He's talking on his phone. The motorcycle man is talking on his phone. He looks around, looks to his motorcycle, looks up to the sky, and looks up here at my window. Talks on the phone, looks to the window. Lightning-fast I back away and shit!—he has seen me! There's no time to waste.

The shots ring out, but the rain outside drowns the sound of them and all I can hear is the pattering drops and I look again by the lamp light and they do fall so strong. The motorcycle man drops to the ground. I don't know where I hit him but I did hit the son of a bitch.

I find myself on my way out of my room, then down the stairs, then out the entrance of the apartment building. There's no one around. I want to see the motorcycle man. He lies on the ground right where he previously stood. I have hit him somewhere in the chest. He is spewing blood from his mouth. But he is still alive and his eyes half-open are looking up at me and they don't look fiery. They don't look villainy. The eyes that are looking at me right now are windows of a soul confused. They're asking me. They look up at me and they look past me, behind me, upward, and I look behind me and it leads me to the window, the jalousies I have left open and the lamp telling me the fierceness of the rain.

I look down at him again, his questioning eyes, and I look at the cell phone that has fallen beside him on the ground. I pick it up, the call is still alive, and I put it up to my ear. It is a woman on the other line, speaking, speaking still, "Is it really raining that hard, honey?" I wish I could tell him her honey has just been shot, probably going to die tonight. I wish I could speak also and tell him how hard the rain really is. There's the lamp up there. I don't suppose I could patent the trick before someone else does?

Man, I hope they catch the shooter already.

Printed in the United States
By Bookmasters